My Story

Only God Will Be My Judge

Lucille M. Griswold

Hamilton Books
A member of
The Rowman & Littlefield Publishing Group
Lanham • Boulder • New York • Toronto • Plymouth, UK

Hamilton Books
4501 Forbes Boulevard
Suite 200
Lanham, Maryland 20706
Hamilton Books Acquisitions Department (301) 459-3366

Estover Road
Plymouth PL6 7PY
United Kingdom

Printed in the United States of America
British Library Cataloging in Publication Information Available

Library of Congress Control Number: 2011937501
ISBN: 978-0-7618-5681-8 (clothbound : alk. paper)
eISBN: 978-0-7618-5682-5

∞™ The paper used in this publication meets the minimum requirements of American National Standard for Information Sciences—Permanence of Paper for Printed Library Materials, ANSI Z39.48-1992

FOR CHRISTOPHER AND GABRIEL

*You both occupy a private place in my heart
and fill it with sunshine and happiness*

Acknowledgments

THANKS to Charmaine Cruise and Huong Nguyen for their generosity in reading my manuscript and offering suggestions. Also appreciated is the invaluable computer knowledge and support I received from Catherine Griswold and Ashley Lewallen. Many thanks as well to Lindsay Macdonald and Piper Owens for their patience, understanding and editorial assistance and to all the other staff from University Press of America for their warmth and care in helping my book come to fruition.

Chapter One

Nine eleven. I would venture to say that everyone knows exactly what those words mean without further clarification. 9-1-1 the same numbers, a different meaning. To me, however, those numbers indicate a new life, a new beginning. The opportunity arose, and I took immediate advantage of it.

It was an absolutely beautiful day on the eleventh of September in the year 2001. I was supposedly on my way to work in one of the Twin Towers Buildings in New York City from my home in Connecticut. Megan and I had purchased the home three years before, and our life went downhill from there. It was a stately home on over an acre of land. The pressure of the huge monthly house payments started to take their toll on me, and I admit my personality changed. I became unbearable to be around not only to my wife and others but to myself as well. If Megan evoked anger in me, I had all I could do to restrain myself from hitting her I was so filled with angst. My young daughter's personality began to show signs of nervousness and anxiety due to the tension between my wife and me. Many times I would throw any small object in sight and sometimes these objects hit either my wife, or my daughter. I knew I was getting out of control, and I wanted out.

I started hiding large amounts of cash and planning an escape from what was for me an unbearable situation. I knew there was no way I could ever get my wife to move to a more affordable house. I attempted many times to bring up the subject of a less expensive home, and I was completely rebuffed. We would end the conversation in a huge fight. It was the same old story. She would mention that this is what we worked for all these years. Our neighbors did not seem to have a problem living here. So, my wife wondered why I was so concerned. My well over six figure salary was supposed to be the boon to a happy life, but I hated going in to the city every day, and I hated my job. Megan just could not understand any of this though I tried many times to explain my situation to her. Counseling did not help either. My wife's one objective was to keep up with the Joneses regardless of any sundry feelings I might have.

I began to carry large amounts of cash on my person. Instinctively, I knew I wanted out, and I was just going to get up and leave one day. One afternoon when my wife and daughter were out, I was sorting through some paperwork when I came across some fake identification papers I had purchased while visiting Houston, Texas on business. My cohorts and I had heard that all anyone had to do who needed fake identification was to go to the flea market on Airline Drive and fork over a small amount of cash. We decided it would be fun to test the theory, and one afternoon when we had a few hours off between lectures, we went to the flea market, and sure enough, we were able to obtain new identifications. We laughed at the absurdity of this, pocketed our new identifications, and I came home and stuck mine in a drawer. Seeing it now, however, excited me with a new enthusiasm. I realized that not only could I leave my family, but I could use my alternate identification card to establish a whole new identity and start a new life.

Throughout high school and college I had always enjoyed helping the local mechanic work on cars. I had taken courses at the vocational school and became a certified mechanic. I would have been content to do that the rest of my life. I knew, however, that my parents aspired to better dreams for me, and being an only son I wanted to please them. I enrolled in college and got a degree in finance. I hated my choice from day one even though the money and status proved to be everything anyone could hope to achieve. I was not working very long when I started to dream of once again becoming a mechanic. I knew that no matter where I moved I would have no problem finding a job in that field. Every day my plan was coming into focus. I personally was no longer sure I would miss my wife, but it did break my heart to leave my daughter that I loved dearly. Frankly, though, our once placid relationship was becoming more and more hostile. Knowing that the cause of this hostility was due to my own antagonistic traits, I began to justify my leaving by thinking my wife would be better off without me. It was, coincidentally, on the day the Twin Towers of the World Trade Center were pulverized on September 11, 2001, that I had decided to make my escape.

Chapter Two

The morning of the eleventh, I left at my usual time and drove to the train station. Leaving the car in the parking lot, I boarded a train not into the city but in the opposite direction out of town. My intentions were to go to a used car lot and purchase another vehicle with some of my cash. I selected a nice 1992 Toyota Corolla and drove out of the lot on my way south towards Tennessee. The sun was shining, and I was feeling great and confident with my decision to leave. I turned on the car radio and overheard something about a plane crashing into a building in New York City, so I turned up the volume. When I realized what had actually happened my first reaction was shock, just like everyone else. For one thing, had I gone to work as usual, I would have been in the building when the plane incident occurred.

Shockingly, as horrible as I initially felt, I began to realize what the other implications for me would be of the Twin Towers' collapse. My family would think I was killed in the building, and no one would ever come to look for me. Incongruously, I primarily began to feel a strange sense of elation. My wife and daughter would be well cared for, and I would be considered an unfortunate victim of this horrible atrocity. The rest of the ride to Tennessee I was glued to listening to the news and silently planning my new life as well. I decided to make Tennessee my destination of choice.

I found a room in a boarding house that would suffice until I got an inexpensive apartment, and I started to roam the town looking for auto repair shops. On the edge of town I saw a rather large facility, and they actually had a sign advertising for a mechanic. I had gotten a buzz cut and dyed my blonde hair (what was left of it after the cut) a dark brown. I felt it still might be wise to camouflage my appearance in case they put pictures of the victims of the New York disaster in the paper or on television.

The job interview did not entail my giving a lot of information. They basically wanted to know if I knew anything about cars and said they were willing to 'try me out' for a few days. They offered me a good hourly wage, and I knew I could be comfortable working there and be able to survive in the town.

A week had passed and just about everything on the news concerned the attacks in New York City and subsequent other attacks at the Pentagon and the plane that went down in Pennsylvania. I was sitting one evening watching television after work. They were interviewing the spouses of the victims of the disaster. I was startled to see a photograph of myself in a picture with my wife and daughter, and then an interviewer began questioning my wife. It astonished me to see that she seemed genuinely sad to know I was a victim when with my deepest emotions I always felt she would have been glad to see me go. Perhaps the horror of the attacks was so shocking to all that my demise in this manner was indeed a sorrow to her. I, nevertheless, in my weird sense of being confident, was still sure I was doing the right thing.

Psychologists would probably have a lot to say about my being completely oblivious to the horrors, the gore, and the heartbreaking details that occurred when our country was attacked that sunny day in September 2001. I could have been one escaping down the Towers' stairwells and confronting the delays in escaping due to the debris, smoke, heat and water on the steps. The carnage and devastation shattered America's sense of security, but I was completely unmindful. The Stock Market even closed for an entire week. The gruesome site of body parts, people jumping out of buildings and the rush of dust filled air never impressed my senses when hearing of the collapse of the buildings. In fact, my life proceeded in quite a normal fashion, if there is such a thing as 'normal' where life is concerned.

The feeling of comfort I acquired in my new job was extremely reassuring. I loved every minute of it. Before long, the owner had asked me to please continue full time. I found a nice apartment on a lake with a relatively low monthly payment compared to the area from where I came. Since both my parents were dead, and I had no siblings, it was easy for me to say I came from a small town in Connecticut and that my wife and child had been killed in a car accident. I also explained that I had been moving around now for a couple of years and had reached the point where I wanted to settle down. The implication I was trying to communicate was that the subject of my prior life was too difficult to discuss. Because people sensed that I was sensitive about talking on this topic, I found most were relatively very nice about not questioning me, and I settled down with a reassurance in myself that I had not experienced in a long time.

Chapter Three

Disbelief, on the other hand, permeated the minds of my wife and child. I, of course, had no knowledge of this nor did I care. My wife had picked up my daughter from school after hearing of the tragedy on the news. Neighbors and friends gathered at the home, along with my wife's mother, waiting by the phone to hear any news about me. Many employees who worked at the Twin Towers had been able to call their families either with words of confirmation they were alright or to say they loved them and always would love them, regardless of what happened.

Many other families, like my own, would never hear from their significant others again. Once the buildings were pulverized and the area filled with rushing smoke, haze and debris, all hope for my survival was pretty much destroyed. The next few days my wife went around in a dazed panic. She was angry, sad, and overcome with a multitude of emotions. She wondered why I never called, but later learned that my cell phone had been left in the car in the parking lot at the train station. Megan began contacting insurance companies and getting out the paperwork from my various life insurance policies, pension and 401K plans, and slowly she could see that financially she would easily be able to continue to live in the big house she so adored. In that sense, her life was not going to change very much. Intuitively, the spark ignited that not having me around was not going to be so dreadful after all. She could spend the money as she pleased, continue to live her flamboyant lifestyle and not have me around to fight with all the time. With the exception of the disturbance in our daughter's life, Megan began to realize that perhaps the tragedy for her was not going to be as traumatic as for most.

Oddly enough, my daughter Tracy's personality also turned for the better after the initial shock of realizing and thinking her father had been killed. The fact that her mother and I were no longer at odds with each other helped in ceasing to set her nerves on edge, and she began to live her life with more peace in her heart. Because I always had to work such long hours, most of the carpooling and other decisions were left up to my wife anyway where my daughter was concerned. When I was working at my other job, this was something I did not like at all as I very much wanted to be involved with Tracy. However, the demands of my job nearly drove me crazy and certainly did not leave me the time to do the things with her that I desired.

Since my prior home was in a large metropolitan area, a lot of our personal business was written about in the larger newspapers that could be found all over the country. I could read about a Memorial Service held in my honor at our local parish church. As time continued on I could also read in the sports pages how my daughter Tracy began to excel in school soccer.

My wife utilized her time fighting for the rights of the victims of the disaster and doing more volunteer work than she ever did while I was living with her. In fact, she became quite the social butterfly. She appeared to be thriving without me. Once the news made me conscious of these facts, I was not completely sure how I did feel about that.

Chapter Four

During many lengthy months after the horrific catastrophe, my wife spent numerous hours with my mother-in-law Catherine who had trouble sleeping even before the dreadful happenings.

As an only child, Megan spent a lot of time driving her mother to doctor's appointments and to the various and many tests she required, and Catherine's health became a huge issue following my demise from their lives. Catherine's back started giving her much pain and she needed an MRI which was traumatic in itself for her. Then the orthopedic surgeon had her going to physical therapy where she would walk out after a session in tears hurting more than before she went in. On her own then, she tried going to a chiropractor and the same issues with pain continued. Then, it was ninety dollars a visit to an acupuncturist.

Stomach pains caused Catherine a few visits to the hospital emergency room and then dizzy spells and depression set in. Megan began to fear she was going to lose her mother now too.

Megan made an appointment for Catherine to see a neurologist. This doctor asked Catherine to list the medications she was taking like the other doctors did on each first visit to the many different offices. There was one big difference in that the neurologist asked Catherine how long she had been on the sleep medication to help her sleep. When the doctor heard how long Catherine had been taking this medication she was quite upset and said she was going to take her off the medication gradually. She attributed the back pain, stomach symptoms, and dizziness to the taking of this drug. When Megan heard this she became quite upset and angered that all the other doctors she had seen did not pick up on the length of time her mom was on the medication. She and her mother did everything right by telling and listing this drug on the paperwork only to have it mean absolutely nothing in the doctor's diagnosis. It took nearly a year, but Catherine did get better once off the pill, and she amazingly was like a new person.

Transporting her mother to the many doctor's visits and tests, while stressful in itself, was a distraction for Megan, keeping her mind off the ghastly events she had experienced. In a strange way, this turned out to be a positive in her life. Megan's days were so consumed with her mother; the other sad events began to be put on the back burner.

Chapter Five

My life was also actually taking a turn for the better. I loved every minute of my work, and I was good at what I did, so advancement and pay raises came frequently. Weekends were spent at the local pub, and I found no shortage of beautiful girls to fulfill every type of desire a man might have. There was one especially beautiful wealthy widow that caught my attention when she used to bring her Jaguar in for servicing to our shop. I understood she had a son about the age of Tracy, and it was quite obvious to me her flirty personality was directed right at me. Oddly enough, her son was also very good at playing soccer.

My boss was a wonderful family man and he and his wife often invited me over and any one of a particular group of girlfriends I might have at the time for pizza or a nice meal and cookouts when the weather was nice. They had a pool in their yard, so summer days were fun at their house. The lake where I had my apartment also was used for boating and swimming, and I purchased a little sunfish sailboat to cruise around many evenings after work or on my days off. I really did not want or need a lot of days off because I enjoyed so much the work I was doing.

In fact, I was feeling as though I had been given an opportunity to be reborn and wondered what professionals would say at my ability to acclimate so easily to giving up an entire life in one part of the country and starting anew in another area, with a different job, and without the family I had known for so many years. I readily admitted to myself that I was feeling no remorse nor regret for my choices. Perhaps the worst part of the whole situation was that I should never have stayed in a position that obviously had been very hateful to me.

The longer I worked and my skills became apparent, my tasks became more specialized. People started bringing in vehicles for restoration purposes, or vehicles that were collector's showcase vehicles that perhaps the owner chose to renovate or paint the exterior. My clientele became more sophisticated, my services were in much demand, and my salary was rising steadily. I was acquiring a reputation for my skills around the country. Men interested in purchasing these collector's vehicles would pay my way to travel with them to different states to help by giving them advice on the purchase of a vehicle.

One day, a customer asked me to go to Connecticut to check a vehicle that interested him that was for sale. The town where we were going was close to where I used to live. While I was anxious to make the trip, I also was filled with trepidation. My looks by now had changed quite a bit, so I really did not think anyone would recognize me. I was still keeping my hair cut short and dark, but I had also put on some weight. The weight actually gave me a buff appearance since I had been more on the skinny side while working at the Towers.

We arrived in Connecticut late at night one Friday and were going to look at the car the next morning. The customer had some special business on Saturday afternoon, so I was free to do as I pleased until I met him at the airport that evening. The car we looked at was a beauty and well worth the asking price, so I advised my customer to go ahead with the purchase after taking it for a test drive and checking it over. Since we both were going our different ways in the afternoon, the customer rented one rental car for himself and gave me the money to rent another one that I could use. He also made arrangements for someone to drive the recently purchased car to Tennessee, and he would have it in a few weeks after some minor work that had been mutually agreed upon was completed.

Saturday afternoon I could not resist driving by my old home. The neighborhood looked as elegant as usual, and my wife had done a great job on the upkeep of the home. Then, I drove past a field, and there was a soccer game being played. The temptation to stop was just too great. I pulled a baseball cap down over my forehead to conceal most of my face, parked the car and sat on the opposite side of the home field. I perused the stands and could see my wife and some other mothers sitting there routing for their children. She really looked good I had to admit. I then heard a spectator yell out my daughter's name. Tracy had grown quite a bit, and I had a certain sensation to just go up and give her a big hug, but of course I knew I could never do that. What a fantastic player she had become. I grabbed a schedule since this apparently was a travel team to see where else I might go to watch her play. Unfortunately, none of the games were near Tennessee, but if I did get to travel again, I tucked the paper in my pants pocket for future reference. I was pretty much able to see the whole game before leaving to go to the airport.

Chapter Six

Tragedies transpire in life, yet often for most people who are not directly involved with the tragedy life continues on with its daily occurrences. For the next several years my life evolved into a wonderful routine, and my apparent transition to a different life materialized quite successfully in my new atmosphere. Friendships occurred, and life events like weddings and births became part of the normal schedule. Unforeseen circumstances, however, would eventually become apparent that would alter the pleasant status quo.

In the meantime, I had become friends with a young bachelor who was the manager of the local bank where I did business. It started out as a casual friendship when I would go into the bank and we would banter back and forth to one another. A few times I had seen him eating at the local café when I went in to eat on my lunch hour. Tom would invite me to sit with him and we would get in some good conversations talking about the stock market, Wall Street and the Dow Jones average. Tom was impressed with my financial knowledge. I explained to him that I was an avid reader on the topic of finances, and in another life I might have decided to work in that field. The more we met casually, the friendship became stronger and we used to plan spending time together during the evenings and on weekends. I told him I had gone to a private school that was no longer in existence as I was always trying to cover my tracks from my past life. However, Tom never really questioned what I said, nor would he have had a reason to check on me. We were friends after all, and I did not appear to have a shady background where he or anyone else I met in Tennessee would feel the need to investigate.

We often double dated with a couple of beautiful girls we had met one night at the pub and with whom we played pool. A lot of the women in this area were drop dead gorgeous or some red hot mamas to be sure. They had these perfect little bodies that would cause any man to salivate. Where the women in the New York Metropolitan area were usually ten to twenty pounds way too thin, and had shoulder bones and rib bones poking out of their skins, these women had just the perfect amount of weight in all the right places like the thighs and boobs. Not only that, they were ideally proportioned and voluptuous. I often hear people talking about a woman's long legs, and I could not help but wonder upon looking at some of those women what was so special about having long legs, especially so if the legs were not in proportion to the rest of their bodies. To me, they just looked like their legs traveled up the body to nowhere, and I did not find them attractive at all. It did not matter to me if women had long or short legs just as long as the legs were in proportion to the rest of their bodies. Well, you can see, I was obviously enamored of these gorgeous gals and the two in particular that began to play pool with us on a regular basis.

I could see though that Tom had become extremely infatuated with Lynn. Their relationship was developing into more than something casual. One night she did question him on whether she was supposed to believe the fact that he was trying to impress on her that he was a bachelor who had never been married. Tom indeed insisted that this was true. Lynn then stressed the fact that he probably would not believe that she was a mother with seven children whose husband had walked out on her when the oldest was twelve years old. Tom loved Lynn's sense of humor and took what she said as a big joke until he looked in her eyes and realized she was not joking at all. Lynn was sure this was going to be the end of a fine friendship, but she knew it was time to put all the cards on the table so to speak. Tom had fallen way too far in love with her already, so much so that he could not just dismiss the relationship because of the fact Lynn had these children. Many people thought Tom out of his mind for him to even consider continuing the relationship, but continue he did. Lynn's children really adored Tom once the relationship became a definite fact. They had been so long without a male figure in their lives, and it turned out that Tom's affection for the children became strong as well. The situation was not always easy, especially in the beginning, because when Tom entered their lives he set some boundaries the children did not like. Fortunately, for them, his easy going personality on top of his handsome good looks prevailed, and they began to develop a rapport that was the envy of any family. Talk of a wedding between Tom and Lynn began to ensue.

I could not have been more thrilled when Tom asked me to be his best man. The whole small town was buzzing about the wedding. Many in the town respected and adored Lynn. They knew the history of how her husband had just walked away on his family one day and never returned. Many years later they did discover from some of the husband's distant relatives that he had passed away about seven years after he left his family. Lynn's children were active on the local school and town sports' teams, and Lynn was doing a fine job raising such good children. Of course, everyone in the town knew Tom as he was such an esteemed leader in the community and a valued business man. The match, though different than the standard in scope, appeared to be made in heaven.

People from all over the small town and the areas in between were to be invited to the wedding. Because of the enormity of the size of the guest list, it was decided to hold the wedding in the Cathedral in a neighboring town. The reception later was going to be at the new and recently constructed American Legion Hall, a very modern beautiful facility, not like the usual brick buildings with a hall. The women in the area worked hard transforming the large room into a gorgeous island paradise. One would not have recognized the interior of the room at all once the ladies were finished with it. As an older bachelor Tom had a lot of money, and he desired to spend a lot of his own money on the wedding and not leave all the expenses to the bride as was generally the custom. I was busy planning a bachelor party. It only seemed natural to want to hold the bachelor party at the pub where Tom and I had spent so many hours with Lynn and other friends.

Chapter Seven

The wedding was held on a beautiful, sunny September afternoon, not unlike the day of the September atrocities of 2001. Stained glass windows of the Cathedral glistened in the bright sunshine. All of Lynn's children were in the wedding, five daughters and two sons. The dresses were of a beautiful blue teal color, though each dress was of a different design to flatter each individual girl's particular figure. I would not have known the name of the color of the dresses if Lynn had not told me. I just knew it was one of the most beautiful colors I had ever seen in a dress or on any dresses I had seen in any other wedding I attended.

Lynn was an absolute beauty with her long curly blonde hair, and I could hear all the women gasping at the splendor of what they called her Vera Wang gown. Tom looked speechless standing at the altar and in complete awe of his gorgeous bride. When both their eyes met, there was no doubt in anyone's eyes of the immense love they had for one another.

I suddenly began to realize that I never had that same connection with my own wife. I wondered just what the attraction had been between us. Could I not have known ahead of time that her obsession with brand name labels and her flaunting names of famous people was essentially a weakness in her character to supplement her for some loss she had experienced when young? Like my parents, Megan was the one pushing me to go into finance, and I was too young and intellectually immature to realize I was being manipulated.

As the bridal party was being introduced to the wedding guests at the reception hall and my name and the name of the maid of honor was called, I noticed to my left, seated at a table, the gorgeous "Jaguar lady," the name I used when talking to the men at the shop.

Our eyes met briefly and I felt something turn inside me that I don't ever remember feeling before. Her beauty was breathtaking as she sat there in a most gorgeous red dress. While she was always so sweet and ladylike with me at the shop, and yes, even a little flirty, in my heart I always felt she was in a league of her own and above me in class and style. Consequently, I never pursued a relationship with her. The moment quickly passed and my attention was focused on delivering my toast to the bride and groom. A brief video was shown of the bride and the groom when they were babies and progressed through the different stages in their lives. They indeed were a handsome couple and appeared destined for one another. As the evening advanced, I had enough drinks to make me feel relaxed and ebullient and to help me really enjoy everything that was going on.

Tom did everything he possibly could to be sure I caught the garter. At this point, I was raring to put that garter on just about anyone with a skirt. Whether it was fate or not I'll never know, but the red dressed Jaguar lady was the one who caught the bridal bouquet. I became like a little kid, talking too much and acting too silly. I kept begging under my breath for God to help me. There was every opportunity to make a good impression on this specimen of splendor, and all I could do was act like a silly teenager. Somehow, we got through this fiasco, and the band started to play an endearing, soft love song. She just stood there as though waiting for me to ask her to dance, and I said something stupid and walked away. For some reason, I could not face her during the rest of the evening I felt so embarrassed.

The bridal party decorated the getaway vehicle with all kinds of signs on the windows, and cans dangling off the rear of the car. Everyone extended their wishes to the blissful couple as they drove away to the airport and their honeymoon. I stood there smiling when unexpectedly I heard this velvety soft voice beside me saying how impressed she was by the toast I gave to the bride and groom. I had enough sense then to at least say thank you and something like, "I'll see you around," and off I walked. I could just as well have not gone to bed that night. Sleep was not on my agenda apparently, partly because of the excitement of a wonderful occasion, but mostly because I could not get Jaguar lady out of my mind. The next day, I was happy to get to work, get under the body of a car, and focus my mind on other things.

Chapter Eight

I really missed Tom while he was on his honeymoon to the Atlantis Hotel in the Bahamas. There was such a need for me to talk to someone about Jaguar lady, and Tom was my closest friend. Sarah, the gal who often played pool with me, Tom and Lynn, was always in the picture, but I felt she was more like a sister than anything else.

One evening Sarah and I decided to go to the Harlequin Dinner Theater together. Sarah wanted to see a particular show, and I had nothing better to do, so I accommodated her request. Sarah was fun to be around. We laughed a lot and had an easy repartee with one another. Parking looked like it was going to be a problem, so I dropped Sarah off at the entrance while I looked for a place to park. The lobby was quite crowded when I finally got inside, and at first I had a hard time finding Sarah. In the distance I thought I saw her talking to someone, and as I walked towards her I noticed she was talking to Jaguar lady. For a moment I stopped dead in my tracks afraid to venture forward. When I stopped, Sarah spotted me and waved me to come forward to them. I did not have much choice but to do what she said. Apparently, I found out later, Sarah and Jaguar lady were good friends having gone to high school together.

Sarah introduced me to Colleen. Her pretty name fit the fabulous face. She had dark shiny hair that had a slight wave and was not too long, nor too short, but just right. Colleen's huge brown eyes lit up when she realized who I was and said, "I believe we met before. Are you not 'garter man' from Lynn's wedding?" Here we were, Jaguar lady and garter man. This evening she was wearing a figure hugging black dress whose skirt flared a little at the hem, and it had a leopard collar. My mind thought of a beautiful sleek feline and my heart started to pound.

The theater lights dimmed indicating the meal line was about to start, so we said our quick goodbyes and found our seats. Her table was catty corner from us, and across the room, so if I looked at the proper angle I could gaze upon her throughout the evening without being obvious and gaze upon her I did. She appeared to be with a group of women, and that made me feel good.

On the way home, I casually brought Colleen up in our conversation in the hope I would learn more about this fascinating creature. Sarah explained how extremely popular Colleen had been in school and how all the guys adored her. She was a cheerleader and active in town sports as well, and she fell in love with the quarterback of the high school football team. What else did I expect? Knowing this, I was further convinced she would never really be interested in me, and I dropped her as the topic of our conversation. We went on to talk about the fun time we both had at the wedding.

The next day Tom called me at work to see how things were going. He explained that they were having such a good time that they wanted to extend their honeymoon for another week and maybe two weeks. I told him that everything at his apartment was under control since he left me in charge of checking it occasionally and collecting his mail. Tom was assured by me not to worry about anything except that the two of them should enjoy themselves. I promised Tom I would notify the assistant manager of his bank. Secretly though, I could not wait for him to return. The atmosphere at the shop just felt good when Tom was around after work or during lunch hour when we would meet and enjoy our conversations which I now missed. I thought those next two weeks would never end.

Chapter Nine

One afternoon, after Tom returned from his honeymoon, I was just coming back from lunch when I saw the silver Jaguar drive unto the lot. Colleen got out of her car and went to talk to the receptionist. My name was called over the loudspeaker to come to the front desk. The receptionist explained that Mrs. O'Brien could hear this knocking noise in her car and inquired if I could please check it. After inspecting the car I detected a problem that was going to require her leaving the car at the shop. I offered to bring Colleen home if she would leave her car with me, and I explained I could probably have it finished by the next evening.

As Colleen sat in the car beside me her skirt rode up above her knees, and I had all I could do to manipulate the car in the right direction. When she gave me the route to her home, I began to realize that she lived in one of the better areas of town. Her husband must have left her well off because I knew Colleen did not work outside the home. The homes were gigantic in size, and the lawns were very green and very lush. In the distance, I could see this fabulous white house with a porch encircling the front and sides of the house. The shutters were black and a bright red door opened. Some young children ran outside giggling and sprinting around.

Colleen indicated that the white house was her home, and I quickly maneuvered the car into the driveway. The children stopped to look at the strange car, but as soon as they saw their mother get out of the vehicle they ran up to her full of excitement and with big hugs. She introduced me to the children. They really gave me the once over, but they were pleasant children and politely said they were pleased to meet me. I told Colleen I would call her the next day and let her know just what the repairs were going to entail. She shook my hand and thanked me. I wanted to hold that soft hand forever.

By late afternoon on the following day the repairs on the Jaguar were complete. I had the receptionist call Colleen to give her the details as to the cost and what exactly had been done. Colleen told Gail that her son's friend would drive him over to the shop and that she would send a check along with him to pay for the cost of repairs. Her son could then drive the car home. When Aaron, her son, arrived, I took him over to the car and explained what had been done and what had been replaced, showing him the piece of the equipment I had removed so they could see its poor condition. I noticed Aaron was dressed in his soccer uniform having just returned from an after school game. I told him I was a big fan of the sport, and he explained they were having a big tournament at his school that weekend and he would very much like to see me there. I told him that since I had now personally met one of the team's players I just might show up at the game. He gave me the times the games were to be played, we shook hands, and off he went. I watched as Aaron walked away. He had his mother's good looks, dark wavy hair, and shoulders that I am sure all the young girls found intriguing.

Some areas played their soccer in the spring, but in our area the sport was played in the fall. Saturday was a beautiful, warm and sunny day in the beginning of October. As I slowly made my way out of bed I thought it just might be a good day to go and watch Aaron and his team play. When I got to the field he spotted me walking on the sidelines and gave me a big wave. I was glad I had come. I was a little disappointed when I did not see Colleen, but the game was exciting and Aaron was proving his skills in the sport on the field. During one of the time outs I saw the silver Jaguar enter the parking lot. I sat mesmerized waiting for Colleen to exit the car. First I saw what I think they called a wedgie shoe hit the pavement with this gorgeous leg, and then the other leg followed. Colleen was wearing a pair of faded jean shorts, and I noticed many men in the area turn their heads as she walked past them. I began to get that excited though uncomfortable feeling again and decided to go to the opposite end of the field where I could look at her from a distance and not have to carry on a conversation. She sat in the bleachers next to what I presumed to be some other player's mothers. A little while later a rather good looking man came by and sat beside her. I wanted to wring his neck. Watching them laugh and talk with one another, the jovial feeling I had been experiencing began to dissipate quickly.

I felt better once the game commenced, and I could focus my thoughts more on the excitement on the field. Aaron made some outstanding plays and his team won hands down. I went over to shake his hand on the way out and refused to look in the direction of his Mom. Just as I was about to reach my car, I felt this tap on my shoulder. There she was, smiling and beautiful. Colleen thanked me for being so prompt in finishing the repairs on her car and also for coming to see Aaron play. This time I did maintain some composure as I vaguely looked for the man that had been seated near her who was now nowhere in sight. I told her she was quite welcome and that the pleasures of watching her son play were all mine while reiterating the fact of how very proud she must be of him. She explained how he was being looked at by scouts and the next year they were going to be making some big decisions for his future. On rare occasions, thoughts of my other life and family filled the core of my being, and that statement jolted me into thinking about my daughter. I realized she was about the same age as Aaron and was probably going to be going through the same course of events. If I ever felt any sadness about leaving, it was always a sadness connected to the loss of not being near, or with, my daughter. This time was no different. Colleen said she hoped she would see me at the next game on Wednesday evening during the following week, and I said I would try and make it. The realization hit me that it was really Colleen I wanted to see much more so then her son.

Chapter Ten

By Tracy's sophomore year of high school she began to think and act like a lot of teenagers do where their parents are concerned. Everything my wife said to Tracy created a big problem between the two of them. Of course my wife did not have the most calm personality, and most of the time she insisted she was always right. For her, there was no room for discussion, and it was always the case that either you do it my way, or you do not do it at all. Neither was there room for compromise or understanding. This created stubbornness in my daughter that often easily escalated to gigantic proportions where she would stomp her way out of the house.

Driving away in anger in her car was just about the worst thing Tracy could do and my wife did not know how to handle this. The two of them would go for days without speaking to each other after a fight. Even worse was the fact that Megan made Tracy's social life her own life. She wanted Tracy and her friends around constantly instead of establishing a life of her own. Tracy did not care to be around her, and this too caused friction.

The time came for Tracy to start looking at colleges and she was also being checked by soccer scouts at her games. Tracy already knew that any college remotely close to her home in Connecticut was going to be totally out of the question. Her comment would be something like, "I need to be away from this crummy town." Or, "I can't stand the people around here, and can't wait to get away." Primarily, what she did mean was that the further away from her mother she could be, the better she would feel. Yes, she loved her mother, but at the moment it was a love/hate relationship.

Megan could not help but think at times like this that it might be nice to have a man around the house, especially so to help her with sending tapes of Tracy playing soccer to the various schools requesting them and to other colleges where Tracy might like to attend. Megan was not electronically inclined and finding reliable people to help in this situation—well, it was next to impossible. Fortunately, one day, another father who was taping his own daughter's performance on the field offered to aid the family by taking videos of Tracy. In return, Megan invited his whole family out to dinner one night.

For parts of two summers the mother and daughter did venture together to check out various campuses within a several hundred mile radius. Megan would have preferred Tracy choose a school close enough where she could come home on the weekends. That was the last priority Tracy wanted, so her interests focused more on schools about an eight or more hour drive away. Sometimes Megan's Mom would go along and those times were great bonding times between the three generations. Tracy loved her grandmother who was always such a support to her and who was forever managing to come up with the most interesting tidbits of information.

Chapter Eleven

I guess I was not realizing how much time I was spending with Sarah. Spending time with her just felt so comfortable that it only seemed natural for me to just go every place with her. We would smooch up a storm sometimes, but I knew that was as far as I ever wanted our relationship to go. Of course, by limiting my exposure to just Sarah, I was also putting myself out of the ring to develop a relationship with anyone else.

Had I felt more secure with myself I surely would have pursued Jaguar lady more, but I just could not get out of my mind that she was way out of my league. She exuded class wherever she was. It appeared that some women never had to try and be part of the boys club with rough language or laughing at off color jokes because they were just comfortable in their own skin being a woman, feminine, yet assertive, comfortable, intelligent and beautiful too. That was Colleen. Her whole demeanor suggested someone special and sincere. However, I still felt she was so far above me, and that was surely because of my own probable inadequacies and insecurities. She was never in any way snobbish nor ostentatious, and always appeared to be so genuinely happy to see me when we would meet on the street, or wherever. I just figured she had no trouble finding good men to keep her company, and I often would see her with different men around town, but I never saw her with just one special person.

Many nights Sarah and I spent time with my boss and his wife playing scrabble, or double dating with Tom and his new bride. Sarah worked at the local hair salon. Therefore, she was privy to a lot of the town gossip. Word started to come in that one of my bosses' children was caught speeding and on drugs. Carl never mentioned anything about the drugs or about his child to me. How does one handle such rumors? I could not help but notice the last time when we were at the house that this particular son looked a little spaced out, but he did not hang around long enough for me to be really sure. Carl's children were usually very well mannered, and when the son left he shook our hands and said he would see us later, but we often left before he got home. As a busy teenager, it was unusual for us to see him when we were there.

One evening when we were sitting out on Carl's patio having some drinks, we could hear sirens all over town. We all remarked that it sounded like it was serious, and we hoped that we were wrong. Our evening ended amicably, and Sarah and I said our goodbyes. On the way home we did notice a police car pass us on the street going in the direction of Carl's house, but police patrols were not uncommon in the area. The police were like a friendly reassurance to everyone as they patrolled the streets of the small town letting everyone know that they were available if needed, and their presence was comforting as they always scrutinized for the unusual.

After dropping Sarah off at her apartment, I watched a little of Letterman on television and was just ready to get into bed when my phone rang. Carl was on the line saying that the family had an emergency, and he asked if I would open the shop the next day. He said he was in a hurry and would get back to me later, but explained not to worry because everyone in the family was fine. I assured him I would open the shop, put the phone back on the receiver and went to bed.

On the local morning television news I heard of a terrible accident near the entrance to town. There was mention of a pregnant lady losing her baby, but I did not catch any names, and the news then gave the weather. I got to the shop early and unlocked all the doors. The mechanics started arriving and we all proceeded getting to work.

During the late morning Carl came in to the shop and asked to see me privately in his office. He explained how his son Steve had been in a horrible accident involving a pregnant mother, and her baby had died. My heart sank as Carl looked so dejected, and also because of the horrific nature of the news. So far no one had been charged he explained as it was possible that the pregnant mother was at fault, and there was an investigation going on. Carl overheard talk that the family was going to sue both Carl's son and Carl for allowing the son to drive while on drugs because of rumors that had been circulating about Carl's son. Steve was still only seventeen. Whether this was feasible or not, Carl did not know, but Carl was beside himself, worried about losing his business, and concerned now about his son's chances of getting into a good college.

I told Carl not to worry about the shop because I would be available to help him in any way he determined to be necessary. Carl said he was going to get on the phone and get a good lawyer. The police were having his son tested for drugs and a preliminary hearing had been set for the case. Neither Steve nor the young mother had been injured, though both were mentally anxious and depressed.

Newspaper reports on the accident were relentless in their not reporting the news but rather more in printing hearsay by the local town gossips. They slandered Steve persistently without any evidence or cause to do so. Everyone, and every report, was sympathetic towards the young mother that had lost her baby. Steve was considered just another young, careless and reckless driver.

Each person that came into the shop was more interested in talking about the accident than in knowing the problems with their cars. They were not able to get a lot of information out of me though. Carl rarely came into the shop for the next few weeks prior to the hearing. His wife and son were really having a tough time. Steve did not even want to go to school and he needed to attend classes since this was such a crucial time for academics in preparation for college.

The court day finally arrived. Carl said I could close the shop that day as he would very much like his friends' support at the hearing. Sarah, Tom and Lynn came with me and we attempted to give Carl and his wife as much encouragement as possible.

The court ruling could not have turned out better. Steve's drug test showed no drugs in his system, but the young pregnant mother had been given an anti-anxiety pill prior to the accident to calm her nerves. Since in the past she had a slight reaction to the pill, she had been ordered not to drive. The police determined that it was the pregnant mother's car that was the cause of the accident and the case was dismissed. Our emotions were mixed. On the one hand, we were thrilled for Carl's family and particularly for Steve. On the other hand, we could see the devastation in the faces of the young woman and her parents and spouse.

Carl invited us all out to eat at the Grey Bull Grill where steaks and drinks were abundant. We all became aware that the routine of daily life could so easily be disrupted and we were thankful that in this case all turned out well. Of course, compared to me, no one knew better how much things could change in one day. My new life was a testament to that.

Chapter Twelve

Things did not continue to go well for Steve however after the court ruling. Going back to school was sheer torment. Everyone there started calling him a baby killer. It did not matter to them that the young mother was at fault. Indications appeared that the court had not ruled in his favor, nor that the evidence was overwhelmingly for Steve and against the baby's mother.

Steve tried to talk rationally, especially to his closest friends, but they were unrelenting in the manner in which they treated him. I will never personally be able to understand such cruelty. It appeared as though they did not even want to know the truth. Steve had always been very popular. Perhaps the students had always resented Steve's popularity, and this was their way of showing their resentment. I wondered if this were a sign of the times in this day and age where people did not appreciate others doing well. When I was in high school my friends always seemed supportive of any accomplishments I might have achieved. These friends of Steve's were just downright vicious and mean and filled with jealousy and envy. Could it be that the youth of today are not taught respect and consideration for others feelings? Yet, how can I blame the youth when we have so many adults searching the tabloids and thriving on any bit of gossip to titillate what may be to them sad and dull lives.

This was a time for Steve to be visiting colleges and filling out applications, but instead depression started to take over. While Steve did not want to go to school, he also knew that his parents would not allow him to stay at home. Yet, as compatible as Steve was always before with his parents, he could not bring himself to tell them what was happening. Had he done so, they might have helped him by arranging for Steve to attend another school or to be home schooled. Steve did not say a word to anyone, and when the attacks upon him escalated he started to just leave classes after attendance was taken and go wandering to the next town, roaming around the malls, or walking around the parks in the neighboring towns. When his parents questioned him as to the type of day he had, he would lie and say everything was great. Children often lie when they feel they cannot talk to their parents because they anticipate what the parent's reactions would be.

Steve's eighteenth birthday was fast approaching and his parents tried to get him to invite some friends over to help celebrate. All Steve wanted to do, he explained, was just to have a quiet birthday with his family. This was so unlike Steve, but his parents thought he was still upset because of the baby dying and decided not to push him to do otherwise.

During Steve's time away from school he began to solve his own problem. He knew that he would be considered an adult soon and capable of making his own decisions. Two days after his eighteenth birthday Steve met with a Marine recruiter and enlisted in the service. Because he was such a good student and a healthy looking physical young man, the Marines were happy to have him join. Steve insisted he did not want to wait until graduation, but was told he needed a high school diploma in order to join. What he was not saying was that he could no longer go back to school and endure the psychological abuse he was getting every day. Regrettably, for the Marines, Steve's lack of emotional stability could have proven to be a real detriment to his career. In retrospect, the fact that Steve was basically forced to return to school to graduate turned out to be a good thing for him, and graduate he did. He essentially kept telling himself that the Marines wanted men who were tough, and if he could not take the daily verbal abuse he would not make a good Marine. Steve did not inform his parents of his decision until a few weeks before graduation. His parents could obviously see that Steve's mid-semester grades had dropped sharply, though they had not realized he was not attending class. Steve fortunately was able to quickly get back on track once he had made his decision to join the Marines.

To say Steve's family was shocked when they heard the news would be putting it mildly. Every day, casualties from the war in Iraq were escalating. Carl thought his wife was going to have a nervous breakdown. Loud, heated arguments broke out among the family members in a family that was usually calm and mild-mannered. Many evenings in the privacy of their bedroom Carl and Barbara would accuse each other of forcing their child to go to war. In reality, neither one of them had anything to do with it. I mentioned to Sarah how I could sense the tension in the family over Steve's enlistment. She wisely reminded me that perhaps trouble had been there all along, since there was the time when Steve was on drugs and the family appeared to be unaware. Maybe their calmness was all just a pretense. I, at first, was angry at what she said, but none of us really knows what goes on in the privacy of one's home.

Graduation day, while lovely, was not the happy occasion that all had anticipated for Steve from the day he was born. Of course they had the big party and the same kids who weeks before were giving Steve such a hard time showed up to enjoy the free food and drinks. Many of the adults could not help but feel a tinge of sadness knowing that going to war could easily be in the future for this fine young man.

The build-up of tension and melancholy before Steve's departure had grown unbearable. Everyone close to the family had tears in their eyes when they said their goodbyes and they all promised to keep in touch with Steve. Oddly enough, but maybe really not so odd, was once Steve had gone to do his basic training, his parents, siblings and friends were able to get on with their daily routines and feel better. Though they were still sad, the tension began to fade away. I could remember feeling the same tension the days before I made my escape from my old life, which quickly faded away once I finalized my decision and left. That is why I was thinking that their change in attitude was really not so odd after all.

Things at the shop began to get back to some sense of normalcy, and for that I was grateful. Carl installed a tall flag pole outside the shop to hang the American flag and show his support for his son and the other young men who were fighting.

Chapter Thirteen

Business at the shop became so overwhelming that Carl decided to make use of the property surrounding our building that he owned and finally build an extension. I especially had became known as the expert on remodeling sports cars and in doing more exotic type mechanical work on expensive vehicles. Our clientele brought in people from great distances that wanted the best for their cars. Carl appreciated what I had done to expand his business and he offered me a partnership.

Naturally, I was elated at this great offer, but along with it came the request that I oversee the building of the extension that was probably going to take a good six months at least. Carl was getting older, and I could see him phasing his way out of the shop, doing more administrative work with the books along with a multitude of many other tasks that entail running a lucrative business. Carl also chose to spend more time with his family. After the episode with Steve, Carl had become more reserved, and it was obvious he was more apprehensive in the treatment of his other children.

Enlarging the business also meant we needed to hire more mechanics. Carl said I would be needed to train some of these new mechanics in working on the more specialized skills for which I had acquired my esteemed reputation. Finding good mechanics was not an easy job and certainly required more thought and investigative work than when Carl had hired me. Our country's pattern had changed because of the terrorist attacks. We had to be very careful that the people we hired were legal residents. How tempting it would have been to pay someone a lower rate and forget about background investigations. We did not want or choose to take the risk that this involved.

Sarah, knowing that we were taking on new hires, mentioned that she had a nephew from another state that was looking for a job. Jimmy had been in trouble with the law and had spent some time in jail. Because of this jail time

Jimmy was having difficulty getting hired in his own state, and she wondered if we might consider hiring him. Sarah explained that he was very good at fixing cars and thought the potential there was a good one. I told Sarah I would discuss his situation with Carl and we would get back to her.

Frankly, we were reluctant to hire Sarah's nephew, because a lot of our clientele put complete trust in our skills and reputation, and we did not want to sully any of their thoughts. In the end, Carl decided to take a chance on Jimmy. He could not get out of his mind how everyone had treated his own son Steve, accusing him even after they knew he was not guilty. Carl realized being a young teen was a vulnerable age and he felt Jimmy deserved a second chance. Jimmy did get his GED in jail so that was one step in his advancement to the good. We would start Jimmy out on the more routine work like changing the oil in cars and chores of that caliber and slowly train him as we observed his work.

Along with Jimmy, we hired three other new mechanics that were mostly older. One was around thirty-two, and two were close to forty. All three had worked as mechanics in other cities and knew of our reputation, so they came to our area requesting interviews. The individual that was close to thirty-two was a little on the quiet side, and I frankly was not sure I really liked him, but Carl had no qualms where Peter was concerned. A foolish reason I was ready to comply with Carl was that Peter was willing to share an apartment with Jimmy. This arrangement pleased Sarah because she was afraid Jimmy might have to live with her for a while.

Enlarging our business caused a great change in the atmosphere around the shop. The few of us that had worked there prior to the expansion really got along well. We praised each other's work and tried to help one another out when one of us had a problem. Two of the new older employees appeared to have a grudge particularly where Jimmy and Peter were concerned. There was constant bickering and criticizing of their work without any offer to help the younger ones to improve their skills. Peter was especially the object of scorn. Because of the strain of working in this type of atmosphere, I became irritable and out of sorts. My social life was becoming practically nil since I was so busy concentrating on construction delays and the countless other problems we were encountering.

Happily though, close to the end of the sixth month, it appeared the builders were actually going to finish on time. This seemed almost a miracle, but Carl and I could not have been more grateful. A big ribbon cutting ceremony was planned and the Mayor and a few councilmen even came out on opening day. Our business put this small town on the map and most individuals were extremely grateful that we chose to expand and remain in the area because this meant that we indirectly helped to build on the town's reputation.

Once the shop was re-opened, to include the new extension, my life reverted back to some normalcy and Sarah and I were seeing each other again more frequently. One Sunday evening when I met with Sarah she appeared rather distraught. A co-worker of Sarah's had a nineteen year old daughter who lived in the same town, had a good job, and was living on her own. The mother and the daughter spent a lot of time together and talked frequently on the phone or sent many e-mails. Twenty-four hours had gone by without a word from her daughter at all. The mother had checked her daughter's apartment and neither she nor her car were around. Sarah tried calling the girl's work place to see if they had sent her on an out of town trip which was not uncommon. The last time her co-workers had seen her though was when she left Friday evening after work. She had told them she was going to the movies with Jimmy, our new young mechanic and Sarah's nephew. Susan and Jimmy began seeing each other shortly after Jimmy moved to our town and they had been introduced. Jimmy explained that when he got to her apartment Friday evening Susan was not there so he went back to his apartment and waited there to hear from her. He fell asleep on the couch and awoke the next morning when the phone rang and Susan's mother was calling him to find out where Susan was.

A week went by and no one heard from Susan. By now a criminal investigation was in full swing. Foul play was assumed, and because of Jimmy's ex-criminal background he was a natural suspect. I was concerned on many fronts. Naturally, I was worried that a young girl might have been the object of foul play, and certainly I was concerned for my friend Sarah and Susan's mother. Selfishly, I guess you could say I was feeling terrible for myself as well since I had talked Carl into considering Jimmy for hire. I was feeling very guilty now about doing so.

Jimmy was taken into custody, but released temporarily because of lack of evidence and the absence of any body. The atmosphere at the shop was unusually strained and Peter appeared to be obnoxious in his treatment of Jimmy. I wondered how the two were surviving living together. When Susan was missing two weeks, the police got an anonymous phone call saying that they overheard Peter saying strange things that might pertain to the missing girl. Peter accused Jimmy of being the anonymous caller, and Jimmy did move out to live with his aunt. Peter was yelling and shouting, using foul language at the garage, saying that just because Jimmy moved out did not mean he would not have to still pay his share of the rent. I had to take Peter to my office and restrain him. He was told that if he ever spoke so outrageously in front of the customers again he would be fired. Like Jimmy, Peter had been questioned by the police after they received the anonymous phone call, but he too was released temporarily.

Talk of the missing girl consumed the town's people. We could not go anyplace where this was not the topic of conversation. I began to wonder when all the horror in our lives was going to stop. It started personally with Steve's accident and subsequent law suit and then followed Steve's shocking enlistment into the Marines. Now, it was Sarah's business partner's daughter who was missing. Having two suspects working at our garage certainly was no consolation either. Just when we began to think our lives would return to some normalcy with the completion of the garage renovations, we barely had enough time to recover when Susan disappeared. Would a nice normal girl choose to just leave everything and everybody she held dear and just take off for another place, or did foul play actually happen to her? I realized this was a strange question for me to be asking. After all, most of the people in my prior life assumed I was a nice normal guy too, and I just picked up and left everything and everyone I knew. So, knowing this, I was hoping that maybe they would find Susan still alive. I wanted to wish that would be so.

Sadly, after another week had gone by, Susan's car was found near the County reservoir hidden in a wooded area. The interior of the vehicle was splattered with blood, but no body was found in that vicinity. Police personnel and helpful volunteers formed search teams to cover a certain radius in and around where the vehicle had been found. Still, after several days, no body had been found.

Susan's mother was not only filled with grief, but she was torturing herself. The last conversation she had with her daughter was a little disagreement, and instead of saying their usual, "I love you," one or the other slammed down the phone in anger. This happened many times before between mother and daughter, but usually the next day they were calling each other back as though nothing had happened. She kept strangely trying to blame herself for the loss of her daughter. Sarah could hear her saying over and over, "Please God, help them to find Susan wandering around in the woods alive. Please God." "Please God, let Susan know I love her dearly and did not mean to hang up the phone in anger." She repeated this over and over until it nearly drove Sarah crazy, and Sarah felt completely inept because there was nothing she could do to help.

After three days of intense searching, the effort to find Susan was called off. Not one little clue had been found. Often I hear of wives missing with no clue as to where they might be. There were two cases in the state of Illinois going on right at this time where the husbands were suspect, but the husbands were running around living a routine life because no corpse could be found. The townsfolk attempted to return some normalcy to their lives, but in their hearts all anyone could think about was Susan.

One evening about a week later, I overheard a news bulletin on the car radio as I was driving home from work. It appeared that I became aware of many horrible instances from news bulletins either on the car radio or on television. Some boy scouts, hiking on a trail, had found some personal items that were hanging off some branches of a tree that might have belonged to a young woman. A few of the boys left the trail (without permission) to investigate, and to their horror found the body of a dead woman. They ran screaming back to their group and to their leaders. Using their cell phones, the leaders reported what the boys had seen. News reports stated the body was about the age of the missing young girl and speculation was that it more than likely was Susan. The young girl had been stabbed several times. I immediately called Sarah and we went to Susan's mother to attempt to reach her before she heard the news on the radio or television, but unfortunately we were too late. Carolyn was so distressed we had to call a doctor who immediately prescribed a sedative. Sarah spent the night with her and the beauty shop was closed the next day. The next morning, confirmation was made that the body was Susan's.

At work the following morning, the two new older mechanics were really on Jimmy's case calling him a murderer and telling him to get his butt out of there and go confess to the police. It was not long however during that morning that the police were back in the shop and took both Jimmy and Peter to the police station for questioning. Surprisingly, Jimmy's story was verified with a few witnesses coming to his aid, and Jimmy was released once again. Peter, however, was arrested and a DNA test was ordered to be performed on him.

People in our small town in Tennessee were thrilled by the Johnia Berry law that requires the collection of DNA samples from anyone arrested for a violent crime. The Tennessee Bureau of Investigation, however, was complaining they did not have enough money to follow through on the law named after Knoxville murder victim Johnia Berry according to a friend of another friend of Tom's who worked for the TBI. With the exception of what some people claimed they overheard Peter saying, most of the case was going to be circumstantial, so DNA proof would help to facilitate a conviction. DNA verification appeared to be the special God-send they all needed. TBI officials had already hired six new technicians to handle an already existing backlog. These new technicians would now be available to start work on new samples.

Chapter Fourteen

With all the shock of the town's inhabitants trying to digest that Peter was a major suspect, everyone was overlooking the trauma Jimmy was enduring. Jimmy had finally begun to think life was treating him well. He fell in love with Susan, and Susan had loved him. This fact was completely overlooked when Jimmy was accused of Susan's murder, and Jimmy now was suffering severe depression and was not coming to work. In addition, he was still living with his Aunt Sarah. He had loved his job at the shop as well, but he could no longer make himself get up to return to work. No one realized that he and Susan were secretly contemplating marriage. Now, his self-esteem had reverted back to where he had been before moving to Tennessee.

Carl knew someone that owned a shop just over the border in Kentucky whom he called and who had agreed to have Jimmy go there and work for him. The shop had a little apartment over it where Jimmy could stay until he became acclimated to living there. Trying to convince Jimmy to leave was difficult at first, but he finally succumbed. Jimmy began to realize that a lot of his daily depression was caused by having everything in the town remind him of time spent with Susan, so it started to make sense that getting away might be a big help to overcoming his sadness and depression.

Now, I was left with the prospect of hiring two more mechanics once again. This time we concurred that both Carl and I had to agree one hundred percent on the men we would ultimately hire. First, though, Sarah and I were going to take the next weekend off to help Jimmy move.

The following Monday I began interviewing again. This time we had more applicants from town and both Carl and I were more confident in hiring those who had lived in the area and whose families we knew. One young man had just graduated from the local high school and his parents owned a hardware store in the downtown area, and they were well respected people. The other man had been working in the auto repair section of the local Sears store and we both felt confident hiring these two men. They were not as experienced as some other applicants, but knowing their backgrounds was a bigger plus to us than experience because we could train them to work to our standards.

That Wednesday afternoon the news was all over town that Peter's DNA sample was a definite positive. Most in the town were relieved to know the killer had been found, but Carl and I were sad to know that we were the ones who had brought him to our area to work in our shop. The townsfolk however were very gracious to us. If anyone blamed us, we never heard them say so to our faces.

Just when we thought our lives might be settling into a pleasant non-intrusive routine, Carl and his wife got news that Steve was being deployed to Iraq. This was a family who supported the President's stance on our country's position in Iraq, but nevertheless, when someone close to you must go to war we all knew that life would not be the same in our community for the duration of Steve's tour.

Chapter Fifteen

Tom and Lynn invited Sarah and me over to play cards one evening. Socializing was like a rare occasion any more. It felt good to laugh and enjoy each other's company. As the women were cleaning up in the kitchen, after we had some refreshments, Tom said to me that he heard the good news.

"What good news are you talking about?"

Tom said, "Hey, buddy, the fact that you and Sarah are going to be married." I sat there in disbelief and must have looked horrible because Tom asked me if I was feeling alright since I looked pale. "Where did you ever get that idea that I was going to get married?" Tom stepped back and gave me a very strange look. "Well," he said, "that has been the entire topic of conversation I have been overhearing between Lynn and Sarah as they talk about dates, and who would be the bridesmaids, and I can't believe you look so shocked."

"I never Tom, ever, discussed marrying Sarah—never."

"For God's sake," Tom shouted, "Surely you must have discussed something with her considering all the time you two have spent together." At this point, the women heard our voices escalating and came into the room. Lynn inquired if something was wrong. Tom and I briefly glanced at each other and attempted to assure the women that everything was fine as we tried to change the subject. The mood of the evening had been altered however. I claimed a headache and said perhaps we had better go on home. Since it was getting late anyway, no one made an issue of our leaving.

On the way home, Sarah did mention to me that it appeared that Tom and I were having some sort of disagreement, but I told her that was silly and just blamed my headache. As I roamed around my apartment getting ready for bed that evening, I wondered what in God's name I did to make Sarah think I wanted to get married to her. The more I thought about the situation though, the more I realized that she was the only women I had been seeing for years now, and I supposed this exclusivity might give her the impression we were going to go further with our relationship. I had to stop it now I knew, but how? I understood instinctively I was going to hurt Sarah. In retrospect, I realized I had been very selfish to not have set some boundaries a long time ago. I just got too comfortable in our relationship, and I honestly could not completely say she was like a sister to me anymore because we did have sex on occasion though not routinely like you would think of someone you were wishing to marry. I suppose all would say I was extremely naïve.

Carl could sense there was something wrong with me and my attitude. I could not help but notice he avoided being near me as much as possible the next day at work. He may not have known what was bothering me, but common sense told him he did not want to find out either. I knew I had to end the relationship because there is no way I could marry Sarah. I just did not feel enamored enough to actually want to live with her on a day to day basis and have the experience of all that marriage entails. Perhaps I was remembering my prior marriage and how we were constantly at one another's throats. I also knew it was more than the worry about living with her. In my heart I really did not love Sarah. If there was a women I could love I immediately thought of Colleen, but Sarah, well no it just was not in me. Yet, I realized we had become so comfortable together I knew I would miss the camaraderie.

Unfortunately, Sarah did call me at work to see if I wanted to go see a favorite movie we both said we might enjoy. As much as I wanted to see the movie, I actually told Sarah I still was not feeling well and would prefer not to go. On the way home after work I tried to figure out in my head how I was going to tell Sarah about breaking off the relationship. I worried about the kindest way I could do this without completely losing a good friend and devastating her in the process. Nothing I could think of seemed appropriate. For two days I kept telling her I was not feeling well, and the third day she offered to come over and make me some soup, but I insisted I wanted to be alone. The fourth day I realized I had to let her know. I was acting like a child, avoiding her at all costs, and this had to stop. Three times I attempted to pick up the phone and dial her number, and three times I stopped before I could do it. Eventually, my finger slipped and hit the redial button (she was obviously the last one I called), and she was so quick to answer I could not hang up in time. I asked if I could go to her apartment and talk with her. Her sweet voice said of course as though she thought I was feeling better and ready to get on with life. This made me feel even worse. Not since I left my home in Connecticut on September 11, 2001 had I been filled with so many emotions. These emotions were much more anxiety filled though then the ones on the eleventh.

Sarah, looking like an angelic vision, opened her front door before I could even push the buzzer. Her smile quickly faded when she saw the somber expression on my face. How on earth was I going to do this? Sarah immediately offered me food and started to go towards the kitchen. I asked her to please just sit down as I had something I needed to tell her.

"What's wrong sweetie?"

I explained to Sarah that what I was about to say was one of the hardest things I had ever done in my life. She just sat there and waited for me to say more without offering any help to ease the situation for me. Her whole body stiffened causing me to take a deep breath as I straightened up my own body. She waited.

"I overheard that you told Lynn we were going to get married." I at least got that much out of my mouth.

"Why, yes, honey, of course I did," was her reply.

Shocked by her honest response I asked, "What made you think we were going to get married? What did I ever say to you that made you think that?"

"Baby," she said, "We already acted like an old married couple, except I would have enjoyed more sex, so I just assumed that was the direction we were going."

This was the moment of truth. Now was the time to be honest. I sat down on the couch, put my hands over my face and took a huge deep breath. "Sarah," I said, "I am so sorry you misinterpreted my actions. I think you are one fantastic person and I planned to be your good friend always, but I never intended for our relationship to go any further than that."

Tears started streaming down her face when she looked at me and said, "You have got to be kidding me, right?" I shook my head and for a moment neither one of us said a word. Sarah picked up a magazine and threw it at me yelling, "How could you do this to me?" She started pounding me on my chest and while I wanted to take her in my arms to console her I really didn't think that would be a wise choice.

I started walking to the door. "I'm sorry," I said. "I was hoping we could remain friends, but it is obvious that is not going to happen." I proceeded to my car.

Chapter Sixteen

At this point in my life, my popularity dropped about one hundred points. Everyone sided with Sarah, and I got a huge amount of hassle from both Tom and Carl. Oddly, only Lynn seemed to understand that it was not all entirely my fault. She called me one evening at home because she said she just had to let me know that often Sarah assumed things to be true without basis. Lynn explained how she often tried to talk to Sarah about her relationship with me and inquired of her if I actually asked her to marry me. Lynn gave details of how she always found Sarah's answers to be evasive. I thanked her for her vote of confidence, but I also said I probably should have had the common sense to know better. Anyway, my social life was now practically nil.

Consequently, as a result of my sad social life I found solace by pouring myself into my work. The car restoration part of my business was booming, so working on the vehicles seemed like the perfect solution. My work also required me to travel several times in the next few months out west and down to Dallas. While in Dallas, I stayed at the estate of a wealthy car dealer and we rode horses while there. This was a fun new past time, and it was my intention to look into riding horses and maybe even buying one when I got back to Tennessee. Perhaps I could learn to love an animal instead of a human, and in that way not end up getting flak for just enjoying the animal's friendship without strings attached.

Many customers surprised me with their knowledge of some ranches in the surrounding areas, and I became more serious about purchasing a horse and also finding a stable where I could board one. The horse I ultimately selected was a bronze beauty. The stable had some training lessons in the care and good grooming of their horses and while cleaning up horse's poop was not the most exciting thing in the world, it was a definite distraction for me, along with the brushing and feeding, and of course the riding. There was another benefit to riding my bronze beauty. There were plenty of real life attractive females out there riding horses right along with me, and this was turning out to be more fun than I ever expected. I enjoyed being outdoors, the smell of the fresh air, and the beautiful Tennessee landscape. Of course, I outfitted myself in new cowboy boots and a ten gallon hat. Putting my whole heart and soul into this new endeavor became my goal.

One day, as I was leaving the stable, who should I see riding towards me on this striking dark haired horse but my gorgeous raven haired Colleen in all her loveliness. Whoa, did her tight shirt and Jodhpur style pants knock my brains out. Those pearly white teeth glistened at me when she came up to greet me. She told me how Aaron was now playing high school football and was just as much a star in this sport as he had been in soccer. Aaron anticipated playing either sport at one of the local colleges, and Colleen was happy he would not be going far away since she knew she was going to miss him terribly. Aaron was such a good help to her with his siblings and around the house. A customer was going to meet me in another hour in town, so I had to regretfully say my goodbyes, but Colleen did say she hoped we maybe could ride together sometime. As much as I wanted to really get to know Colleen better, I was also apprehensive about starting a new relationship. However, I had the common sense to tell her I would look forward to riding with her.

The next occasion when I saw Colleen, I was just arriving as she was leaving. I secretly changed the hour I went to the stables hoping I would see Colleen, never knowing that she was actually doing the same thing where I was concerned. This time she inquired how Sarah was since she had seen us together that night at the theater. I explained that Sarah and I had a falling out and were no longer seeing each other, and this really appeared to spark an interest in her. I was sorry to see her go.

Chapter Seventeen

A few years after nine eleven quieted down, and our country was fully involved in the Iraq war situation (though technically Congress had never declared war), news from Connecticut dwindled, and my knowledge became less on what was going on in the lives of my family members. I knew that my daughter was excelling in soccer by reading the sports pages, but once soccer season was over I knew absolutely nothing at all about her, nor did I know anything about Megan's and Tracy's personal lives.

Had I been involved with them, I would have known that my straight A soccer star daughter fell very much in love with a black football player. My wife did not know quite how to handle this situation. She had her dreams for Tracy, and none of her dreams included the love of someone of the opposite race. Megan claimed she was not prejudiced but concerned that her daughter and friend would be the object of ridicule. Her first inclination was to prohibit Tracy from seeing her friend Smitty, but it quickly became apparent that Tracy would have none of any type of restriction where this lover was concerned. However, much of what concerned Megan about the relationship was indeed coming true.

One would think that our country was well beyond the racial strain that existed during the 1950's. This, apparently, was not necessarily so. The young people appeared to have developed more prejudices than society would have deemed possible. Students started calling Tracy and Smitty names, and despite the old saying *Sticks and stones can break my bones, but names will never hurt me*, the names they especially were calling Tracy stung her to the core. As a popular child, she had never experienced any type of backlash in her social life. Being a star athlete, Tracy was more used to being praised instead of scorned. This new experience began to take its toll on her school work and on her placid personality. Never did it occur to Tracy though to stop seeing Smitty. That was not an option where she was concerned.

Just when her grades should have been important to enhance her college applications, Tracy's grades were dropping drastically, and she often would not show for club meetings like the National Honor Society. A conference with Megan was scheduled by Tracy's teachers. Megan was shocked to hear how poorly Tracy was suddenly doing. The only thing that did not waiver in Tracy's life was her commitment to Smitty.

When Megan got home and confronted Tracy, the two of them got in a nasty fight, and Tracy stormed out the door. She did not come home that night nor for three days later, and Megan was sick with worry. Smitty's mother contacted Megan and told her that Smitty was missing as well. To make matters worse, there had just been a big news story the week prior to this incident where another young couple had committed suicide. The children left a note stating that because the parents were refusing to let them see one another, they could not continue on with their lives. This was a parent's worst nightmare. Megan actually wished for the first time in years that she had a man around to help her decide what needed to be done. All of a sudden, being a single parent was not all that it was cracked up to be. Megan did not even have the help of a father, or father-in-law, uncles or any male influence that she could turn to for advice.

On the third afternoon after Tracy disappeared, and after three days of Megan calling everyone she knew to include the police, Megan was sitting at the kitchen table distressed beyond comprehension with her elbows on the table and her head obscured in the palms of her hands. She was startled when the front door opened, and her daughter entered the room. Tracy's facial expression could not be determined as she walked in the direction of the kitchen towards her mother. For a moment, the two females just stood there staring at one another. Mixed emotions filled Megan's heart with a combination of anger and joy. On the one hand she wanted to kill her own daughter for the angst she had caused her mother, but then she also wanted to embrace her with relief knowing that now Tracy was fine. Ultimately, they both reached for each other with a heartfelt embrace.

Megan motioned for Tracy to sit down at the kitchen table as she walked to the stove to heat some water for tea. "I am happy you came home Tracy. I missed you terribly and was scared out of my wits for your safety," Megan led the conversation.

"I'm sorry Mom, but no one seems to understand my feelings, and I just got so frustrated I could not take it anymore."

The mother looked at her daughter, and she tried to imagine being in Tracy's position. Heaving a huge sigh, Megan finally said, "You know darling, I am not going to fight your love for Smitty anymore. You are welcome to see him any time you want, and as long as you are in my home Smitty will be a welcomed guest here as well." These simple kind words from her mother were the incentive Tracy needed to settle down with a peace in her heart she had not realized for a long time. As time progressed, her school work began to improve. The two teens just seemed to enjoy one another's company watching movies at home, riding bikes together for exercise, and talking about their plans for college. Megan began to realize she was going to feel fine and more accepting of the fact that Tracy wanted to go to a school far away from home.

Chapter Eighteen

The abundance of work at the shop really kept me busy. The situation I had leaving Sarah no longer was the focus in my life. I believe it was harder for Tom and Lynn because they could no longer invite the two of us over at the same time for those fun evenings we often shared together. That was just not going to work. They continued to invite us each individually at separate times, but the ambiance and the mood were just not the same. I understood though that Sarah had quickly attached herself to some other new guy in town. Hopefully, this new guy would not turn out to be the jerk I had been in our relationship.

Steve, Carl's son, was coming home on leave in a few weeks and they planned a pool party for the occasion which was going to be filled with sadness as well as joy. Steve would be deploying to Iraq shortly after his leave was over and none of us wanted this to happen. The war became more personal when you knew someone that was actually going to be involved.

The weather could not have cooperated more the day of the party. As I drove into the driveway the smell of grilled hamburgers permeated the air and I began to realize just how hungry I was. Steve never looked so good. His sharply defined tanned muscles burnished in the sunlight as he came up and gave me a huge bear hug. Steve seemed perfectly fine with going to war. In fact, one might even guess he was looking forward to the adventure. The strain of his leaving though was quite obvious on the faces of his parents. Everyone attempted to keep the conversation topics light and, as was usually the case with any occasion celebrated by Carl and his wife, the party was a lot of fun and enjoyed by all. I was exhausted by ten o'clock that Saturday evening after having done a lot of swimming and diving in the pool and wrestling with the others in the pool to capture a greased watermelon. By ten thirty I was on my way home and actually contemplating going to church in the morning.

As a child, my parents brought me to church every weekend, and I made my first holy communion and confirmation which meant I attended all the classes leading up to those occasions. Somehow, this does become ingrained in you whether you want it to or not. It even occurred to me to maybe go to confession, but in my heart I knew I could not come forth with what I had done about leaving my family. First of all, to go to confession one must be really sorry for their sins. I still did not feel sorry, and that perhaps was a waning factor in my personality. I often tried to justify my actions by talking to myself out loud; trying to convince God that everyone seemed to be doing just fine. So, what was the harm in what I had done? Perhaps, I considered, if I started to become more involved in my religion, God might somehow be more willing to forgive me. Hence, my desire was to go to church that Sunday.

Unobtrusively, I found a seat in the rear of the church Sunday morning, quietly knelt down on the kneeler, and said a few prayers. Overheard in the foyer of the church as I bowed my head in prayer was the softest, sexiest, sweetest voice whose familiar lilt awakened every fiber in my body. Instantaneously, I knew it was Colleen. My God, I thought, she is Catholic too. This was one unexpected plus to going to church that I had not even begun to dream about. My original reason of penance and piety towards God was quickly being overturned by lustful images of this woman who always seemed to create such havoc in my being. I kept my head bowed as I peeked towards the aisle when she and a few of her children walked down to get a seat. Stunning as she was always, I could not keep my eyes off of her nor get my mind back to worshiping. This time I was not going to avoid her. I would somehow get in a conversation with my fellow parishioners at the end of Mass until she walked by and could spot me in her view. This became a compulsion and was my personal mandate.

I heard the priest say, "The Mass has ended. Go in peace." I actually enjoyed singing the last hymn as the procession, headed by the priest, exited the church. I could see Colleen gathering her paraphernalia from the pew and checking on each child as she got them ready to leave. However, I kept singing as others were already leaving the church. Just as Colleen was leaving her pew, I immediately put the hymnal on the rack and stepped into the aisle myself. I got in a small conversation with the priest, and my timing could not have been better since it was about that time that Colleen's girls were beside me. Startled when she saw me, Colleen gazed into my eyes and said, "What a pleasant surprise. How are you?" By then we were walking down the stairs and the girls were asking if they could go to the Corner Coffee Café down the street for some sticky buns and hot chocolate. In their sweet uninhibited way, they invited me to join them. Colleen jokingly told them they should not be inviting every strange man that talks to their mother to come along with them. The girls reminded her though that they had seen me the day I took her home in my car. Leave it to the children to have the memory of elephants. Colleen then did ask if I would like to join them. Thinking how good a nice hot cup of coffee would taste at that point I said, "Sure, why not?"

With the girls in tow, conversation was not hard to come by and they had tons of questions for me. Before we knew it a whole hour had gone by. This time I was going to be the aggressor and invited Colleen to go horseback riding with me the following Saturday. You could have bowled me over when she said yes. The next week was the longest in my life as I waited for those seven days to pass.

That Saturday, I was to meet Colleen at the stables since she was going to be dropping off some of her children for art lessons first. It appeared we had a lot in common with her being a widow, and supposedly I had also lost my spouse. We talked about how hard it was to lose someone close and what it was like trying to deal with the everyday problems in life while being consumed with grief. Colleen did explain how she was fortunate to have her mother nearby who was a splendid help to her, but lately her mother was not up to par health-wise which was an added ache and burden to Colleen. She was also concerned about the possibility that some day she might have to put her mother in a nursing home. We both agreed life and its decisions were not always easy to endure. We just naturally appeared to be drawn together like most metals are drawn to magnets.

We met at the stables for the next few weeks enjoying our Saturday rides together. Aaron was going to be having his athletic banquet at school and Colleen asked if I would like to go and keep her company. I had reached the point now where I was never going to refuse anything she asked of me, so I was delighted to go. This occasion was different though because now others were seeing us together in a public place, and we did get a lot of stares from those in attendance. Actually, for me this was a good thing. I wanted everyone to know that this beautiful creature chose to spend her time with me. How lucky was that? We started spending more and more time together, so much so that news got around town we were now a couple. We enjoyed time taking the children to the amusement park or Disney movies, and the evenings were ours to savor and enjoy. I was also being asked for more advice as Aaron was putting in his college applications and getting offers for football scholarships. Every time my opinion was taken as gospel, my manly image flourished.

Chapter Nineteen

Colleen was completely altruistic. I personally don't believe she realized how beautiful she actually was, but beauty alone was not what endeared her to people. If someone needed help in town you would find Colleen there unobtrusively giving of her services. Once her husband passed away, and she realized that monetarily she was not going to have a problem, her children became her main focus. As long as she was home when they arrived from school to be available for talking, transporting to various events, or just being with them for support, the rest of the day she felt should be used in doing charitable work. Nothing of what she did was ever too much in her own mind. As a completely selfless person, she often felt that whatever was done was never enough.

One weekend afternoon, I had gone to the stables to feed my horse and do a little riding. Colleen was busy that day doing volunteer work at a local rehabilitation center. The sky had a strange luminous, light-greenish grey appearance, and on the television in the lounge area of the club house, I could hear the beep, beep, beep of what usually meant an impending storm. I really did not pay that much attention to what the message was since I was on my way out the door to leave for my apartment. Something appeared really odd in the atmosphere as I drove along the country road in my car. I could not fully understand what was occurring that was so different. It was then that I saw the funnel cloud becoming visible in the distance. The cloud appeared to be zigzagging across the sky as though playing hop-scotch and a strange feeling besieged me. Once I heard the reverberation of the wind sounding like a roaring train, my nervous instinct turned out to be full blown fear. I remembered hearing someplace that if you are in a car during what I realized now was a tornado; one should get out of the vehicle and lie down in a ditch. There were some ditches on the side of the road that were not really deep but as this funnel cloud advanced closer to me I followed my first instinct and stopped the car and immediately dove into the ditch and covered by head with my arms. Words cannot express my excruciating fear. The noise became louder, and as I was covering my head with my arms I actually saw my car being picked up and moved to the other side of the road. None of what happened took very long time-wise and eventually the noise was gone, and calm overtook the area. For a moment, I felt frozen in time and was not able to move. I slowly began to emerge from the ditch. I could not believe the devastation around me, though in this particular area there were just one or two farm homes and mostly land with some toppled trees. Miraculously my car, though it had been picked up by the wind and moved, had no damage.

The car started up immediately, and for this I was grateful. The closer I got to town though and observed the chaos all around me it looked like Tennessee had been hit by an atomic bomb. Houses looked like matchsticks, and I was barely able to trace my way home. When I arrived on the street where my apartment once stood I wished, at that point, I was not home because my apartment was no longer there. People were outside trying to gather what personal items they could. Others were locked together in an embrace crying or just plain relieved to be alive. Some of my neighbors came up and gave me a hug. Everything seemed surreal. I searched the ground for a while but quickly realized that I was left with pretty much nothing more than what I had on my back. Having my car was a blessing because those of my neighbors who had been at home at the time of the storm, and whose cars were parked in the lot, lost not only their homes, but their cars as well. I decided to drive over to Carl's home to see how they survived the storm. One would not have known that only a few miles away everything was normal and serene. The storm never reached the area of Carl's home, and Carl was fine.

When Carl opened the door he had this astonished but relieved look on his face. "I just heard on the news that the tornado hit your part of town and was just about to call you. Thank God you are okay." The reality of what had occurred finally hit me, and for the first time that I can remember since I was an adult I had tears in my eyes. I left my wife and my daughter and never shed a tear. I knew before I left my apartment area from talking to my neighbors that fortunately all were accounted for and no one had died in our complex. There were numerous deaths however being reported on Carl's television. So, here I was an adult male overcome with emotion, but no one I knew had been physically damaged by the storm. The tears would not stop. Carl led me to the couch and Barbara, Carl's wife, offered me a drink. They sat stunned as I told of my experience driving home from the stables and the ultimate destruction of my apartment.

My cell phone was buzzing. Colleen's sweet voice on the other end bounced me back to a degree of composure as I told her I was fine, but that I no longer had a place to live. The rehab center escaped damage she told me, but a mile down the road Colleen explained were many casualties, and she had stopped by to aid the victims in her usual selfless manner. She explained how she had the spare room with bath in the basement of her home and she insisted I come to stay with them for the time being. I felt helplessly grateful and accepted her invitation. Colleen explained she did not know how long she would be. Her mother was taking care of the children with Aaron's help, and fortunately they were all fine. Overhearing our conversation Carl motioned I should stay with them for a few hours anyway and join them for dinner. I told Colleen I would come over in the early evening, and I actually told her I loved her.

Chapter Twenty

Anxiety, nervousness, tension, jumpiness, agitation, edginess, restlessness all became words of description to explain the inner turmoil I was feeling. I had always been rather cocky in attitude, and experiencing these feelings made me numb and depressed. Colleen suggested I seek treatment for this disease of fear as I liked to call it, but I foolishly rejected any such suggestion. Having Colleen's children nearby was a wonderful jolt of serotonin to my system. Even in one's most depressed moment the children came up with things that always made me laugh. As the days wore on, the symptoms I experienced became less prominent, until and unless signs of a storm appeared imminent, and then in a flash the signs would all resurface.

Staying in the finished and attractively comfortable basement of Colleen's home, while accommodating and pleasant to me, was just not going to cut it for me for too long a time. I knew exactly where I wanted to be in that house, and it was not in the basement. Just going up to the kitchen in the morning for a cup of coffee and seeing Colleen in her short shorts and messy hairdo drove shivers up my spine. Once in a while when the children were not around, which was not often, I would grab Colleen, pull her up against me, and we would embrace in a delightful, long, and sweet kiss. Of course this just served to tease me all the more.

Colleen's Mom was spending more and more time with us at the house too and Colleen was considering whether or not to sell her Mom's home and move her out of that home where Colleen had been raised. It became quite noticeable that Mary was showing signs of dementia. As I tried advising Colleen with decisions about her Mom and aiding her in how she should handle all of this, it became quite evident to me that my own fears slowly were beginning to subside. Often, when we stop focusing on ourselves and become engrossed in trying to help someone else, our own problems tend to fade away and appear not as significant. This was certainly happening to me, and the feeling was good.

One Monday, when Mary had stayed in her home, a neighbor friend there had called Colleen and said her Mom was acting strangely. Colleen asked me if I would drive over to Mary's house with her to see if we could help Mary understand that perhaps she should now come and live with Colleen until they could find her a place in a nursing home. This was a tough decision for all, and we were expecting resistance on Mary's part, so we knew this was not going to be easy. Either way, Mary at least was going to come back to Colleen's for the week. We both wanted to observe Mary's actions personally and compare them to what the neighbor had been saying.

We walked up the pathway after parking the car and knocked on her mother's door. After waiting what seemed like a reasonable amount of time for Mary to answer, Colleen went around the side of the house to look in the window. Her mother was in the chair watching television. Mary tapped on the window, but we still did not get a response, so we figured Mary had fallen into a deep sleep. Colleen used the key she had to let us in, but we could immediately see that Mary's position in the chair did not appear normal. Colleen ran over to her and yelled, "Mom, Mom," and the limp body fell forward slightly. We both realized that most likely Mary was dead. Colleen screamed to me to call 911 as I was already dialing the number. Colleen attempted CPR to no avail, and I thought she too was going to collapse.

The ambulance and medics were there in a short time and confirmed Mary's death. Colleen heard them calling the police and got extremely upset with them, accusing them of thinking a crime had been committed. I could tell her nerves were shot, and explained that everything they were doing was normal procedure. Several hours actually went by before the funeral parlor van arrived to transport the body away. We stood there standing like lost sheep in a meadow that had been separated from the rest of the herd when we watched them wheel the stretcher towards the van. I had already called Colleen's neighbor asking her to please take care of the children. Colleen had called Aaron and told him what had happened and asked him to please help the neighbor explain that their grandmother was very ill and Mom would be home shortly to explain to them what happened. Colleen thought it might be better if she personally told the sad news of their grandmother to her children.

After the medics and all others were gone, we drove back to Colleen's house for Colleen to explain to the children about their grandmother's death. The older girls were extremely upset, and we could see that the younger ones did not quite comprehend what was going on, but somehow they instinctively knew to just sit quietly and watch the others cry. Colleen had to go to the funeral parlor to make arrangements and decided to take Aaron and two of the older girls with her to help decide what clothes Grandma should wear and plan a service. I stayed behind to take care of the other children.

It was around seven o'clock when Colleen and the children returned, and I had dinner waiting for us all to sit down to eat. By then, neighbors had been dropping by with casseroles and baked goods, so it was obvious there would not be any shortage of food the next few days. Neighbors in fact came in and did the dinner dishes and played with the children. Their help was extremely invaluable. Around ten in the evening, things died down and we got the children ready for bed. It was only after the children were all asleep that Colleen broke down. "My mother has been around all my life. She was there to support me when my husband died, to help me with the small children at that time, to comfort me always. I talked to her daily, and I just don't think I will ever be able to continue on without her. Furthermore, I don't even know where to begin to start doing so." Gazing at my eyes Colleen asked me how on earth I survived losing my wife and child so tragically. She wondered what I did to learn to cope. "That was why I moved around so much," I explained. "I just could not stay in one place, but I did not have small children at home where moving would upset their lives. In your case, the more stable you keep things for them, the better off they will be." Here I was giving advice on something I never experienced. I had lied so much now that telling my story seemed so natural to me, and the strangest part of it all was that I experienced no feelings of guilt whatsoever. I was becoming immersed in my own lies to the point of believing and essentially feeling they were true.

To have the sun shine so brightly when your mood is so depressed was incongruous. The day of Mary's funeral, under more ordinary circumstances would have been enjoyed and savored for its brightness, clear blue skies and delicious warmth. Inwardly, however, Colleen was almost wishing the clouds would roll in and gray the atmosphere to fit her solemn mood. A lovely portrait of Mary was displayed near the casket, and it was obvious to all that Mary was a rare beauty even in old age. Partly because of Colleen's selflessness and the fact so many admired her, and knowing Mary had also been a generous loving women, the service was packed with people of all ages from all over town. All the grandchildren stood up together and each had something special to say about their grandmother. While some of the comments were so innocent, and others created giggles among the congregation, most of them were especially endearing. Having the grandchildren speak so adoringly about their grandmother was the highlight of the day.

Once we were back at home, the sunshine and pleasant day turned out to be a blessing. The children acted as children normally do when they are young, and without a care, by changing their clothing and running outside to play while Colleen rested.

Chapter Twenty-One

Since I had taken a few days off to help with the funeral, I had a lot of catching up to do at work. The past few months had been unnerving with the tornado, the loss of my apartment, Mary's funeral, and trying to make a home away from home in the basement of Colleen's house. It was almost a relief to be back at work doing something I loved and joking around with the guys. My mind though was still not settled. My heart ached when I would observe the grief Colleen was enduring. I also needed to decide if I just wanted to take a loss on my apartment or to attend the meetings of the condo board to investigate the rebuilding of the units. I knew what I really wanted to do, and that was to ask Colleen to be my wife.

After work that evening, I stopped by the church for a prior scheduled appointment to meet with Father Girard. I wanted to see what was going to be involved in planning a wedding in the church before popping the big question to Colleen. To be outright lying to the priest seemed a sin of such major proportions. I did not even want to fathom the consequences of what I was saying as I told the Father that I had no record of my life as a child to know if I had been baptized or not. The school I attended was no longer in existence, and any paperwork my parents might have had was never recovered by me when they died. Father Girard said we could only approach everything as though I were not a Catholic, and asked if I would be willing to go through the sessions where I could receive the sacraments. I knew this was the path I would have to take in order to get Colleen to marry me, and I quickly agreed to do as the priest suggested.

There was a note for me when I got back to Colleen's house saying she was at a conference at school with the younger children, and my dinner was being warmed in the oven on a low heat. I manufactured a plan to take Colleen to a special dinner the next evening and asked Aaron, who was upstairs doing homework, if he would babysit for us. My intentions were to bring up the topic of marriage at the dinner.

Colleen appeared totally relaxed when we entered the elegant old church dining facility where the interior had been designed into a restaurant with about twenty tables. I had made reservations at one of the corner tables towards the rear that had the most subdued lighting and was the most secluded table for two. The flickering candles enhanced Colleen's beautiful skin and caused an enchanting sparkle in her eyes. She immediately grasped my two hands across the table, holding on to them, and expressed her thanks to me for helping to give her much needed strength and being by her side during a most difficult time. While I was going to wait until after we enjoyed a few glasses of wine to tell her of my plans, this just seemed like the perfect opportunity to express my feelings. I looked straight into Colleen's eyes and said, "Colleen, I want to always be by your side. It would mean the world to me if you would be my wife."

"I thought you were never going to ask me this question," she said. "I had a feeling you still missed your wife and daughter so much that perhaps you would never marry again." Slightly taken aback by her statement and the frankness of the way she said it, I believe I was more surprised than Colleen.

"I rather thought the same thing about you," I replied. "In fact, I never thought I measured up to your classy persona and stature. I knew from the first time I saw you that I wanted to be with you, but never had the guts to confront my emotions and do anything about them."

The remainder of the evening was just sheer enchantment. I explained how I had already been to see Father Girard and clarified how I was going to do whatever was necessary to be able to marry her in the church. This simple statement delighted her, of course. The rest of the evening we were exhilarated and full of excitement as we discussed dates and how we would tell the children, plus other minute details. While it was not my desire to go back to her house and sleep in the basement, I had no intention of jeopardizing my relationship with the children by starting now to sleep with their Mom. The time would come soon enough.

Chapter Twenty-Two

The next few months were filled with a multitude of things to do. I was attending meetings with my condo planning board, and work at the shop was busier than ever. Colleen was also very involved in planning a wedding, selling her mother's house, deciding what to do with all of her mother's furniture and other interior belongings, plus Easter was just around the corner. Some of the children were still young enough to believe in the Easter Bunny and Easter to me this year was really going to be exciting because of the children and the fact I would be receiving the Sacrament of Confirmation.

Aaron had also decided to attend a college about three hours away from home, though still in Tennessee, so plans were being made for him to leave home soon. One weekend, Colleen got a babysitter and we drove to the school with Aaron for a student/parent orientation. While the students were kept busy being shown the campus and entertained at some functions, the parents were busy hearing lectures about the school's policies and procedures. Safety was a big concern with recent shootings on college campuses and mothers were especially worried about their daughters' safety walking alone on campus. Young girls were urged to really not walk alone if they could help it, but they were comforted with the fact that there were blue security lights every so many feet to report problems should they find it necessary. Aaron's group of students consisted of mostly the athletes who had to report earlier than the rest of the students. Not all of the orientations were held at the same time. The date Aaron's orientation was scheduled worked out the best for all of us what with my last minute planning for my confirmation, the classes I was taking with the religious education mentors, and the selling of Mary's house.

Any spare minute we did have was spent at Mary's house sorting through her belongings and Colleen attempting to decide what should be saved for her, for the children, and what should be given away or sold. It was a daunting task that was often tinged with sadness when a certain item would bring back memories from the past of happy or sad times. With persistence however, we slowly but surely got the job done. Since Colleen had a house full of furniture of her own, with the exception of a few special pieces of Mary's furniture, the rest of the furnishings were going to be sold at an estate sale the following Saturday, and then our task would be complete. Luckily for Colleen, a serious buyer also materialized that same week. They came from out of the area and were only going to be in town for a short time this trip, so the realtor asked Colleen if they could have a look at the house, even though we had boxes piled high and the home was in disarray. Oddly enough, the mess did not seem to make an impression with the people who made an offer Colleen could not refuse. She also liked these people a lot which made selling the house easier. The home held such a unique place in Colleen's heart it surely would have devastated her to see it go to someone she disliked.

The Saturday afternoon after the estate sale seemed like the perfect time for both of us to do some horseback riding. It had been many weeks that we had done so, probably as long as back to the day of the tornado. The younger children were at a party, so we took advantage of the gorgeous afternoon. I could not help but notice though as we drove past the countryside where I had my encounter with the tornado that I started to feel some trepidation. I was happy Colleen was with me to distract me in order for me not to focus so much about what had happened. It felt good to see my horse that others had been so kindly taking care of for me. Once they heard about my tornado incident, the loss of my condo, and the death of Colleen's mother they all just chipped right in to help. Riding high in the saddle with Colleen and her horse trotting beside me, I felt a certain unexplainable peace as I became enraptured by the beautiful surroundings.

The day after Colleen and I had agreed to marry, we gathered the children in the living room to give them the news. The older two seemed genuinely pleased. The younger ones, on the other hand, were extremely blunt. Little Christine asked me if that meant I could now sleep in her Mommy's bed.

"Well, yes dear, that will be true."

"Will that be fun Mommy, or will he take up all the room that you like for yourself?"

Colleen glanced at Aaron who had a big grin on his face as did Susan whose cheeks appeared somewhat blushed. Their look inquired of their mother how she was going to get out of answering that question. Fortunately little Bobby at that time walked up to me, climbed onto my lap and said, "Can I call you Daddy now?" I actually got tears in my eyes, but I gave Bobby a huge hug and told him that would make me very happy, and he could start to call me Daddy right away. Then the little ones all stood up dancing and clapping around the room, yelling "Yea, yea!" I could not have felt better if they were my own flesh and blood. We all decided this called for a fun celebration, and we piled into two cars and drove off to the Cold Stone Creamery where the children kept begging us to put money in the tip jar so they could hear the helpers sing. We kept the ice cream scoopers busy that night.

Of course the guys at the shop had a field day with me, teasing me mercilessly. "Hey, Jaguar man is going to marry Jaguar lady," they kept saying. Jaguar man now became my new name. She is some "HMM - HMM lady, and we wouldn't mind some of her ourselves," they kept teasing. "It will be a cold day in Hell before that will ever happen," I would yell back.

The biggest decision now for us was if we really wanted a big wedding or just a small gathering among our children and a very few close friends. Both of us were leaning toward the small gathering. We knew we wanted to be married before the end of summer and before Aaron had to leave for school. My insides were going crazy not knowing if I could last that long with not having Colleen close to me. The more I felt that way, the harder I worked. All the men at the shop claimed I must have been on some type of amphetamines the way I was working them to death, and myself included. At home, any little thing that needed fixing around Colleen's house was completed in no time at all, and Colleen remarked how she was surely going to enjoy having a man around the house for more reasons than one.

Chapter Twenty-Three

Easter was early in the spring, and the experience of celebrating the holiday while living in the house with small children was sheer enjoyment. Colleen and I had gone out to buy all kinds of jelly beans, chocolate bunnies, peeps, and stuffed animals. After the children had gone to bed we placed the candy in beautiful baskets wrapped in decorated clear wrap tied with huge colorful bows.

The Saturday morning before Easter Sunday we had a light lunch and ate hot cross buns while the children all sat around the kitchen table dying hard boiled eggs. I could never in my life remember all the wonderful fuss put into any holiday. Colleen was an animated figure of enthusiasm that spread to everyone in the house. I almost ached with joy just being in her presence. In my heart, I was trying to comprehend my own feelings because they were so exactly incomprehensible, especially to me.

Perhaps it was all the religious instruction I was getting, but I could sense a change in everything about me. I honestly never felt I had done anything wrong, even though I had in the past gone off and left my wife and child. However, I began questioning more my relationship with my first wife, and I began to ponder just why I did marry Megan. I realized now I never felt the same way about her that I certainly now felt about Colleen. Did Megan and I marry for the wrong reason? Is one expected to know when they are so young? Somehow, I knew though that had Colleen been around when I met Megan, and I felt about her as I did now, there would be no question in my mind at all that I would want to spend the rest of my life with Colleen. The point became more obvious that Megan and I really married because everyone else was doing the same, and she was just as good as any other girl I knew then. What we lacked was this sensation that floods your body with tingling emotion which is exactly what happens to me every time I am in Colleen's presence. This must be the feeling of people who have long and happy marriages I am sure. There is this physical attraction that infuses the soul, so that no matter how disagreeable your relationship may be at times, neither would ever think of leaving the other because to be apart would be so much worse. Having this feeling is a validation towards happiness and helps during troublesome times to keep people together regardless. I inwardly know this must be true. Is this why I was feeling no remorse? The church would seriously condemn me if they knew what I had done and in what I was now doing in receiving the sacraments. Yet, I felt so justified in all I was doing, without any shame whatsoever. Part of my not feeling guilty I am sure was that I did not leave my prior family destitute, so I felt no sense of abandonment. I left them plenty of assets to enjoy a pleasant life. I was the one that, except for the cash I had stashed away before leaving, started off my new life from scratch. As a mechanic, I made an extremely comfortable living, and with my financial knowledge I managed to again have some good investments that I could use to treat my new family abundantly and with honor. Money was not going to be an issue either way though because Colleen's husband had left her well off too. Also, she had now inherited some more wealth from her own mother's passing.

I had such an abundance of love for these children and their mother, much more so then I ever had for Megan and Tracy. Every one of them had gone to Mass that Saturday evening and watched me become confirmed. Aaron was my sponsor.

Easter Sunday was so much fun. We had hidden the colored eggs all over the yard and even had some colored plastic eggs that we filled with small toys and money. I made sure Bobby got his share of the hidden eggs too while the other children were running around wild and at great speed. Then the children insisted that we cover our eyes while they hid eggs for us to find. Strangely, this was fun too. After a wonderful dinner of ham, scalloped potatoes, corn, salad, jello and all other kinds of good stuff, we all kind of sat around and just enjoyed a pleasant afternoon.

The next thing on our agenda was to be our wedding in May. The scheduled date was to be early in the month so as not to conflict with Aaron's graduation from high school. Plans were well under way for this event as soon as we got finished with the Easter holiday. Arrangements had previously been made with Father Girard to conduct our service on a Friday evening. We decided that all the children would participate in what was finally decided would be a small wedding. The plans were to invite a few of Colleen's closest friends as well as Tom, Lynn and their children, and of course Carl and his wife Barbara and their children.

Susie, Colleen's best friend, owned a dress shop in town and her wedding gift to us was to supply all of Colleen's children with their outfits for the wedding and tuxedos for the little guys and Aaron. Tom was going to be my best man and Susie the matron of honor. Susie was also going to watch the children while Colleen and I honeymooned for two weeks at an exclusive Resort in Arizona. Plans were to have the reception after the wedding at the church restaurant where I had proposed to Colleen. The owner had rented the entire restaurant out to us for the evening of the wedding. The tiny and intimate size was perfect for our small group. While it appeared that most of the details had already been made that Easter evening, there were still minor details that had to be finalized such as the menu for the reception; decorations, flowers, and I wanted to select the perfect diamond.

The following Monday after work I stopped at the local jeweler. I knew Colleen already had a ring from her first marriage that she wore on her left hand, so I asked the jeweler to please help me design a ring that was totally different in style. I selected an emerald shaped three carat diamond and while I am not good at describing what the jeweler did with the precious stone, I do know that everyone that was in the store at the time gasped at the beauty of it, so I was extremely pleased. Now, I had to find some way to control myself until the actual day of the wedding materialized.

The waiting proved a little easier than I expected because there were bridal showers for Colleen, where I was given the job of babysitting, dress and tux fittings for everyone, and selecting the menu for the meal at the reception. We then began to worry that we actually did not have enough time to do it all.

Chapter Twenty-Four

I could no more explain my state of being that I felt on my honeymoon to anyone than a Buddha could explain to the ordinary person the meaning of Nirvana. All I know was that it was everything I might ever ask for, and more. We delighted in sleeping together until late in the morning, and I frankly cared less about ever leaving that bed, but hunger finally overtook us. Many times we just ordered room service and stayed right in bed, but then we began to look at the beautiful sunrises, and after a few days ventured outside where we would lounge by the pool, and we even did some horseback riding. This was definitely experiencing heaven on earth.

Several evenings we talked to the children on the phone, and I melted every time I heard Bobby refer to me as Daddy. "Daddy, whacha doin?" "Daddy, you sleepin in the same bed as Mommy there? Are you goin to sleep in her bed back here when you come home Daddy?" "I luv you Daddy and Mommy."

The children were so adorable at the wedding walking towards the altar. Some of the girls spread rose petals on the white cloth preceding Colleen down the aisle. The only sadness was felt by Colleen as she wished her mother could be there to witness this perfect occasion. Aaron could not have looked more handsome either, and Colleen was so proud of the man in had grown up to be.

Of course you would say I was prejudiced, but I never had so much fun at any other wedding reception I attended. We had a three piece orchestra to provide soft sweet music while we dined, and then they let it all hang out when we got up to dance. Everyone at the reception danced, and no one showed any inhibitions whatsoever. We just all knew each other so well and were used to acting like overgrown kids, joking and being so silly that it really did not matter to us how we looked dancing because none of us had to worry about a snooty so-and-so relative mocking us or putting us down. We even paid the orchestra and the restaurant extra money to let us stay an additional hour and a half. By then, even the wait staff and kitchen help were joining us on the dance floor, and the children had a blast. What a wonderful culmination of everything leading up to this special day.

I realized soon after we returned home from the Honeymoon that life living in the basement of the home was nothing like being upstairs with the rest of the family. There was just no way to be alone—ever! Little feet followed the two of us everywhere we went, and the noise level from boom boxes, television sets, and just children yakking away at times reached epic proportions. I made a mental note to make sure Colleen and I had a special date night once a month at least. If we could not get away for the whole weekend, than at least we could attempt to get away for an overnight. The children had not had a man around the house most of their young lives, and I became their new toy in a way. They even wanted to follow me into the bathroom.

Our first weekend at home, I foolishly thought we would sleep in late, and I would then make everyone a nice big breakfast. That proved to be a big joke when around six o'clock the gang of children piled into the room and pounced right on the bed, squeezing their tight little bodies exactly in the middle between the two of us. I made another mental note to be sure and put a lock on our bedroom door. Yet, despite all the chaos, I felt for the first time in my life I knew the understanding of what made a house a home. Instead of bickering over money, and yelling at one another, as was usually my experience in Connecticut, this home with all the noise, all the activity, all the lack of privacy, was a loving and happy, precious home.

Chapter Twenty-Five

Megan and Tracy were spending a rare Saturday afternoon together at home in Connecticut. Time was drawing near for Tracy's graduation, and Megan had been accepted at a college in Tennessee. Megan rather acknowledged by now the fact that Tracy had chosen to go so far away from home. In one sense, she felt the experience of a different region away from the huge Metropolitan area where they lived might actually be good for Tracy. Maybe it was the fact that Tracy had grown more mature, but once their huge fight over Tracy's decision to date Smitty had subsided, Megan and Tracy were finally beginning to enjoy being together more without the constant bickering that had haunted both of them most of Tracy's life.

"I am really thinking of getting a job outside the home, Tracy," Megan said.

"Why now Mom would you choose to go to work after all these years of volunteer work and helping out at the schools?"

"Well, honey, believe it or not, I am going to miss you terribly. I am already beginning to feel the beginnings of the empty nest syndrome."

"Going to work outside the home is not always so great either. You have pretty much had your own choice of a schedule throughout most of your adult life, so getting a job is not going to be easy. I rather think you might find a regular nine to five job stifling."

"Actually Tracy," Megan replied, "I have been working for our local Gazette paper for many years writing stories about people from around our area, and they are losing their full time reporter who used to be in charge of that department. They have asked me if I would like to take her place as head of the department. I am not going to have a rigid schedule, and it is work that I already know I will enjoy."

"Wow, Mom, I didn't realize that. I think that is fantastic, and I change my mind and say go for it."

"Thanks, honey. Hearing that from you gives me more confidence in my decision and helps to validate my feelings."

They started planning their trip south to Tennessee at the end of the summer and arranging shopping days to coordinate around Tracy's summer job so they could get ready for Tracy's first year at college. After a while Megan began to get a pensive look on her face that did not go unnoticed by Tracy. "Whatcha thinking Mom?"

"I have been thinking very hard lately Tracy, and many long hours too, about our home situation before your Daddy died. I know the circumstances in this house were rather harsh before nine eleven. Your Dad and I were constantly squabbling, and I recognize this had to be hard for you to have to listen to constantly. For a long time I could see it affected your personality. I want to apologize to you for that period in our lives. I always blamed your father for all this fighting, but as I get older I begin to understand that I was equally as much to blame. Perhaps I was even a little selfish in my attitude towards life at that time. Monetary objects and a ritzy lifestyle seemed so much more important to me, more so than a loving peaceful home, and I am so sorry that you were the object of our differences and actions. I must admit, I always felt comfortable with this lifestyle and our beautiful home, and even though I will be living alone I intend to stay right here. I hope you will visit often once you are married and gone and that while you are in college you will bring home lots of friends."

"You don't have to worry one little bit about that Mom. You might be sorry you said those words." At that statement they both had a good laugh.

"One thing I hope you will understand is that Dad's and my relationship was poles apart, and we both should have gone to counseling to see if we could work out our differences. Please don't think that all married people acted the way we did. I know there is a good man out there for you, and when you find him learn to respect each other's opinions. I have been reading a lot on this topic, and often young girls seek out men just like their errant father instead of looking for love in the right places. They are willing to tolerate bad behavior perhaps because they feel they can rescue the individual and make them conform to what they think they want. Please don't do that. Not that your father ever treated you poorly. I just feel our constant arguing had to be hard for you to cope with most of the time. I have also been approached many times by other men since your father has been gone, but I felt I never wanted to get involved another time. Slowly, but surely, my thoughts are changing. If the right person were to come along, I would no longer push him away."

"I think I understand Mom as I reflect back about how adamant I was about dating Smitty. If I am honest with myself, while I know in many ways I was crazy about him, in many other ways I knew I was dating him just out of spite to you, to society, to my friends and to all men in general. Smitty will always hold a special place in my heart as I really did like him a lot, but love him—well, I just don't think I really did, but I just don't know. We will always be good friends and for me someone's color will never make a difference in my life."

"Why don't we go out and do a little shopping now and have a late lunch," Megan offered, and Tracy was quick to respond yes. Just mention the word food and off Tracy would go. They piled into Tracy's jeep and went to the Mall. Tracy always did the driving when the two of them went anyplace together. "I am going to miss you kiddo, but I sure as heck am proud of you too, that's for sure."

"I am going to miss you too Mom."

"Yea, right," Megan replied with fake sarcasm, and at that point they turned on the car radio and followed their usual routine of singing in harmony when driving together.

Chapter Twenty-Six

My life with Colleen started fitting into a pleasant, serene pattern. I still enjoyed my work tremendously, but now going home was the best part of my day. This kind of love was fantastic, though I must admit I was consumed with thoughts about my newest wife every minute of every hour. To me this had to be what true love was all about. One might call it an obsession, but I had no objection to being obsessed by this gorgeous woman. When I say gorgeous, of course I do mean that to me she was the most beautiful creature this side of heaven, but her whole demeanor exuded beauty from the sweet sound of her voice to the way she moved her body. Plus, Colleen was just a good all encompassing person, kind and considerate to everyone. What made me feel particularly good was the day she told me how she too was constantly thinking of me one hundred percent of her time. How great it was when I would turn my car into the driveway at the end of the day, to have the little ones run out the front door toward me with such excitement yelling "Daddy, Daddy."

Some Friday evenings we would get together with our adult friends to play cards, scrabble or some other games, but a good majority of the time we just chose to stay at home relaxing in the den with the children surrounding us. One Saturday evening, we were all relaxing in the den. Some of us were playing cards and others were watching an awards show on television. I believe I had dozed off, so when the house telephone started to ring it was as though a commercial on television got really loud, as they often seem to do, jarring me awake abruptly. Since the phone was on the table near Colleen she picked it up and said, "Hello." We all drew our attention to her wondering who would be calling us at this hour on a Saturday. Most of us probably thought it was one of Aaron's friends though he was at work. We heard Colleen say, "Oh, Carl, no." She listened a little longer and said, "Yes, he is here. Let me give the phone to him." She handed me the phone and whispered it was Carl while shaking her head that the news was not good.

"Hi Carl, what's up?"

"It's Steve," he said. My heart immediately began pounding as I naturally thought Steve must have been killed in action in Iraq. In actuality, the problem was the next worst thing that could have happened, though fortunately Steve was still alive. I understood that Steve's leg had been blown off by a car bomb and they were transporting him to a hospital in Germany. Carl was of course calling to notify us and to make arrangements for me to keep things running smoothly at the shop. He was also arranging to get help for the care of the children while Carl and Barbara flew to Germany.

Needless to say, the rest of our evening was consumed with thoughts for poor Steve. We had feelings of anger for the veracity and reality of war where a perfectly youthful and healthy young man could be mutilated in such a horrible manner as to have to spend the rest of his life under less than perfect circumstances. Then our hearts ached for Carl and Barbara, appreciating the agony they must be enduring at this point. We wanted reasons and questioned why it had to happen to Steve, but in reality we knew that this was now a fact about which we could do nothing but give Steve and his family support. Colleen had tears in her eyes as did some of the girls.

I made arrangements to take Carl and Barbara to the airport the next morning. After our initial greeting, when I picked them up in front of their home, the rest of the drive to the airport was quiet and somber with each of us wrapped in our own thoughts. At least the weather was a good day for flying, and this was especially important to Barbara who hates flying under any circumstances.

We did not have the heart to do much of anything else the rest of that Sunday and literally just sat around in somewhat of a stupor. I did make a few phone calls to tell the men at the shop, and some of Carl's other friends. Just talking about the situation was hard to do. Many wanted answers to their questions which I did not have.

When Carl called the next day after seeing Steve, they said they were surprised to see him appear to be in a rather good mood. They could not be sure if this were a front or perhaps the result of some of the medications he was taking. Every person they met in Germany appeared to be very gracious and compassionate from the time someone met them at the airport, to the hours spent in the hospital among a caring staff of hospital personnel. Steve would probably be in Germany for a few weeks and they of course would stay there during that time. I assured Carl not to worry about the home front as we had everything covered. After the predetermined time span, Steve would most likely be transferred to Walter Reed Army Medical Center in Washington, DC.

Colleen and I immediately started working on a plan with Tom and Lynn. The idea was to create an arrangement where we could take turns going to Walter Reed for the long duration of care and rehabilitation that was surely going to be required for Steve. We figured that Carl and Barbara would not want to both be at Walter Reed together for the many weeks required for Steve to be there, so we thought that one of the women would go with Barbara the week she would go, and the week Carl was to be there one of us guys would go to be there with him. This was going to be a long and arduous task, but we felt it was imperative that we do so.

Carl nearly broke down with emotion when I explained our plans while talking to him the next day on the phone. Obviously Steve's injury, the change in the time zone, the lack of sleep, being in a strange area without the rest of the family, not eating properly, the heartache of everything, all combined to work on Carl and Barbara's fragile nerves. It was crucial at this point they too not break down completely. We tried thinking of various things to do to keep them focused and motivated for their son. The task was not an easy one.

A young woman college graduate that was home from college, having just received her Bachelor's Degree, heard about the news and offered her babysitting services. The young lady was the daughter of Lynn's friend from her church. She would rotate babysitting at the homes on the weeks the mother of that home was with Barbara at Walter Reed. Barbara's children were older and their home was near the shop, so they always had someone around in case of need. All three families offered to contribute to paying the babysitter even though she said it was not necessary, so that was one obstacle that was out of the way.

Carl and Barbara had been notified that the average stay at Walter Reed for most of the recruits injured in Iraq was up to ten months. Once Steve was back in the states at Walter Reed, the plan we had all prepared appeared to work fine with only minor glitches. Some communication problems occurred when talking with case managers and civilian care coordinators who while being civilian sometimes did not appear to understand the system. The amount of paperwork alone required for a typical soldier was frustrating because of the fact that there were so many different Army commands involved.

We all felt we needed to learn a lot about Steve's problems if we were going to be beneficial in helping him get back to leading a somewhat normal life once again. Steve's injury was an above the knee amputation. Since this is an amputation in the thigh the whole body weight cannot be held on the stump, but a person is able to sit with this type of amputation. We learned that pre-prosthetic training was going to be extremely important with this type of injury, but Steve's youth and good health would be a great advantage in this endeavor. We had to look for signs that Steve might gravitate towards a depressive state of mind. Though being depressed was not unusual, this stage, however, is often crucial for the healing process. The same time period when some patients are feeling a multitude of emotions happens to be the period when the prosthetics are fitted to many patients right after the wound is closed and the stitches are removed. Not uncommon for a number of patients is the phantom sensation they feel as though the limb is still present. Feeling you still have a leg when none is there plays havoc with your brain. This sensation usually does disappear with time. In the meantime, there were concerns for burns, and blisters from the friction of the prosthetic. Many of the soldiers, the wives of the soldiers, and mothers expressed a desire for some type of "Handbook" that could explain the life of the patient and what the patient could expect to happen while it was occurring. Barbara especially was frustrated at not finding the information she so desired, so she bombarded everyone in sight with tons of questions.

As the months flew by, we all began to gain a certain confidence that while tragic indeed, Steve had the type of personality that in the end was going to help him rise above and beyond all obstacles and overcome them. This was a good feeling.

Carl and Barbara knew enough people through their business where they could pull a few strings and have Steve transferred to a hospital in Tennessee once it appeared he was capable of being moved. This would certainly facilitate being able to see Steve and hopefully help to elevate Steve's mood. The fact that Steve would be close to family and friends was also a positive in the move to Tennessee.

While undergoing the many weeks spent in Washington, and being extra busy at the shop, we were also busy planning a party for Aaron's high school graduation and arranging our schedules so we would be sure to be home for that special event. As often happens in life, we were combining happy and sad times together, and under the circumstances everyone seemed to be handling things well.

I could not have been more proud of Aaron than if he had been my own flesh and blood relative on the day he graduated. I don't feel I was at all prejudiced when I thought Aaron to be the most handsome of all the graduates. He won just enough awards to surpass the pride we already had in him. Since it rained very hard the day of the graduation, the party after graduation could not be held outside. The house was large enough to easily accommodate the large group of people who attended. With the use of tents and the garage areas, the rain proved not to be such a major factor. Aaron took two weeks off to go and spend time with Steve. Aaron's presence turned out to be a real morale booster for Steve.

Chapter Twenty-Seven

Not only had our pleasant lives seen upheaval and stress, the world situation was full of mayhem too with a huge housing market decline. Illegal immigration was a hot topic blistering tempers all over our country, while the war in Iraq was still going on with some saying vital improvements could be seen, and others condemning the whole process. Primary elections for choosing a new President were making history every day all over the United States, and this appeared to be happening with perpetuity. Why did our country feel we needed the length and expense of such a long political process when in other countries they can accomplish the whole course of action in a matter of weeks? For the first time, we had a black person running in the primaries for President alongside a woman. Shootings were happening on college campuses, in homes, at the Mall and fast food restaurants. If one were to listen to the news every day they could be consumed with anxiety and/or depression. Some of us found it better not to even listen to the news, so at least when we were home life could be pleasant and comforting.

Not that everything in our lives was a bed of roses by any means. Two of the newer hires at our expanding shop just could not seem to get along. One afternoon I had to meet with each one individually in my office. The only thing I could extract from either one of them was "attitude." Something serious was happening between the two, but they were not about to tell me. I told them both that either they would learn to get along, or they would be fired. Their attitude was not productive and it tended to upset everyone in the surrounding area. Firing anyone would not be easy for us either since finding employees educated enough to have the knowledge it takes to work on these expensive cars was getting extremely hard. One of the men had children, and I really hated to have to fire anyone, but neither could we tolerate the turmoil they created amongst each other and the rest of us, not to mention the customers.

For a few weeks after our talk, things at the shop appeared to be on a more even keel, and I was grateful I had the talk with the guys. Unfortunately, the peace did not last. Apparently, one of the two guys was having an affair with the wife of the other man with the children. Details of this affair became apparent to me when I was having lunch with Tom at the café. A friend of Tom's wife worked at his bank and the gossip among the bank personnel was running rampant.

Knowing this information however was not an advantage for me because I could see no purpose it bringing it up to either man. What they did outside the shop was their own personal business as long as it did not affect them while they were at work, yet I could sense the situation was reaching a boiling point. Colleen stopped by the shop one afternoon to pick up some personal papers I needed for her to take to the bank that were of interest to both my personal and business life. Colleen actually obligingly offered to do this errand for me since there was a deadline that needed to be met, and I was not sure I could get away from the shop.

The wise guy who was having the affair immediately said some sexist remark upon seeing Colleen. Her appearance did have a way of setting off even the most complacent male, but the man who had the children just could not take listening to the jerk. He said, "That is the bosses' wife, so keep your mouth shut."

Wise guy of course said, "You are not my keeper, so stop telling me what I can say and not say." Pops, as the young father was called, stood their glaring, and the jerk said, "Are you looking at me," mocking what the actor Robert De Niro had said in a movie. Words continued to fly back and forth while fists began to thump and hard punches were made. The guys were rolling around on the ground, banging against some of the expensive cars and blood was spattering everywhere. Colleen ran screaming for help. I could hear the commotion while I was tending to business on the phone. The noise escalated as Colleen ran through the doors. "Come quickly, two of your guys are in an awful fight." Several of the other guys had heard Colleen scream and they were already attempting to pull the two apart, but some of them were getting slammed in the face and beginning to bleed themselves. The guys just were not stopping. Colleen had the sense to call the police. Fortunately, the police did show within minutes along with an ambulance. Even the police had a difficult time pulling the two men apart, but they eventually succeeded.

Of course, that was the last straw, and the men were both terminated immediately, but I later had second thoughts about Pops who was basically a good worker. I began putting myself in his position thinking how I would feel if a co-worker of mine were having an affair with my wife. I had also heard he was defending Colleen that day and that is how the whole fight started.

Besides, he was a good worker and one that we needed at the shop, not to mention I was concerned about him feeding and taking care of his family. Individually, the guys were beaten badly enough that they were both taken to an area hospital. With the fury I was feeling I was not about to visit either one while in the hospital, but when I heard that Pops had been sent home, I picked up the phone to call him that evening. My intentions were to reinstate his employment, but I sat there only holding the phone and not dialing. I began thinking that while Pops was a good and efficient employee he was also often mean and hostile when someone disagreed with him. I could not deny, however, that Pops was mature with adult responsibilities, yet because he reached a mature age he should have acted in an adult way. What he had done in defense of my wife might be considered by any macho male something to be commended. Yet, we needed someone in the establishment that would not use his temper when it came to solving problems. The day I had the two men in my office to talk was not the first time for either of them. Ultimately, I put the phone on the receiver and decided it was time to fire both men. Businesses are never easy to run, and that is exactly what Carl and I had, a business that needed to be managed efficiently. It was not our responsibility to supervise someone else's failures and temperament. Life can be tough, yet adults had to stop making excuses for failures in their actions that they continued to perpetuate, especially so when they actually knew better.

I began thinking that Carl and I could start grooming Steve to work in the shop. In fact, the more I thought about this idea the more I became entranced by it. Steve's leg injury did not affect his brain after all, and he already had excellent knowledge of working with cars from the many hours he and Carl tinkered on simple car repairs when Steve was a youngster. As a cub scout, Steve spent many hours with his Dad carving and sanding wooden cars, and also they would repair and redesign old bicycles. I could not wait to tell Carl, who when he finally heard about it was also ecstatic by the idea. Giving Steve something to envision for his life in the future was the turning point for Steve in the way his attitude changed in his thoughts about a more positive recovery. There were so many pluses in having Steve work with us. Naturally, he would feel comfortable about familiar places and things and could afford a good living doing this type of work. It could only be a plus having someone in the shop that was real family to Carl and as good as family to me. Strangers often cry nepotism when wealthy families hire their own relatives, but why not I ask? If you put all your life savings into running your business than who is better to hire but your own relatives? At least this is true for those family members whom we know to be competent and efficient. Perhaps nepotism had no place in government jobs, but when the business involved your own money, I felt this to be a wise decision.

Chapter Twenty-Eight

In spite of all the disruptions and upheaval in our lives, I can't remember ever being so happy. My existence revolved around Colleen and our beautiful children. Our dispositions blended well, and our powerful love for one another was beyond comprehension. We still, on occasion, had the opportunity to ride the horses, or rather we squeezed in the time, but most of the time was spent with the children doing family things. I would miss her terribly the weeks she went with Barbara to Walter Reed. During those times she was away, it became quite apparent to me just what she did every day around the house so willingly and without complaint. On those days, I would come home and the bed would still be unmade, and the clothes I took off were still on the floor. I had no problem about picking up my own clothes, but Colleen always managed to get to them before I did. The laundry basket got full of all of our dirty clothes. We did not hire the babysitter to clean as a maid would do because she needed to transport the children to their various activities and keep watch over them, so the cooking and all the other preparations that needed doing around the house were left up to me, or Colleen, when I was away. Obviously, Colleen was much better at keeping things running smoothly even though on most days she too was gone most of the day.

In all the years since that day on September 11, 2001 when I made my decision to start a new life, my intentions were to never speak of what I had done again. Lately, however, in my comfort zone with my new life and family, I had this uncontrollable urge to want to tell someone, and the one person I wanted to tell the most was Colleen. Thoughts about our conversation consumed my mind on the rare occasions I was alone. Surely we were so much in love that once she heard my explanation she would understand my situation fully. Or, would she? Would Carl and Tom think I had deceived them all these years by not telling them I had been married before? What would they really think about my leaving another wife and child and under the worst type of circumstances imaginable? Was our friendship stable enough now that they would not judge me?

Perhaps it was because I now became more religious that I had these feelings of wanting to confess everything. My new family and I were very active in our church, and we attended Mass every week. Yet, I did not feel comfortable going to the one place where I might receive the most forgiveness, and that was in the confessional with our parish priest. My religion now gave me a reassurance I had never experienced before. I suppose when one is happy, it is easy to follow the rules and restrictions of a religion. When the rules go against something in our lives we choose to do where the church may not approve, we then start making our own rules and saying to ourselves, "Why do we need religion anyway?" This was a period in my life when I found my religion as a strengthening process to my disposition, soothing me when I prayed, and I felt that indeed my prayers were answered every day I got to spend with Colleen and these precious children. Possibly, this is why I was getting these urges to tell someone, anyone, just what I had done in my previous life. Maybe I was having some inner experience of guilt feelings. My internal conversation would banter back and forth and say yes tell someone, then no you had better not. Back and forth, back and forth that at times I felt I was becoming a fanatic about the whole situation.

Could it be I felt by confessing to those I loved I would console a feeling I didn't realize existed? Was I selfishly trying to ease some innermost guilt? Unconsciously, I must have suffered more from what I did than I ever wanted to admit. I was brought up with a reasonable amount of morals, and one cannot deny the influences that form when we are young and impressionable. Knowing what I did was wrong must have instinctively been working on my inner being the entire time after the episode occurred. How easy it would have been to just blurt it all out to my wife those many intimate moments we were alone together with just the two of us. Often Colleen would look at me and say, "Darling, you seem preoccupied, is something wrong?" Obviously, my concerns and desires were beginning to control the way I acted, and it influenced my outward appearance as well. Two or three times I started to tell my story to her, and fortunately in those instances something happened to interrupt what I was going to say, and the matter was dropped.

Something most unusual occurred that gave me a complete change of mind. A "breaking news" bulletin came on the television telling of a Governor being caught in a scandal with prostitutes and a call girl ring. The indignity of it all was a complete disgrace to his family, to his constituents and to all those who had put their support behind him. Television pundits had quite a day with the telling of this story, and it did not help that a young woman almost twice as young as the Governor had a fling with him around Valentine's Day. I felt as though I had been zapped in the head as I watched the turn of events and the headlines in the newspapers. Every available news station carried this story. I finally grasped the full force of what would happen if I told my own story, even if my intentions were only to tell it to family. I could no longer be sure they would accept what I had done. I fully realized that what I had done could have easily been highlighted in the same manner as the Governor's story and perhaps even worse because my story was so deeply personal to a lot more people who had suffered during the demise of the Twin Towers on September 11, 2001. This account, in essence, would be a story that would be of interest around the world. I vowed that day, then and there, that I would never, ever tell my story to anyone no matter how much of a desire I might have to do so. I had a good thing going, and I was not going to jeopardize it. As a sort of relief of finally coming to this decision, I decided I wanted to take Colleen away for a long weekend to show her how much I appreciated her love. So much of our time lately and been taken up with our visits to Walter Reed, and getting Aaron ready for college. We began neglecting our relationship and falling into the trap of many other married couples. I promised myself I would no longer let this happen.

Chapter Twenty-Nine

Colleen was thrilled when I showed her the reservations to one of the top ten Bed and Breakfasts in the nation. She was full of excitement as she packed her clothes. We were not normally the type to visit B&B's, but since this one was so highly rated, especially by a very popular television host, I thought it would be fun to try something different. Colleen whole heartedly agreed.

With the family situated and all the plans falling into place, we drove off for what turned out to be a very pleasant long extended weekend. We could spot the beautiful mauve colored Victorian structure several blocks away with its white wrap around porches filled with white wicker rocking chairs. The description of our room stated it was the honeymoon suite that had an original claw foot tub in the bathroom. We were not disappointed when we checked into an extremely spacious suite with king sized bed, lounge chair, and a multitude of windows draped with lace curtains that created an illusion of soft, bright lacey shadows.

If there were any drawbacks, it was the fact that the buildings had no elevators and we were forced to carry our luggage up thirty-four tiny steps. With good planning of our trips up and down the stairs, we managed this problem just fine. Shortly after we arrived, the establishment served tea and crumpets. We met and conversed with a delightful couple as we enjoyed the goodies. Not more than two hours later they were serving wine and cheese and fruit in the dining room which you could take out to the Victorian parlor or outside on the porch. Having a late afternoon tea every day and then the wine and cheese certainly did not keep us from going out to eat later every evening though.

While one can enjoy the ambiance of an old Victorian structure you do give up certain modern day amenities as was made clear the next morning when Colleen planned to luxuriate in the tub. The size of the tub looked like it was better able to fit a pygmy and once Colleen managed to step in she had difficulty getting out of the tub, and of course being soaking wet did not help. Plus, the shower curtain surrounded the inside of the tub causing the curtain to stick to your body when you were taking a shower. Colleen became frustrated trying to figure how to remove herself from the tub, and the fact that she started laughing hampered the removal efforts even more. I finally had to go to her rescue and we both got laughing so hard we both slipped into the tub. This situation brought us even more amusement when we related the story to friends once back home again.

Sizing up the other guests each morning was an enjoyable pastime when we went down to breakfast. This facility was large enough where if you missed breakfast it would not have mattered. We had heard of some places where the owners appeared quite insulted if you were not there at breakfast time. However, the first day's breakfast was so delicious we certainly did not want to miss any of them. You could immediately tell those who were friendly and those who were not. One couple came down with books that they immediately opened upon sitting down. The message was obvious, that we do not want any small talk, and we do not have time for socializing. The other guests had no problem leaving them totally alone. Others were just delightful and friendly and could not be more accepting of others. Breakfast time provided us with some good laughs, and then the rest of the day we spent doing as we pleased.

The days were spent walking on the boardwalk and visiting the shops in the small town. One afternoon, I decided I might like to do a little fishing at the lake and Colleen said that would be fine as she would like to enjoy reading out on the high porch deck overlooking the water. When I returned from fishing, I peeked out at her on the porch, and she was really concentrating on reading her book. I snuck up behind her and gave her a kiss on the neck. She looked up at me, and her lips found mine and our kiss was warm and delicious.

I inquired of her, "Whatcha reading honey?"

She answered with a question. "Do you think it is ever proper to lie to someone?" Her question rather shocked me as I wondered from where the question surfaced.

"Why do you ask?" My God, did something happen where she learned how I came into her life? After I finally decided I was no longer ever going to mention what happened, was I now being confronted with the very thing I wanted to forget?

"Oh," she said, "I am reading the *Memory Keeper's Daughter* and the husband tells a huge lie in the book, but in some respects I can understand why he did it." Relief overcame me as I had her further explain the details of the story. Somehow, I knew though that the lies I had been telling were not of the type to be forgiven, and I was glad when she suggested we go to our room to enjoy more pleasant things with one another.

As we were driving home, we promised each other to try and take small trips like this more often in the future. We both felt rejuvenated and wonderfully alive.

Chapter Thirty

Aaron appeared to be enjoying his new freedom at college. He had only been home once after we took him, and we did not expect him to come home again until the next family holiday.

One evening when I returned home from work, Colleen said she had heard from Aaron and he and a bunch of the other students had a free weekend from sports, and they were going to visit a friend on the east coast. While we really did not want him to go away, we knew as parents we had to let him spread his wings, and he was of an age where we really had no more authority over him except essentially to pay his bills.

What I did not know at the time was that the friend on the east coast was actually my daughter and they were all going to Connecticut. Megan was thrilled to be having a group of Tracy's friends come by to stay for the long weekend. The house certainly had enough bedrooms to accommodate them all, and Megan even decided to rent a limo to take them all into New York City to see a play on Broadway. Except for Aaron's visits to see Steve at Walter Reed Hospital in Washington, DC, Aaron had never been to the east coast before, so he was naturally excited. What were the odds that Aaron and Tracy would be attending the same college?

Before Tracy left for school, she and her Mom took a cruise together to the Western Caribbean, and their last big celebration was a wonderful bonding experience for the two of them. Every evening they enjoyed dressing up to eat a five course dinner in the fancy dining room, and then they would go to see the live shows in the ship's theater. From there each evening they would go dancing. The ship provided enough paid escorts, or gigolo's as some people liked to call them, that were specifically trained to ask women of all ages to dance, so they were not at a loss for men with whom to dance. Besides the escorts, the women attracted enough other men on their own to also keep them dancing until the wee hours of the morning.

When it finally came time for Tracy to leave for college, the separation was hard for the both of them. The two women had weathered tough times together with the loss of their husband and father to one of the world's worst tragedies. They found it rough during this period just trying to cope with life and with each other. At a time when they were most at peace and had finally begun to enjoy one another as not only mother and daughter but as friends as well, it seemed ironic that this was the chosen time in their lives when they would finally have to be separated. Somehow, they got through those horrible days of saying goodbye and now this was going to be Tracy's first weekend home. Megan could not have been more excited about the upcoming visit and the fact that Megan was bringing along some friends.

We talked to Aaron on the phone, but as usual with kids, you did not get any more information except the bare essentials. We knew he was going east and that a group of them were going together. He promised he would keep in contact by cell phone, and implied that he was too busy at that time to give further details. Colleen and I looked at each other, rolled our eyes and shrugged our shoulders. He did mention they were going to see a show on Broadway, and he appeared genuinely excited about that.

As promised, Aaron remembered to call when he arrived at his destination, but he didn't say where he was, he just whispered into the phone, "Wow, Mom and Dad, you should see this mini mansion," as he called it. "This whole area reeks of money." Then he said he had to go because they were being called outside to eat at a barbecue with some of the neighbors. That was the end of that conversation.

When the weekend was finally over, and we knew Aaron had safely returned to school, strangely, Colleen and I both felt a lot better. I say strangely because in reality we had no better control over Aaron away at college than we did with him on the east coast, but perhaps just knowing we could reach him quicker when he was closer to home put our minds at ease. Aaron said he had a fabulous time, and we were happy for him. Soon Aaron would be home for the semester break, and we were all looking forward to his visit. Since he had made the long trek east, he did not ask to go to some warmer climate this year for spring break, and we did not encourage him to do otherwise. We missed Aaron, and we were looking forward to spending time with him.

Chapter Thirty-One

Steve was finally released and would be coming home. He had learned to walk quite well with his prosthetic leg, and when he was wearing long pants it was hard to tell Steve ever had a problem. Everything about his appearance seemed quite normal, with the exception of a slight limp when he walked. Carl and I worked together to configure a dolly where he could lie under the cars to do repairs and yet be able to get himself up easily after he was finished. I could not help but think how beautifully not only Steve, but his whole family, coped with the many problems they had been forced to face. I never heard words of complaint from any of them, and they could not have been happier to know that Steve was now going to be at home. They would no longer have to worry about him fighting in a combat zone.

The big test was going to be with Steve's high school sweetheart. When notified of Steve's injury she did not react in a way we thought was normal and barely stayed in contact with Steve the entire time he was hospitalized. Yet, Steve assumed everything was going along just fine.

We heard rumors that Stacey had been seeing other guys once Steve went to Iraq, but Steve apparently did not know about them. The one guy she was seeing the most left town just about the time Steve was discharged causing Stacey to start showing up at Steve's home. Carl remarked to me that Stacey appeared to be very abrupt when talking to Steve. The times she arrived and Steve's prosthetic device was not on she almost cringed and walked away. Steve, though, was completely unaware of any differences in Stacey's attitude. It was obvious he still adored her.

There would be nights that Stacey was supposed to come over to Steve's, and he would be all excited sprucing himself with clean clothes, and combing his hair, only to wait hours for her to come. Stacey would never show, and if he tried to reach her she did not answer her cell phone. Much later in the evening Stacey would call and say she was sorry she didn't make it over to the house. She stated she had a horrible headache, and when she rested she fell asleep. Steve always believed everything she said to him.

However, every time a group of Steve's buddies, both male and female, would come to visit in a group, Stacey was always among them, and she would never complain of headaches at those times. It was obvious to me she did not want to be alone with Steve; she just did not want to miss out on the group fun. Often family members or friends would notice Steve try to touch Stacey in an affectionate manner, and she would quickly avoid his contact. We were all worried how long this façade could continue. No one had the gumption though to mention any of this to Steve. Right now, if Steve seemed unconcerned and was happy, that was really the most important scenario.

One of Colleen's daughters was working out at the gym one afternoon and overheard a conversation between Stacey and one of her friends. Stacey was saying, "Steve's repulsive to me. I could never marry him."

"Then, why do you keep leading him on for heaven's sake?" the friend inquired.

"It is none of your damn business what I do where Steve is concerned," was Stacey's reply.

"Maybe not, but I just don't understand how you could be so selfish in leading Steve on all this time. We all know too that you have been dating other guys when you feel like it. Steve is too nice of a guy for you to hurt him like that, and any girl would be lucky to have him. He does not deserve the likes of you."

The other girl walked away, not waiting for Stacey to reply. Colleen later told me of the conversation, and it made me sick to my stomach. Steve would be devastated to think that Stacey felt the way she did. After all the months in rehab and the many months spent with a psychiatrist, we wondered why Steve had to love someone who obviously was not going to reciprocate that love. We could find no solutions though. We also felt it better to keep this overheard conversation to ourselves and not tell Carl and Barbara. They had enough on their minds already.

Steve was doing remarkably well working in the shop, and his easy going compatible personality was conducive to creating a pleasant working atmosphere. In fact, it was a joy when he would arrive every day at work. His smile was contagious, and it appeared everyone was in love with him except the one person who should be, and that was Stacey.

One day, a beautiful young female reporter from our town's local paper came into the shop to inquire about Steve for an article she was writing about soldiers who had experienced the war in Iraq. She had heard Steve worked at the shop and said she did not mean to disrupt the business, but inquired if she could just have a few moments to set up an interview time with him some evening at a place of his choice. I called Steve over to meet her, and he was using his crutches as he had been working under a car and chose not to wear his prosthetic device. The young reporter did not flinch in the least. Her eyes lit up when she saw Steve's face. There was no doubt Steve was a handsome man and he had this flirty way of looking at the reporter that made her appear flustered. Steve said he would be happy to be interviewed by her and set up a time to meet her, for the first time, for fifteen minutes the following night at his home.

We all teased Steve after the reporter left. Steve picked up his crutch as though he would sock one of us with it as we all scattered in different directions. Guys can be like little kids when they get together, and we were relentless in our teasing of Steve. We were calling him a big war hero and Mister Popularity, and we just carried on repulsively. Fortunately for Steve, a customer came into the shop and things settled down again.

After the first meeting with the reporter, Steve remarked to Carl that the reporter looked so familiar to him. They got out Steve's high school yearbook and sure enough her picture was in it with his class. She was a beauty even then, but she apparently was not in with Steve's group of friends, so he just remembered her gorgeous face, but not her very much. He could not wait for their next meeting while he wondered where she had been all his life.

Steve even set up an appointment on an evening he hoped Stacey would be there as he wanted her to meet the reporter. However, that was one of those nights Stacey claimed a bad headache and she never showed at the house. Steve did find out that the reporter remembered him very well from high school. She insisted Steve was always way too popular for her, and besides they were both going steady with other people at the time. For a strange second Steve almost felt a tinge of jealousy when he heard someone else had been dating her.

One night when the two were meeting and Stacey was not supposed to be there; Stacey arrived unexpectedly and was taken aback when she saw Steve in deep conversation with the pretty girl sitting beside him. Stacey made a really nasty remark and Janice, the reporter, handled her with such class by apologizing herself as though she had said the nasty things. "I am so sorry," said Janice. "I didn't know Steve was expecting you, and he did want me to meet you." Both Steve and Janice were shocked by Stacey's offensive remark when she essentially used a nasty four letter word saying, "Go, F--- yourself."

Stacey never heard Steve talk to her in such a loud argumentative voice as he did when he screamed, "Stacey, what in the Lord's name are you saying? Don't you ever let me hear you talk that way to any of my friends again."

"Oh, so she is your friend now? Well, what about me? Am I chopped liver?" Stacey yelled back in a whiney type of voice. By now, Barbara and Carl had entered the room. Steve tried to explain what Janice was doing at his home, but Stacey just became more repugnant. "You can have him," Stacey shouted at Janice, "I don't want his broken body anyway."

Janice stood up shocked, and Steve stopped dead in his tracks as though he had been punched in the face. Carl came forward and grabbed Stacey by the arm and escorted her to the door while she screamed swear words the whole time. Obviously, the interview session was over, with Janice repeating over and over, "Oh, I am so sorry, so, so, sorry," as she picked up her briefcase and started walking towards the door. Barbara put her arms around the shocked girl and asked if she needed someone to follow her home because she looked pretty shaken. Janice assured her she would be fine and whispered in Barbara's ear her concern for Steve's state of mind.

"Come back tomorrow dear," said Barbara. "Steve is going to need someone like you to reinvigorate him after that terrible blow."

Chapter Thirty-Two

Sadly, Steve appeared to be back to square one, exactly where he had been right after his leg was amputated. Carl was extremely concerned how those horrible words were going to impact his son. Steve would not go to work the next day and just stayed in bed. In fact, Steve did not go to work for the whole week following, and he refused to meet with, or see anyone.

Janice did come to the house the day after the incident as Barbara had requested, but Steve was in his room and would not come out. Colleen dropped by to see Steve, and so did I, but he wanted nothing to do with any of us. Not even the younger children in the families could get a reaction from Steve.

Barbara went in to talk to him one afternoon and told Steve she was going to call a psychiatrist. Steve, who always respected his mother, cried out to her, "I don't need a damned psychiatrist; all I need is to be normal again." Barbara was overwhelmed and walked out of his room. At this point, knowing the way he felt, even if they called a psychiatrist to come they could not be assured that Steve would see him or her.

Everyone had advice, but what piece of advice was the correct one? Some urged everyone to be gentle, and Steve would eventually come around, yet others thought the best way was to be harsh and tell him to get up and out and stop feeling sorry for himself. Neither extreme seemed appropriate where Steve's parents were concerned. They did call several professionals for advice and even that was not consistent. They felt so alone and helpless.

Stacey kept mouthing off all around the town, but she was dealing with the wrong people. Carl and his family were well adored in town, so much so that the townspeople started to retaliate in voice and manner when Stacey spoke her abusive statements. Stacey began to feel so humiliated when the townspeople hit back, that she finally left town to go live with an aunt in another city, and as far as everyone was concerned it was good riddance.

Steve, on the other hand, was just not getting any better. Janice called the house several times and talked to Barbara showing genuine concern but to no avail. Steve did not want to see anyone, especially another pretty girl. Janice began to realize what she was feeling for Steve were not the feelings of a reporter. In high school she always adored Steve from a distance, and she was quickly beginning to realize that, leg or no leg, she was just as crazy about him now as she had been years earlier. She did want to finish her story on Steve, but what she really wanted was just to see and be with him. Somehow, her inner gut feelings told her she would be able to help.

One late afternoon, Janice decided not to call Barbara that day. Instead, she was just going to go over to the house and worry about the consequences after she got there. Barbara appeared to be so happy to see Janice and invited her inside. They had a pleasant chat in the den and Barbara offered Janice some cookies and lemonade which she enjoyed more than expected. Janice realized only then that she had not eaten all day she was so concerned about her visit to see Steve. Fortified after eating the good treats, and reinvigorated, Janice asserted herself and asked to visit Steve in his room. At first, Barbara hesitated, but ultimately Barbara began to think that at this point Janice's visit could not do any more harm than what had already been done. Barbara showed Janice to the room and Janice knocked gently on the door. Steve didn't answer, so she slowly started to open it. Steve was sitting on his bed looking out the window with such a forlorn look on his face Janice almost turned around and walked out, but she did not.

"Hey G. I.," Janice spoke softly, "What's so interesting out that window?" Steve's body stiffened. While hearing Janice's pleasant voice felt so good, his body also went into combat position. He was never again going to let some girl ever get near him, and he totally ignored Janice.

"I really would like to spend some time talking to you," Janice stressed.

Steve growled, "I am not giving any more interviews. You can forget that story about me."

"Well, Mr. Boss man, I am not here to interview you. I just wanted to visit," Janice said more determined than ever.

"Well, you know something? I don't want your visit, or anyone else's, so just leave."

"You know Steve; I'll leave if you want me to, though you are hurting my feelings. I hope you realize that not everyone thinks the same things about you like your Stacey did," Janice retaliated. "Maybe it is time you think of how you are hurting other people and stop focusing so much on yourself. I have feelings too. I was just here to spend a nice quiet afternoon with you and you order me to leave. What kind of person are you becoming?" With that statement Janice started walking towards the door.

She almost got outside the door when she heard this hushed, deep, male voice say, "Stop!" Janice almost did not turn around since she did feel slightly offended by Steve's earlier remarks, but she was drawn back to him like a magnet. Janice walked back towards Steve and sat beside him on the bed.

Quietly, Steve said, "I'm sorry I talked that way to you. I have just been feeling so lousy and inferior and ugly and mean, miserable, dreadful—you name it."

"Oh Steve, I don't think you are ugly, not even one little bit. In fact, to be honest, when I look at your shoulders and into your beautiful eyes, I just feel weak all over."

Steve stared at her half shocked and said, "Don't say those things to me just to make me feel better. I just can't take it anymore. Stacey's statements to me made me feel like I had been hit in the stomach with a grenade."

"You know, Steve, I realized these past weeks after our interview that I have had a crush on you ever since I would see you across a room in high school. I could care less if you are missing a leg. Just to look at you gives me butterflies in my stomach," Janice said as she grabbed Steve's hand. Steve's body began to relax a little as he turned to look Janice in the eyes. Janice could not resist his look and leaned her lips towards his where she planted a soft lingering kiss. After all the months in the hospital, and in rehab, this was just the medicine Steve needed as he parted his lips, and their tongues started playing with one another. At this point, there was a knock on the door and the two pulled quickly apart.

"It's Mom, Steve. I wanted to ask Janice if she would join us for dinner this evening, and Steve it would be great if you came down and joined us too in the dining room for a change."

"I would love to have dinner with all of you. Thank you for asking," Janice replied.

Steve said he would think about joining them. Janice was feeling so full of emotion at this point, she got up off the bed and went and sat on the wicker rocking chair across the room. "Please join us Steve to keep me company with your parents." All Steve really wanted was for Janice to come back to the bed, but dinner was going to be ready shortly, and he just had to get up and move before he went crazy over this girl.

Carl and Barbara were enormously thrilled when Steve followed Janice into the dining room. The food was delicious, and it was amazing to see Steve's spirits lifted as he joined the conversation.

When Janice finally left for home, Barbara could not help but whisper in her ear, "I don't know what magic powers you have, but you are welcomed to come back often and please continue to bring those powers with you." For the first time in weeks it appeared that Steve might recover after all.

Chapter Thirty-Three

What a relief to all when Steve started coming back to work at the shop. Things were getting on a more even keel once again in all our lives. When I got home one evening I suggested to Colleen that we have Tom, Lynn, Carl and Barbara over to play some cards. Friday night seemed like a good night, and when we called the others they were as ready as we were. All the weeks of us taking turns going to Washington to the hospital and the upset in everyone's routine could have taken its toll on everyone, but we were all so determined to help out that we managed it all very well. Nevertheless, we all needed a good fun night out, and that Friday was great.

As we played cards, ate and drank, we talked about Aaron coming home in a few weeks for spring break and about how we all had a child or two that would be in the upcoming school play. Then Carl mentioned that Steve was actually now thinking he was ready to move out on his own and was looking for a place. I mentioned that the construction on the condos near the lake where I lived before the tornado was coming along nicely and some units were already available to rent or buy. Perhaps Steve could even buy one since he managed to save money while in the service. Barbara had also been told that there was a Wounded Warrior Housing Initiative that negotiated extremely low prices on new homes. Perhaps Steve would be able to take advantage of that to buy a condo or small home. The others remarked that they had forgotten about those units and became excited about that prospect, thinking it a good idea.

We all started joking around that Steve probably wanted his own space to be alone with Janice, and we contemplated if they were going to move in together. Barbara rather thought that Janice was not the type to move in with Steve without being married. Yet, we tried to explain to her that even if we didn't like the idea, Barbara should not be surprised if Janice did move in with Steve because the young kids of today think nothing about that type of situation.

Everyone wanted to know if Aaron had a girlfriend in college. We laughed and said that if he did we would probably be the last to know. We mentioned his trip to the east coast with a bunch of his friends and about the good time they all had from what little we did hear.

Business topics and the economy did break its way into our conversation with the housing slump appearing to affect people that we all knew. Fortunately, our little group did not have a problem in that regard, but being business people, or managing a bank like Tom did, we were all concerned about a trickledown effect. All in all though, the conversation was jovial and it was quite late when everyone decided to go home. I was ready then for some down time with my wife.

Getting ready for bed I noticed a famous ladies' magazine on the end table mentioning a story line of using props for sexual pleasure, and telling the readers to fantasize about others to enjoy pleasure with one's spouse. Colleen and I got a big laugh out of all of it. We just felt that anyone that had to go to those extremes were not really in love with their mate. Why would you, first of all, want to think of someone else when the person you had with you was so much better? Also, who needs fake things to arouse pleasure when for us just being near each other was like an electric current ready to spark? It appeared that today people were searching in all the wrong places to find sexual excitement when they had the best in their own backyard, so to speak. Movies had people immediately jumping into bed, naked, seemingly destroying all the enjoyment leading up to the ultimate sensation. I remembered a movie I saw a few years before that took place around the forties. The husband walked into the house and saw his wife, fully clothed, in those long plain dresses that average housewives wore during that time period. The wife, fully clothed, as I said, was bending over and cleaning a bathtub. The husband saw his wife from that rear position and one did not have to guess twice what came across his mind at that moment. Today, imagination did not appear to enter the picture in relationships. Our relationship was super. We had each other, and that was enough, and our evening could not have ended on a better note than that.

Chapter Thirty-Four

The next morning as I walked past the bathroom mirror, I saw this shock of white and immediately reversed my step to take a second look to see what it was. I could not believe what my eyes were seeing. My hair, which had grown and was now soft and wavy, was totally grey. I just stood staring in disbelief when Colleen walked in and made some remark about my certainly being pleased with myself as I stood there blatantly idolizing the image in the mirror.

"Frankly, Colleen, the color of my hair stunned me. When did this happen, and why didn't I notice it sooner?"

"Perhaps we were just consumed with life and all it entailed the past few months," replied Colleen. "Honestly, though, I did notice it several weeks ago and just kept forgetting to mention it to you. I was thinking how very different you looked now than when you first moved here. If anything, I think you get more handsome everyday, which is so unfair. A lot of women just look older, and not necessarily better, with grey hair, but men just get more distinguished looking."

"Well, thanks Babe," I said, as I pulled her towards me. It was at that point that the little ones came running in the room ending our few minutes of a romantic connection.

At breakfast that morning we discussed taking the family to the amusement park near Aaron's college on Saturday of the next weekend. We would spend the day there with the little ones and in the late afternoon visit with Aaron and take him to dinner. The children jumped up and down full of excitement. Not only was it going to be fun for them to go on the rides, but they loved their big brother and could not wait to see him.

We called Aaron later in the day and while he said he had to work the night shift at the club that weekend, he would have plenty of time to meet with us for dinner and would look forward to it.

The rest of the day Colleen and I split up into two cars, each bringing some children with us to do some errands. We promised each other and the children that we would meet at *The Golden Cow* for some ice cream that afternoon around three o'clock. Afterwards, we would go home and get ready to go to the Saturday evening mass at our church. I had so many good things going for me in my life it wouldn't hurt to go and give some thanks to God.

Chapter Thirty-Five

The following Saturday the children were up way sooner than was necessary. However, I could tell from their hyper antics that there was no point in telling them to go back to bed, so I just got up too.

A few minutes after leaving the driveway we must have been asked at least a hundred times if we were already near the amusement park. I wished I had half of the children's energy. We finally did make it just as the park was opening, and at that time there did not appear to be a lot of crowds. Everyone barreled out of the van and started running towards the ticket booth.

Talk about exhaustion, there was not a minute we were not on the go. We went on every roller coaster, merry-go-round, teacup ride, Ferris wheel—you name it. I don't know how the children did not get sick since they consumed a ton of food from popcorn to cotton candy, hot dogs, hamburgers, chips, ice cream, and soda. They screamed in the haunted house and got lost in the maze where I could hear a whimper or two. I felt in many ways like a kid again. We did enjoy a brief respite in the air-conditioned theater watching a magician perform. Of course, none of them wanted to leave when it was time to go, but we just had to mention that Aaron would be waiting for us, and that was enough of an incentive to get them back in the van.

When we first met Aaron, we all took a tour of his room since many of the younger children had not yet seen it. Some claimed the room was too small, while others said they could not wait to go to college and get a room like their brother's. They all got a kick out of seeing their pictures on Aaron's desk and on the walls of the room. Quite obviously, Aaron had warned his roommate that we were coming, so the room was pleasantly in order.

Some of the children rode with Aaron on the way to the restaurant. The majority had decided they wanted to go to *Rocky's Steak House*, so that is where we went. *Rocky's* was the kind of place where big pails of peanuts were set on every table and peanut shells were smashed and scattered on the floor. The lines were outside and around the block and this restaurant did not take reservations, but we were assured the wait would be no longer than thirty-five minutes. With Aaron to amuse the children everyone tolerated the wait quite well.

Finally our name was called. At that moment as we were walking to our table, I noticed someone staring at me from across the room. This woman looked vaguely familiar, and I did not think too much about it except that it was nice to be looked at by someone so very pleasant looking. Yet, I could not get her looks out of my mind. Did I know her from church? Perhaps she had come into the shop, or she worked at the bank. The feeling was a nagging one for a few minutes, but then we got involved seating everyone and ordering our food, and I forgot the incident.

Had I been able to speak to the woman I would have found out that while all these thoughts were going through my mind, this women was having a feeling of déjà vu herself. The moment she saw him across the room she could not take her eyes off of this man. Tracy looked at her Mom and inquired if something was wrong.

"Why do you ask sweetie?"

"The look on your face just appeared desperate Mom."

"To be honest with you honey, I saw a man across the room that looked so much like your father, it rather threw me into a strange state of mind. I guess I could describe his looks as how your father might look now as an older more distinguished gentleman with grey hair."

"Wow, Mom, when we get to our table why don't we order a nice stiff drink for you. I would have one too, if I were old enough."

"I like that idea, Tracy."

The rest of the evening was spent with some of Tracy's friends, who joined them at the table, and Megan's thoughts turned elsewhere.

Chapter Thirty-Six

We were happy that daylight savings time had already begun as we drove home that evening. The ride was pleasant because most of the children fell asleep in the car immediately after we got on the road. They were happy and content to know that Aaron would be coming home the following week for a break.

When we got home, Colleen and I just popped the children in their beds with their clothes on after removing their sneakers. We were all just too exhausted to do otherwise. Briefly, as I lay down in bed, the image of that woman staring at me in the restaurant crossed my brain, but only for a minute because I dozed off instantly once my head hit the pillow.

For a change, things around the house, at the job, and in the lives of our friends appeared rather normal, and the main excitement the whole week was the anticipation of Aaron's homecoming.

How strange that Colleen felt the house needed a thorough cleaning with clean sheets on Aaron's bed and everything put in its place as though Aaron would object otherwise. I kept my mouth shut about all the cleaning though. If it made Colleen happy then so be it, and I guess it is always nice to come home and see the house shine, along with the happy faces of all who lived there.

By Thursday of that week as I returned home from work and walked into the house, the fragrance emanating from the kitchen and spreading throughout the house was heavenly. The smells were delicious with the aroma of brownies and banana bread baking in the ovens and pasta sauce heating on the stove. The gals busied themselves assembling large pans of lasagna. They were also boiling eggs and cooking a ham right along with our food for dinner that evening. I snuck a couple of brownies as I passed through the kitchen on my way upstairs to shower and change my clothing after giving everyone a kiss.

When I returned downstairs, there was a big discussion going on between the older daughter and Colleen. Apparently Colleen was setting down some rules that our daughter did not like. Normally, I tried not to get involved when this type of situation prevailed between the children and their mother, with the exception of the little ones. The younger children accepted me like their real Daddy from day one, and if they needed disciplining, I did not think twice about just doing so without first consulting with Colleen. But in this situation, I knew by instinct to just stay out of the whole thing. Arguing was a rare occurrence in our household, but I noticed that Colleen got more back talk recently from the girls then she ever got from Aaron. Fortunately, as I turned the corner into the kitchen the oven timer went off, and the little ones bounded behind me complaining to be hungry. The discussion between mother and daughter was stopped, at least temporarily, and I was thankful for that. All those good smells in the kitchen had made me hungry too, and at this point all I wanted to do was sit down to eat.

Aaron would be arriving around eleven o'clock the next morning and we were all anticipating his coming home.

Chapter Thirty-Seven

On the flight back to Connecticut from Tennessee, Megan had hoped to get some sleep since they were on the go all weekend. Also, she felt she was getting a little old to be keeping up with those teenage college students. She settled into her seat after drinking a little ginger-ale to calm her nervous stomach. Laying her head against the backrest she closed her eyes, but sleep was not forthcoming. Her mind kept racing back to that man she saw across the room in the restaurant.

Just when Megan thought she was beginning to get her life under control she observed that strange man and her whole applecart was upset once again. She remembers hearing it said that most people have a look-alike person some place in the world, and this man surely did look like her husband. The resemblance was uncanny. Of course, his hair was a different color and the style was different, but those eyes—those eyes. She told herself to stop the nonsense. So what if he looked like her deceased husband, she wondered. Why did it bother her so much anyway? This was not like a ghost of him for goodness sake, so what was causing her this frustration?

Maybe she was bothered so much because, thinking back; she never grieved the way she thought was proper after losing a husband in such a horrible manner. They had been having a lot of arguments, and frankly her life turned for the better once he was gone. However, she was still caught in the ghastly tragedy of that horrible day when the Twin Towers collapsed despite her lack of mourning for her spouse. She not only lost her husband, but the father of her child, and all the other friends she knew that perished that day. While putting up a brave front for Tracy, Megan was caught in the whole horror of the situation, yet she never really felt overly sad that her husband was gone, and for this she always felt a certain amount of guilt. Through the years the guilt dissipated quite a bit, but now it all came back to haunt her again.

Every time she closed her eyes his face reappeared to her. Maybe she should have ordered some liquor to drink, or do anything to focus her mind on something else. She kept chastising herself over and over, thinking how stupid it was for her to be focusing on an individual because he resembled her deceased husband. Megan was beginning to feel dim-witted, so instead of trying to sleep she got a book out of her bag and decided to read instead. Her restlessness continued through the entire flight until the plane landed. Only then did she become preoccupied with retrieving her luggage and hailing a cab.

Once home, Megan unpacked and took a nice comforting hot bath. Fortunately, she fell asleep without any problems. The next day she was back at work, and life was back to its pleasant routine with no more memories of her departed husband.

Chapter Thirty-Eight

Saturday morning I took the little guy with me to buy some donuts. He selected just about every kind in the glass cases and proceeded to eat one in the car on the way home. White filling oozed out of his mouth, unto his clothes, and all over his hands. I reached over with my finger as I was driving and scooped up some from his clothes and promptly licked the cream. It was delicious. He was oblivious to me and really absorbed into eating that donut and was ready to reach in the box and grab another when I said, "Whoa, Buddy, why don't you wait until we get home because it is almost time for Aaron to arrive."

"Shucks, Daddy, I'm still hungry, but I'll wait."

The girls met us at the car and immediately scooped away the box of donuts. I picked up Jeremy holding him out before me so as not to get cream all over myself. I took him directly to the kitchen and was washing him off when we heard Aaron's car pull into the driveway. Jeremy was off in an instant, too fast for his own footsteps, consequently falling down the two steps leading from the kitchen to the den. He let out a curdling scream and when I saw his little face it was covered with blood. Everyone came running to see what had happened, and the girls started screaming too. Colleen had approached us by then with a cloth that she pressed against Jeremy's mouth. Once some of the bleeding was under control, it was obvious that Jeremy was going to need stitches. Confusion filled the house as Aaron was coming in with some of the kids bringing suitcases, and Colleen and I and the others were rushing around trying to get ready to take Jeremy to the emergency room. This was not the homecoming we had anticipated for Aaron for sure.

Jeremy reached out to Aaron as they were passing in the living room and Aaron asked, "What's the matter Buddy?" Jeremy started crying loudly all over again, and I asked Aaron if he would like to come with us to the emergency room of the hospital. The girls started complaining they didn't want

Aaron to leave and the whole situation was a bit of a circus. Colleen finally raised her voice just enough to get everyone's attention as she told everyone to calm down. She told Aaron to stay with the girls while the three of us drove to the hospital. Jeremy's wound was still bleeding profusely as Colleen exchanged towels trying to put pressure on the site of the cut.

Fortunately for us, the emergency room was not crowded that morning. Though, with the way Jeremy was bleeding he probably would have received preference from the triage team anyway. The doctor on duty happened to be a friend of ours which helped to put Jeremy at ease and frankly me too.

Back home, the girls were attempting to clean up the blood that had gotten on the rug while Aaron put his suitcases in his room. When he came back downstairs they all sat down to eat donuts. The girls made some bacon and eggs with fresh orange juice. Everyone ran to grab the phone when it rang, but Aaron got to it first only to find out it was someone soliciting money. Aaron managed to get the solicitors off the phone when it rang again immediately, and this time it was his parents. Colleen explained that the skin that went across Jeremy's upper lip and the side of his right cheek had quite a gash that would require about twenty-two stitches. They were going to wait for a plastic surgeon to come in to take care of Jeremy since everyone was worried about Jeremy having a scar on his face. Colleen asked how things were going on at home as she said to Aaron, "I am so sorry honey we had to leave you so soon after you arrived. What a mess this whole thing is."

"Don't be silly Mom. Things like this can't be helped, as you always tell me. I have everything under control here so don't worry, and tell Jeremy we all love him."

It took the plastic surgeon over an hour to get to the hospital, and none of us ever found out why. We didn't even bother to ask why he took so long when he did arrive as we were just so happy to see him. Jeremy had been given something to calm his nerves and once the doctor did arrive things progressed a lot faster. By the time the doctor finished with Jeremy, and I saw all the stitches on our child's beautiful face, I almost felt sick to my stomach. Up to this point everything that occurred just appeared to be surreal, but all of a sudden the situation became reality, and I felt a little dizzy and overwhelmed. Colleen, with the strength of most women I know, appeared to take it all in stride. The doctor assured us that he was good at his profession and any scar would be minimal and would fade in time.

By the time we arrived back at the house it was already three o'clock in the afternoon. The children were all gathered in the den watching a video. Of course Jeremy immediately got a ton of attention. The television was turned off while everyone listened to Jeremy tell about his exciting tale at the emergency room.

Chapter Thirty-Nine

After dinner, the children were playing on the swings outside in the large backyard and started catching some bugs in a jar as daylight began to fade. They were disappointed that the bugs did not light up like the lightening bugs that would surface later in the summer months. Once darkness prevailed we all went inside, made some popcorn, and began to relax in the den. We told Aaron about Steve's new living arrangements and he was all excited about going to visit him in his new place the next day.

All of a sudden Aaron jumped up saying, "Wow, I forgot the pictures of when I was away," as he ran upstairs to get them.

When Aaron returned downstairs with the pictures we all tried to grab them at once, then we decided to look at the pictures one at a time and pass each one to the next person to see thinking this might bring some kind of order to the process. I saw a young, cheerful group of children in their late teens happily enjoying themselves. The picture of the huge white limo, the front of which looked like a Hum-Vee, really impressed the youngsters. Considering all the bad vibes people get from our youth today it was such a pleasure to look at this wonderful group of teens that I knew were not only good students, but many spent several hours a week working for charitable causes.

The girls were asking Aaron if any of the pretty girls in the pictures were his special girlfriend. Aaron denied having one special girl at this time saying he was having fun enjoying all of the beauties. Then I saw a picture that nearly stopped my heart. My body instinctively jerked and moved abruptly and uncontrollably backwards as though astounded, and those next to me looked up to see what was wrong. My head kept reeling the words internally without my voice verbally speaking them, "Oh My God, Oh My God, Oh My God!!"

Colleen immediately ran over to me. "This is the second time in a month you have had this strange reaction honey. What on earth is wrong? I really think you need to see a doctor."

There were no words coming out of me that could explain my actions. I had just seen a picture of my home in Connecticut with my former wife and daughter standing in front of it. While the two women looked a lot different, there was no denying the house was mine from the color scheme, to the tiny gargoyle statues placed in the flower garden. Slowly, I began to comprehend that when Aaron went east, he had gone with his friends to Connecticut to be with my daughter and wife and to stay in my house. I started to shake while attempting to tell everyone I was just fine. I wanted to look at more pictures to confirm what I had seen, yet I did not want to draw attention to my special interest in them.

"I'm fine," I said. "No need to worry. Let's get back to looking at these fun pictures." I managed to keep my feelings under control, and from my perspective at least, the rest of the evening seemed rather normal. Around eleven o'clock, all the children were in bed. Colleen said she was going upstairs, and I informed her I would be up shortly after I turned off the lights in the kitchen. On my way back through the hallway to the stairs I noticed the packet of pictures on the table. At first I was going to walk on past them, but curiosity got the best of me, and I grabbed the packet and went back into the kitchen so Colleen might think I was getting something to eat or drink. I made sure to sit down before opening up the folder to remove the pictures. Now I knew who the woman was in the restaurant that was staring at my eyes when we went to see Aaron. After realizing how physically close we were at that time at the restaurant my heart started to palpitate. I looked at the rest of the pictures. Several of the pictures showed the interior of my house too. I noticed a few changes like maybe a piece of furniture or two had been eliminated or replaced, but for the most part the house appeared pretty much the same. It looked great to be honest. My daughter Tracy was emerging as a real beauty and so absolutely astonishing, tall and lovely. My only hope was that Aaron would not see her as the beauty she is and become more attached to her in a personal way. What were the odds in this world of these two children ending up at the same school? Had the school been a Princeton, Yale or Harvard I could more fully comprehend this happening, but a small intimate college in Tennessee?

Colleen called down to see if I was alright and to ask if I would be coming up soon. At the sound of her voice I immediately shuffled the pictures back in the packet as though I were a small child caught in the act of doing something mischievous and went up to bed. Sleep did not come easily to me that night. I feared my happy life as I had been living it the past number of years was about to see some big changes.

Chapter Forty

Fatigue finally took over and I immediately fell asleep. I was surprised to see how late I slept the next morning. Since we had not gone to Mass on Saturday night the family was all in a buzz getting ready for church. Jeremy was the one who came in to awaken me saying, "Daddy, you better get up soon, or you will be late."

"Hi Buddy, what's the rush?"

"We are all going to church, come on, come on, and get up Daddy, now."

By then Colleen had entered the room. I assured her I was finally up and would be ready on time. I appreciated the distraction of getting out of the house and going to Mass while at the same time also feeling selfish as I prayed for a fix to this strange predicament of my wife and daughter resurfacing again in my life. We met Carl and Barbara outside the church with their brood and we all decided to go to *Peggy's Waffle House* for breakfast. The place was lively and there was a thirty minute or so wait, but we were so busy catching up with each other and for them especially with Aaron, that those thirty minutes just flew by.

When we all said our goodbyes, we knew we would be seeing them around 6:30 p.m. that evening for the picnic we planned in Aaron's honor. The rest of the afternoon was spent getting ready for the picnic.

Aaron had gone over to see Steve's new condo and he kept raving about how good looking Steve's girlfriend was and calling her a true beauty. When he returned, all Aaron talked about was some day having a neat place like Steve's all to himself. We assured Aaron that the time would come soon enough.

The weather could not have cooperated more, with the sky a gorgeous cerulean blue color. The warmth of the sun felt delicious on my body. I momentarily had forgotten about the picture incident until I saw Aaron walking towards Carl and Barbara with the pictures in his hand. “Oh, no,” I thought. “Not this again.” I began to feel anxious as though I had been given a jolt of electricity or a shot of caffeine. I walked towards the grill and started putting the hamburgers and hot dogs on to cook hoping the distraction would get my mind off the pictures.

Barbara could be heard saying rather loudly, “Holy Cow, look at the size of this house Aaron stayed in,” as though the rest of us had not already seen the pictures. “These people must make big bucks.” Then the conversation turned to the fact that Tracy’s Dad had been killed in the September 11th, 2001 incident. The conversation quickly turned somber with all kinds of questions and imaginings. I asked Aaron to take a minute at the grill while I went inside the house to take care of something. Before I collapsed, I just had to get away. I walked up to my bedroom into the adjoining bathroom and put the commode seat down and sat on it. Resting my elbows on my knees I covered my face with a damp towel and heaved a big sigh. I took a couple of very deep breaths and sort of meditated. Feeling a little better, I got up and took an aspirin out of the medicine cabinet and quickly swallowed it along with a glass of water. Looking out the bathroom window it appeared as though the group was on to something else, so I composed myself and went back outside. The timing was good because the food on the grill was done and everyone was anxious to sit down and eat. By now the fullness from the food we had eaten at *Peggy's Waffle House* that morning was gone, and we were all ready to “dig in” again.

Chapter Forty-One

Once Aaron returned to school, life seemed to settle down to something more predictable. My mind was working overtime though with constant thoughts of how my prior life was thrown into my present life. I could not believe the uncanny situation. What would I do if Aaron should find Tracy more attractive than the current feelings he now said he had for her? What in God's name would I ever do? Suppose they got engaged and then wanted to be married? In both those supposed events there just would be no way I could avoid being in contact with my wife and Tracy. Tracy, in fact, would— well I just better not go there.

With all these events happening, I began to feel this was God's way to punish me for what I had done. Yet, those pictures showed a happy mother and child and a beautiful house. They apparently were doing well without me in their life. Was what I had done then so very horrible that God could never forgive me?

Fortunately, or unfortunately, I am not sure, other events occurred to take my mind away from my past and more into the present. It just seemed that no family was immune from some sort of crises in their lives anymore. We could not blame our family's situation on a mother who worked outside the home because Colleen was a stay-at-home Mom. Two of Colleen's daughters that were very much like my blood related daughters were now in high school. One, Susan, was a freshman, and Casey was a sophomore. They appeared to be happy children, were well adjusted, active in sports and well-liked. We never would have anticipated a problem from either one.

What we did not know was that Casey was associating with her supposedly well respected friends from apparently esteemed families who turned out to be not so well adjusted after all. These were all children who came from families where money was not an issue. Many of the girls had part time jobs, but even if they did not, all they had to do was ask their parents for any needs or wants they had, and the money would be made available. Most of them did come from families however where both the parents worked, and they were left alone after school for many hours until one or both parents came home. At ages ranging anywhere from fourteen to sixteen, society seemed to agree that this was an age range quite suitable to have children be left home alone, and no one questioned the many families who did so. Consequently, these were the homes where the girls would like to congregate after school. Since most of the girls up to now had good reputations, no parent questioned the girls meeting at these homes after school. We knew the parents, and the girls always seemed so very nice that no one anticipated a problem. The school session was coming to the end of the year, and most of the sports for a majority of the girls were finished. Except for the upcoming finals, the girls pretty much had perhaps too much idle time on their hands. About five or six of them congregated usually every day for the past few weeks in one of the homes where the parents both worked.

The afternoon sessions started out basically harmless until one rainy afternoon. A few of the girls were sitting around listening to music. Some were dancing, and a few were talking on their cell phones while they cooked popcorn in the microwave. Once the popcorn was finished, they all gathered together with the girls that were listening to music. One of the girls took something bright out of her purse and showed it to the group. The glistening object was a gorgeous piece of southwestern jewelry, all silver looking with turquoise stones. "Wow," the group remarked in unison.

One of them asked where Jill had purchased the bracelet, or she wanted to know if it had been given to her as a gift? Jill told them they would never in a million years guess where she got it.

"Well, get to it Jill," Casey remarked, "Where did you get it?"

"I took it from the store called *Abigail's* in the middle of old town," Jill replied.

Most of the girls gasped. One said, "You mean you stole it, when you say took it?"

"I would not call it stealing. Anyway, those stores carry tons of insurance just in case someone does steal their stuff."

"Yes, but that just means they add the cost onto the price of the object."

"Don't be such dorks," Jill replied. "Honestly, this has been the most exciting thing I have done in a long time. You all have to try it to see what I mean."

Some of the girls shook their heads no, but others seemed excited to give it a try.

"Ah, come on guys, you are all here and saw this. It is only fair that you all support me. Don't be such 'fraidy' cats. We don't look like the normal group of kids that take things, so you will find it rather easy to do."

Casey brought up the fact that Jill and all the girls had enough money to just go to the store and buy what they wanted. She wanted to know why they would want to resort to stealing?

"Oh, for heaven's sake Casey, you are such a 'goody two shoes' and always afraid you are going to get caught doing something against your parent's wishes. You don't have to get your parents to approve everything you do. Grow up and do things you want to do, and if you do it right you will get such excitement that you would never get from just going into the store and buying it."

Fortunately, Casey did not need to say anything back to Jill because someone else interrupted the conversation, but her self-esteem dropped considerably as she wondered if she really were a goody whatever it was that Jill called her.

The group of six girls finally all decided that each one was going to select a day and on that day *take* something from *Abigail's.* As it turned out, Casey was going to be the sixth and last one to participate. They would all then meet every day back at Jill's house and show what each girl was able to take without being caught.

Later that week, back at Casey's house, she heard the words, "You certainly are looking somber. Where is that beautiful smile that is usually so forthcoming from you every day?" Colleen could not help but notice that these last few days Casey appeared to be out of sorts, and she was mentally attempting to calculate if it were that time of the month for her daughter.

Casey played actress by putting a forced smile on her face for her Mom. She so much wanted to tell her Mom what the girls were doing, but she also knew that if she did so all her friends would criticize her and call her a blabber mouth. "I'm fine Mom. I have just a little headache maybe. I could use some food. What's for dinner? It smells so good, like chili."

"Chili it is Babe. Would you please cut that French bread on the counter into slices and get the salad out of the refrigerator?" At this point, others started sauntering into the kitchen and within a short time they were all sitting down to dinner in the dining room. Everyone dug in after grace was said.

Chapter Forty-Two

Casey actually began to get excited after the fourth girl came in that day with her acquired piece of jewelry. They all sat around 'oohing' and 'aahing' at this small piece of treasure. "Oh, I was so excited. It was just so easy. The store lady had a nice conversation with me when I entered and then got a phone call. I went to the opposite end of the store and slipped these earrings into my pocket. My heart was racing. I felt as though I had won a big prize in a contest. The price tag said the earrings were worth over $200.00. I then walked slowly around looking at other things in order to make it appear I was still browsing. I later waved good-bye to the owner and calmly walked out. I was still anxious until I got in my car and drove away. Oh, gosh, this is just the most fun I've had in a long time."

One of the group finally asked, "Well, now that we have this beautiful stuff, what are we going to do with it? If we wear it out and around, our Moms are sure to notice."

Jill said that for now they should just hide it at home in their rooms and wait until everyone had gone through the experience. When that was done, she said they could all help to decide what would be the best thing to do. Perhaps they could take the jewelry to a pawn shop in a neighboring town and get some money for it. Even if the money did not amount to anything much, it would be more than what they had when they started. The girl who had just stolen the earrings said she wanted to keep hers and save them in a drawer until she went to college.

"That's a possibility too," said Jill, "but, we still have two more girls needing to take their turn."

The fifth girl also was victorious in her thievery and was ranting and raving about how great she felt and how much fun she had taking a necklace. Casey, while still unsure she was doing the right thing, was nevertheless caught up in the excitement. Tomorrow was her turn, and she was anxious to show the group of girls she could be successful too.

That same evening when the owner of *Abigail's* was getting ready to close, she asked a co-worker where the silver circle necklace was that she had just put out in the showcase. "Did someone buy it today?"

"Not from me," said the co-worker.

Abigail checked to see if she had put the necklace in another showcase, but quickly realized there was a void in the space in that showcase too. In fact, the more she looked at the showcase she began to notice that other objects were missing as well.

The co-worker said she had noticed some of the girls coming into the store every day this week after school and she was wondering if they possibly could be taking things when in the store.

Abigail shook her head no. "I know most of those girls, or at least their parents. They are not the type to do such a thing."

"Well, no one would have suspected the actress Winona Ryder to do such a thing either, but she did and big time. Perhaps we had better pay more attention during the after school hours tomorrow, just in case."

"I suppose you are right," Abigail agreed. "Neither of us will take a break for the two hours after school lets out tomorrow, and we'll observe those who come in the store during that time."

Casey had a hard time sleeping that night. She was both excited and frightened at the same time. This whole experience distracted her so much that she neglected to do her homework. The next day in French class when called upon by the teacher to answer a question, Casey was completely oblivious of the answer so the French teacher asked her to stay after class for a brief moment.

"Your school work has not been up to par Casey, and your class participation has been nothing to brag about either. Are you having trouble understanding this part of the lesson?"

"No, I'm fine," Casey replied. "I promise I will do better."

"Well, if you don't do better, you're grade is going to drop from an A to a B, or lower, and I will be calling your Mom. You are going to be a junior next year, and if you want to go on to college then this is not the time to have your grades drop."

"Please don't call my Mom. I really promise I will do better." At that, the teacher said she hoped this was true and she released Casey. The rest of the school day Casey did make an effort to pay more attention in class, but it was getting harder and harder to do as the school day was coming to a close.

Outside the school building, after school, the other girls waved and gave Casey the victory sign of the middle and pointy finger shaped into a "V" a la

President Richard Nixon. Casey waved goodbye to her friends, got into her car and drove into town.

Her heart began to palpitate as she parked her car in the vicinity of *Abigail's.* She tried walking casually into the store, but her knees did feel like they might buckle. Nevertheless, she made it into the store and said hi to Abigail and her co-worker. When the two ladies asked if they could help her, Casey said she was just looking around and thanked them. The two women really were not that suspicious of Casey. Her mother was a favorite when she came into the store, so they really did not anticipate a problem. Casey was cursing under her breath that she had the rotten luck of two women being at the store when the other girls only had to deal with one. She wandered over to a far corner and spotted a gorgeous bracelet that she began to hold in her hands. It was expensive, but not as expensive as the jewelry locked in the glass cases. Casey began to wonder how the one girl got the $200.00 necklace, since most of the very expensive jewelry required a saleslady with a key to unlock the case, but this bracelet was around $50.00. She immediately pocketed the bracelet and proceeded to pick up another item trying to appear nonchalant. However, Abigail spotted Casey putting the bracelet in her pocket and nodded to her co-worker to keep an eye on her while Abigail took her cell phone out of hearing distance where she dialed the police.

Casey put down the other object, smiled at the lady, said goodbye and started for the door just as she noticed a police car pull up in front of the store. She did not know if she should keep walking or turn around and go back to the store. Surely the police were not there for her after all. The co-worker held the door open for Casey to leave, and she started to walk faster to her car when she heard a male voice say, "Young lady, will you please come back here?"

"Are you talking to me, sir?"

"Yes, I am. I would like you to walk back into the store with me."

Casey experienced a fear she had never felt before. She could feel her limbs shaking.

The officer asked her to reach inside her pocket and remove everything that was inside it. Casey put her hand near her pocket, but then she just froze and sat there.

"Please remove the items yourself, or I will have to do it for you," he said.

Slowly she began to remove a few pieces of tissue and a dirty mint, and then out came the bracelet. Casey burst out crying and asked if she could call home which he allowed her to do.

Susan answered the phone, and Casey told her what she had done saying she was so afraid to tell their Mom. "What shall I do Susan?"

"What a dumb thing for you to do. Did those stupid girlfriends of yours put you up to this?"

"Susan, don't lecture me now. Please help me."

"Well, obviously I am going right down to the basement where Mom is doing the laundry and tell her."

Chapter Forty-Three

Colleen had apologized profusely to Abigail when she arrived at the shop. The policeman did go against protocol and let Casey drive in her mother's car as they followed him to the police station where he filed a report. Since this was the first time Casey ever had any trouble they released her to go home with a stern warning never to attempt to do such a thing again.

When Colleen called me at work, I was beside myself with worry. As soon as I finished with the job I was doing I left to go home because by that time Colleen was already bringing Casey home with her. I tried to comprehend why Casey would do such a thing. Never was there a child loved more by all of us. Do some children going through the adolescent early teen stage automatically develop low self esteem because of peer pressure? What was the thrill in stealing from someone else? I looked up kleptomaniac on the computer. The first sentence said that it was important to distinguish between kleptomania and shoplifting. Shoplifting may be impulsive or planned, but it is deliberate and motivated by profit. People who shoplift may steal for the thrill of it, on a dare or out of anger. Patients with kleptomania do not generally plan the theft in advance, take items of little or no value and are remorseful but feel unable to stop. It appeared as though women were more likely to be affected by kleptomania than men. Anxiety, guilt and depression are more often found in people with kleptomania.

I felt confident that Casey was not a kleptomaniac, and her shoplifting was probably more precipitated by a dare or out of anger for someone. I just could not believe Casey had an irresistible compulsion to steal. While I was on the computer, Susan walked in and inquired about what I was doing. I explained how I just could not understand what made Casey do such a thing.

"Oh, Dad, that's an easy one," said Susan. "Casey has been hanging around with a very snobbish group of girls who have nothing better to do after school then to congregate at each other's homes where the parents are out working. I would be shocked if anyone of them ever spent any of their time doing charitable work or helping others less fortunate than themselves. They are extremely label and brand conscious and would only consider shopping at stores like *Nordstrom's*. They are all so shallow and not really at all like Casey. Even if they all just went out and got a job despite not needing the money, they would be better off instead of sitting around concocting ideas that are going to get them in trouble."

"If that is so, Susan, why did you not say something to Mom and me about Casey's friends?"

"Because, Dad, I did not think Casey was so stupid that she would follow every little thing the girls suggested to her."

At that point in the conversation Colleen and Casey returned home. Casey broke down in tears again. I gave her a big hug while asking, "Why, baby, why?"

"They told me it would make me feel good. They all did it without a problem."

"Who are they Casey?"

"You can't make me tell that Dad, nor you either Mom."

For that split second, the parents let Casey's statement slide until a moment in time when her disposition would be more under control. As it turned out though, Casey never had to "rat" on her so called friends. The girls were foolish enough to steal from a store where they were well known and Abigail thought back to the other girls who came in during the week and gave the list of names to the cops along with a list of other missing merchandise.

While I had been hugging Casey the phone rang, and I overheard Colleen talking to Abigail. That is how we established who was responsible for helping to instigate Casey. We knew the problem was ultimately Casey's own fault, but we up to that point had not been able to figure out just what would cause her to falter as she did.

As soon as Colleen put the phone down on the receiver it immediately rang again, and this time it was Jill's Mom. She was shouting so loudly at Colleen the rest of us could hear the conversation. She was calling Casey all sorts of horrible things and asking how she could be so crude as to implicate all the other girls. Colleen rarely ever raised her voice, but she did this time.

"Now you wait just one damn minute. Abigail was the one who gave the girls' names to the police and up until the time she did my husband and I had no knowledge of who else had been involved in what Casey was caught doing, so you just stop your preaching right this minute." Jill's mother just slammed down the phone and all of a sudden I had some inkling what might cause Jill to want to do something so outrageous.

At this point, I could care less about the rest of those girls. Quite obviously we were not going to be allowing Casey to spend any more of her after school time with them anyway. In fact, Colleen made that quite clear on the way home from the police station. She told Casey that for the rest of this semester and school year she would be coming directly home from school every day and she would, understand, would, find a useful purpose for being at home during that time whether it was to clean a closet, to study, or to help make a meal, but you will come home and you will not be allowed to spend any more time with that group of girls. Colleen also suggested Casey find herself some new friends.

That evening when Colleen and I were talking downstairs, after everyone had gone to bed, Colleen explained how she was so mixed up she was feeling a variety of emotions.

"I am ashamed to say that one of my emotions is embarrassment. Everyone always said I had such lovely children, and now I feel like a failure. Children all over the world do things that get them into trouble, so why as a parent should I feel embarrassed? Is it a reflection honey on our parenting skills?"

"Don't be foolish," I said. "Many parents go through a lot worse things. We all try our best and sometimes it just doesn't work. I think what hurts more is that she got so much love in this home, that I can't help wonder why she went seeking excitement someplace else? Yet, I know that kids will be kids, and it is how we treat Casey now that will ultimately be the important issue on how she survives this scandal and gets on with her life. Parents whose children live routinely and don't upset the apple cart cannot take full credit because their children do not happen to get into trouble and appear content with the status quo. Terrific parents are the parents who stand by their children when they do get in trouble, to pull them up when they are down."

Chapter Forty-Four

Returning to school after the weekend was hard on Casey, but her parents were not going to let her neglect her studies because of her foolish actions. She felt as though she could see and hear people whispering about her as she walked among the students, and the other five girls were downright nasty as they did not want to believe that Casey did not tattletale on them. It helped having her sister at the same school. The two sisters promised to meet at lunch time. Susan brought along her friends who treated Casey with respect and basically ignored stating anything about what she had done. By the end of the week the kids were on to something else, and Casey's life appeared to be returning to normal.

A most unusual thing happened when Colleen essentially forced Casey to go to Abigail's store on Monday after school to apologize to the owner.

"I am so sorry Mrs. Smith," said Casey, half shaking and half starting to cry.

"To be honest with you honey, I am sorry too. This is not something I would expect of you, and I frankly feel even worse for your wonderful parents. I also know however, that sometimes children make big mistakes, and they should not have to suffer for those mistakes the rest of their lives. I have a suggestion for you about which I would like you to think. I want to show you I still have some faith in you."

"What suggestion, Mrs. Smith?"

"I could use another person for the few hours you are off after school to tidy up the shelves and wait on the customers if we are busy. I would like to offer you this opportunity to work for me at minimum wage too. What do you think of that offer?"

"Are you serious? You are not joking with me, are you?"

"I am very serious. I want you to know I have faith in you, and we can show the gossips in this town that you really are someone to be trusted."

"Wow, you are awesome!" Casey gave Abigail a big hug. After Abigail decided Casey would start the next day, Casey ran out of the store to tell Susan who had been waiting for her outside. Only then did Casey become concerned that her mother might be upset because she had mentioned that Casey should come home to do chores.

"Well, what a wonderful show of support for you Casey by Abigail. I always had such respect for her, but this time I am overwhelmed by her generosity. Of course I will let you work in the store," Colleen said. "My main objective was for you to not spend time at the home of any of those girls, and to keep you busy as well. This certainly will solve both problems. However, though I doubt they would, if any of those girls come into the store, you are not to talk to them except in greeting, and you must be sure to have only Abigail wait on them."

"The way they have been treating me Mom I really don't ever want to have anything to do with them again. This has helped me to see their true side."

After this incident, I noticed the girls were both treating their mother better and there was a lot less friction in our home. I guess sometimes out of something bad we get rewarded with something good. Anymore, it appeared that just about every family we knew had their minor catastrophes with children the ages of Casey and Susan. Our catastrophe was a shock to our system, but we handled it well and survived for the better.

Chapter Forty-Five

The next weekend Colleen and I were going to attend the 50th Wedding Anniversary of Carl's parents. Since it was in the neighboring state of Kentucky, we decided to get a hotel room and stay overnight. We both needed the opportunity to get away. Steve's girlfriend was going to stay with the children. She was such a sweet person, and all the children loved her.

The party was held at a Mansion on a lake. All the decorations and the beautiful landscaped grounds were especially pleasing to the eye. The party was a champagne brunch. Drinks and hors d'oeuvres were served outside on the deck overlooking the lake before we entered the main ball room. They had close to one hundred people attending. Many of them were old friends of ours as well as many of Carl's parents' friends too, so we all had such a fine time reminiscing. Inside the main dining room, tables glistened with floral arrangements on top of mirrors with soft appealing colors interspersed with gold to signify fifty years.

There were stations of food in every corner, with a man to make omelets, another with pastas and roast beef, ham, bacon sausage, scrambled eggs, pastries, Belgian waffles, pancakes, fruit, cheese and too much more to mention. A huge ice sculpture surrounded a flowing fountain of champagne, plus there were many other offerings of drinks, both alcoholic and non-alcoholic.

Often, you will hear on talk shows people suggesting all types of things about people who are married a long time. Some claim they could not possibly still love each other, nor have sex any more, yet those same people will brag about their own relatives married for a long time. In listening to the conversations around the room, many of the happy couple's friends had also been married a long time and truth be told those couples looked darn happy to me. I believe all the negative talk comes from people whose own marriages were not a success, so they refuse to believe any other people could be that happy for such a long time.

The disc jockey made a few announcements of welcome, and the children said some beautiful things about their parents. Then the disc jockey started the music and we danced to a variety of tunes late into the afternoon when the wonderful party ended. Everyone lingered around saying their goodbyes and gathering their memorabilia to bring home and show their families and friends.

I was absolutely thrilled to have my wife all to myself the rest of the evening, and we made good use of our time in the room. We were grateful not to get any unsettling phone calls from home, and we managed to sleep late before packing and leaving for home the next day.

I put the car phone on speaker phone, made sure we had enough gas, and we played some soft music while enjoying the scenery when the phone did ring. It was Aaron calling from school. We were both so excited to hear his voice.

"How are you sweetie?" Colleen said.

"I'm great Mom. You sound like you are on speaker phone."

I interjected that we were.

"Oh, Dad you are there too? Where are you two anyway?"

Colleen told him we were driving in Kentucky on the way home from Carl's parent's 50th party.

"Oh, cool. How was it?"

"It was a great party honey," Colleen replied. "So, when are you coming home since the semester is about over, and how were your exams?"

"I feel like I did pretty well in my tests, well at least I hope so. I'm calling to tell you that since we don't have to be out of our rooms until the end of the month we decided to help Tracy load up her car and drive and follow her back to Connecticut so she won't have to go alone. Her mother is flying in to also help, but she was so grateful when we made this suggestion."

I swerved over the yellow line out of shock.

"Easy, easy," Colleen interrupted.

I mumbled something about spotting an object in the middle of the road, which of course was a total fib. I also started getting one of those anxiety attacks again, yet was trying without much success not to show it.

Aaron asked if anything was wrong because after Colleen said the words "easy" there were two times we both sort of stopped talking, and Aaron just heard silence in the car.

I had to know some details, so I asked him about his plans.

"We are just going to follow Tracy and her Mom back to Connecticut in a caravan, help her unload her stuff, stay with them a few days, then return back to clear out our own rooms. Then I will come home for the summer."

My mind was trying to absorb everything he said. I guess it will be ok I thought. What harm can come from Aaron doing this? They have no way to make any connection to me just because Aaron would be going to Connecticut. Did they? The palms of my hands were sweating, and I told Colleen I was feeling terribly sleepy and asked her if she would like to drive for a short time.

Thinking that if I made a fuss about Aaron going on this trip I would only draw attention to myself, I made a quick decision to say that if he followed his plans as he described them, and he came home when we originally expected him, that it was fine to help out Tracy and her Mom. I prayed there was no hidden agenda I could not comprehend. Was my son falling in love with Tracy? Oh, Lord, this just could not be, please no, no, no, no, no! I glanced in Colleen's direction to make sure she was in agreement about Aaron making the trip. Of course, Colleen was delighted. What is it about these mothers that fall 'ga-ga' over their sons meeting eligible young ladies. I believe Colleen did think Aaron had a crush on Tracy. By now I had pulled to the side of the road. We sat there for a short time finishing up our conversation with Aaron before proceeding on home.

Colleen continued to listen and sing along to the songs on the car radio while she drove. I, on the other hand, sat there and drove myself crazy with all sorts of suppositions. Again, I cursed the fact that these two children somehow crazily ended up at the same university. Please let me believe Aaron when he says he just likes Tracy as a friend. Please! What would I do if this situation turns out otherwise? At the rate things were going, both Megan and I were bound to meet up one of these times. This just could not happen at all. Even though my looks had changed, Megan lived with me long enough that there was no way she would not recognize me. I could tell that just by the way she looked at me across the restaurant that evening when we were not even close to one another. I felt like pinching or hurting myself to get my mind off all these negative thoughts. I had to stop this right now, or I was going to have a nervous breakdown. As though my body were listening to my thoughts, I literally did become tired, and I fell asleep without my even realizing it. The next thing I knew, Colleen had pulled the car into our driveway. The sleep I had helped me to relax, and once the children ran out to greet us I was relieved by the distraction.

Chapter Forty-Six

I had been doing a lot more administrative work at the shop, but that Monday when I went in to work I decided to do more hands on work to keep my mind off of yesterday's phone conversation. With the high price of gas these days, people were choosing not to buy big gas guzzler cars anymore, and they were more willing to keep up repairs on the vehicles they already owned.

Eager to get down and dirty, I began working under a sports car that one of the other guys had started fixing. I asked him to repair the worn leather on the front seat while I worked under the car for a while. Our shop had the capacity to also do leather repairs which was a convenience to our customers as they did not have to take their cars to special leather repair shops.

However, I was not under the car very long when I had these horrible back pains and could barely get out from under the vehicle. One of the guys helped me to stand up, but the pain was reaching an unbearable point. This definitely was going to shoot a day at the shop because the only thing I could do at this point was to go home and get some rest. How I was able to drive home I don't know, but I was rather happy when no one was there. At this point, all I wanted to do was take a couple of pain pills and lie down in bed.

I slept quite a few hours and was awakened by Colleen coming into the bedroom saying, "What on earth is the matter honey? Are you ill?"

"I just have a horrible back ache. While I was able to sleep well, right now it is obvious the pain is not going away. Could you call Dr. Johns and make an appointment for me?"

Fortunately, I was able to get an appointment early the next morning. The orthopedic doc named Dr. Johns could not really find anything wrong but did order an MRI or Magnetic Resonance Imaging. I was surprised when he asked me if I had been under a lot of stress lately since apparently that often causes a lot of back pain. My first reaction to the question and the subsequent answer I gave was that I did not have any stress at all. Only later I remembered all these anxiety attacks and inner fear I was getting over the "wife situation" and I thought, oh great, now the problem is going to manifest me in ways I would never have anticipated.

My MRI was scheduled for the middle of the week, but there was no way I could go to work before then because I felt so absolutely miserable. How strange that I got anxiety attacks every time I heard news of my prior wife, but being enclosed while getting the MRI did not bother me at all. They scheduled an appointment for me on Friday of that week where the doctor examined the MRI results but again found nothing wrong except some usual deterioration and spots of arthritis that might get worse in the future. This news should have made me happy, but since I was still in so much pain, any happiness I might have felt was muted by my suffering.

After many weeks on mild pain pills and physical therapy I still felt incapacitated, so the doc decided to give me a series of shots to see if this would help alleviate the pain.

I started reading up on back pain and found one book that recommended learning some relaxation techniques that supposedly could help to remove back pain. Thinking I had nothing to lose at this point, I started practicing what they suggested and also began the series of three shots. The shots were a great success, but I felt if my tension were to continue I had best learn to relax myself as well. At the moment, until I could determine Aaron's real intentions for my daughter, I was definitely going to need to learn these techniques, or I was sure the back pain would resurface.

When I did return to my job, I left the under the car body repairs to the younger men and went back to doing the administrative work.

Chapter Forty-Seven

Aaron was home for the summer by now, but because of my involvement with my back problems I really did not get an opportunity to discuss the trip to Connecticut with him. He started his summer job immediately, so often we passed each other in the house with my going to therapy or him leaving for work.

When Aaron was not working, he spent a lot of time at Steve's house. We had assumed Janice had moved in by now, but Aaron said Janice told Steve she would not live with him because she knew it would upset her mother. That statement surprised me that she would be concerned about what her mother might think. In this day and age it was very rare for young people to think of others more than themselves. Aaron did expect Steve was going to ask Janice to marry him, so it was good to think another wedding might be in our future. Steve had already told Aaron, if and when the wedding occurred, he wanted him to be his best man.

When I returned to work at the shop, I had a lot to keep my mind busy. The vocation of car technician was getting more intense in the past few years and I appreciated the diversion from worrying about how to deal with the factor of my "old" family coming back into my life. The past decade saw rapid changes in automotive technology, so it was important that we kept the guys working for us qualified and knowledgeable on how to do good work on the cars brought in for repair. We were constantly upgrading our facilities and equipment because of this rapid speed of automotive technology, and we continued to send our technicians for training. There were certain shingles we wanted displayed on our facility such as the ASE certification (Automotive Service Excellence), NAPA Autocare, and Parts Plus Car Care to name a few. Our customers continued to come back year after year for routine maintenance and upkeep in addition to any car problems they might have, and our hope was to continue this ongoing relationship. We were proud of our customer service, and I was constantly observing the employees to make sure their work and attitude were up to par. Consequently, when I was at work, I was just fine, and rarely gave the Connecticut family any thought.

Anymore though, back at home it seemed that every little thing made me think of Megan and Tracy. One night we were all sitting down to dinner and the discussion finally got around to Aaron's trip east. Actually, it was Susan and Casey that showed the interest, so I just sat there taking in the conversation. Aaron said that several of the guys took turns driving with Megan and Tracy on the long trip to give them a break while two other cars of his friends followed behind. With that amount of help involved, it did not take long to unload Tracy's stuff and situate it in the house. Aaron told how the first night Tracy's Mom ordered pizza for everyone and they all relaxed around the house.

"Oh, yea, Dad," Aaron said. "I saw a picture of Tracy's Dad and he looks a lot like you might have looked when you were younger. I just couldn't get over how much the two of you resembled one another."

I took a sip of my iced tea to clear my throat and tried sounding nonchalant. The drink was of no help though. My voice sounded squeaky when I said, "No, kidding."

"Sure did. It was almost eerie!"

"Well, I have heard it said that everyone has a double some place. I guess her father is my double." How easy it was getting for me to lie to everyone.

The little guy laughed saying, "Maybe that's your ghost Daddy. Tee Hee."

He made everyone else laugh, and once again the conversation got averted and we were on to something else. These past few months have been hell for me. Was it ever going to end, or was it going to get worse? How I would love to be able to predict the future. Then again, maybe the status quo was better right now.

Chapter Forty-Eight

Thefts of gasoline were becoming more prominent since gas prices had reached sky high proportions for the United States. While all of us were affected by these prices, in actuality our business was profiting indirectly because of this fact. Several areas in town had suffered thieves puncturing the tanks of vehicles while using a container to catch the fuel. Pickup trucks and sport utility vehicles were the most vulnerable given their height. Newer vehicles had plastic tanks that were easy to drill and had less of a chance of a catastrophic spark. Preference for drilling, as opposed to siphoning, may have also surfaced because of a design change in the tanks of vehicles that now have check balls which prevent spills in rollover accidents, and this consequently makes siphoning more difficult. Many of the thieves were using cordless drills. The heat and friction generated could have easily caused fires, so police were very much concerned.

Supposedly, some of these thieves might even attempt to resell the "liquid gold" as many were calling this crime of opportunity. Gas tanks were becoming a cache of valuable loot. This type of crime was first seen during the Middle East oil embargo of the early 1970's. I knew from prior experience that the cost of replacing a tank on passenger vehicles would run anywhere between $300 and $400 dollars, and the plastic tank on newer vehicles could run as high as $500. There was so much work at the shop because of these crimes that I was back to helping with repairs just to support our shop in keeping up with the extra volume of work. Accordingly, I became immersed in work again and my own personal travails were easily set aside during this time.

Working long hours meant I missed a lot of goings on at the house. The children were always so involved in multiple activities where I usually enjoyed either taking them or watching them perform. I felt as though in some ways I was reverting back to the time I spent working in Connecticut that was so time consuming I lacked the time and enjoyment of participating in Tracy's life. I also knew, however, that the long working hours were only going to be temporary. Hopefully, with increased police surveillance, there was not going to be another rash of gas tanks being drilled for a long time.

Many nights during that time period when Colleen and I hit the pillow, we had no problems quickly falling asleep because of our extreme exhaustion. I cherished the time we spent talking to each other in the quiet of our room after everyone had gone to sleep. That was how I kept on top of everything that was going on in all our lives, but lately I was not privy to any of that information. I, of course, was tired because of the many long hours at work since we decided to work overtime to keep on top of the overload of vehicles needing repairs. Colleen, on the other hand, was exhausted by just having to do everything herself without any help from me.

After several weeks of hard work and exhaustion, life began to settle down and we were all out back sitting on the deck one evening after dinner. It became apparent just how much news I was missing when the talk turned to Steve's wedding. I was astonished to hear that the wedding had already been planned for a few short weeks away. Steve and Janice wanted a simple wedding. In fact, they were to get married officially in the Catholic Church rectory with just their parents in attendance there. Afterward, they were going to repeat their vows in a reenactment outside in Colleen's backyard under the white trellised gazebo. Just a few close friends and family were going to be invited, and of course Aaron was going to be the best man.

Chapter Forty-Nine

Colleen and I had signed a pre-nuptial agreement when we got married. Her husband had left her well off, and I had no intentions of taking any of that away from her. I had established a strong portfolio of investments myself after receiving insurance money from the tornado and the ultimate sale of my condo. Plus, as co-owner of the shop, I was what one would easily now call wealthy. My financial training was a big asset in running our business, so I guess I could thank my parents for that. The property Colleen's house stood upon was outstanding, and the backyard gazebo area would definitely be a great site for the wedding. I understood tents had already been ordered for the reception to be held after the wedding, and they were getting a dance floor brought in as well. When those women set their mind to something, they accomplished it with sheer will and determination. Bridal showers were already being planned for Janice. The bride and groom were fortunate in the fact that because they were being married at the rectory they did not have to go through the lengthy wait that having a wedding in the church would entail. They worked along with the priest in order to pick a day that was convenient to both of them and to the priest as well. All involved wanted to be sure the priest could be in attendance not only for the wedding itself but for the reception after as well.

Of course, Steve also had been busy working late hours at the shop like the rest of us, but he was thankful for the overtime money. Feeling a little left out of all the planning, I asked if there was anything left for me to do. I found out that Carl and I were in charge of ordering the liquor and soft drinks for the occasion and finding a bar tender.

Many of the flowers in the yard would be in full bloom when the wedding occurred, so there was no doubt everything was going to look fabulous. My biggest concern would be the weather that day, but no one else seemed too worried about that.

We lit the fire pit and started making *s'mores,* the delicious little graham cracker treats with chocolate and marshmallows that I learned about after marrying Colleen who had said they were often made at Girl Scout camps. While we all sat around eating the goodies and chatting, I heard the girls telling Aaron how cute they thought Tracy was. I overheard him say, "She loved you guys too and said she would have loved to have two sisters like the two of you. I told her she had to be crazy."

The girls got Aaron in a bear hug and started to wrestle him for telling Tracy she was crazy for wanting sisters like them.

How would the girls know what Tracy looked like I wondered? Was Aaron showing more pictures of the two of them together? I wanted to ask but was afraid of doing so until Casey said, "Will she be back here again before she returns to Connecticut?"

OOOh, NO, what did I just hear? Was Tracy actually in my house? No, it could not have been. I tried telling myself to stop getting crazy, but then Colleen interjected how very sweet she thought Tracy was. I could feel the pounding in my heart.

Susan then brought up the fact that Tracy agreed with Aaron when she said to me, "Tracy really did think you looked so much like her Dad when she looked at the family pictures on the piano."

"Was Tracy in our home?"

"Yea," Susan replied. "In fact she was here a couple of times on the nights you were working late."

I knew this time I had to compose myself, or the family was going to notice a pattern of my getting nervous every time the conversation was about Connecticut, Megan or Tracy.

"Oh," I spoke softly so as not to let out that squeaky voice once more. "Is she planning on visiting us again, and why was she here this time?"

"She was here to spend the week with some girls on her school soccer team. They brought her over here to say hello to me along with a couple of the guys who had gone on the trip to Connecticut with us. They were going to try and come back here this evening, but I know she is leaving tomorrow, so I seriously doubt it now. But, who knows? The night is young."

I shook my head to indicate I heard what Aaron said, but then I just sort of froze in my seat contemplating a thousand things I should do. Oh, I hope they don't come here tonight. Yet, if they do, I need to make an excuse and get out of here. After about ten minutes, I again spoke softly and said that I was feeling tired and since it was nearly ten o'clock I thought I should be going up to bed. The younger children had stayed up longer than normal, and Colleen had already taken them upstairs to bed a few minutes before, so I did not have to deal with any suspicion from her. The girls gave me a hug and we said good night. Should Tracy come in later that evening, I could safely pretend to be asleep though I knew a good night's sleep was not going to happen to me that evening. Thank the Lord Tracy was returning home tomorrow. I lucked out this time by working overtime. How would I manage another future visit?

Stop the questions I told myself. Practice relaxation techniques. You do not want your back to start hurting again. I never would have anticipated this happening in a million years on the day I left Connecticut. Do people in the witness protection program go through these same types of occurrences?

Chapter Fifty

I was happy Steve's wedding was fast approaching. Exhilaration filled the air and my body was feeling partially exhilarated too. The five days leading up to the wedding there was constant movement. Delivery trucks were bringing white chairs to set up on the lawn around the gazebo. There were bolts of white netting to be used to wrap around the tent poles. Huge pots of fern were deposited all over the yard, and I heard that fresh flowers would be coming in soon. Carl and Barbara were at our house a lot checking things off their list and meeting with the caterers to show their choices of where to set up tables of food. With the exception of helping Carl with the liquor, I began to happily relinquish any other duties. This wedding after all was really about Carl and Barbara's son and they were only using our yard for that purpose. The more this information sunk in, the more I began to relax and enjoy the excitement realizing that was all I had to do really, to just sit back and enjoy.

I did babysit several evenings while Colleen attended numerous showers in Janice's honor. Brightly wrapped gifts with large colorful bows were dispersed throughout the house, courtesy of Casey and Susan who were also invited to the showers. I loved my family and thrived on all this excitement. I had heard that Tracy did stop by our house her last night in town, so I was very thankful I had thought up the pretense of going to bed when I did, though that night I hardly got any sleep at all. Now that I knew she had gone back to Connecticut, I could better immerse myself in the anticipation of the big day to arrive.

Steve was so fortunate to find such a lovely girl. He had really settled down and had accommodated himself so well to his incapacity of missing one leg. When he wore long pants one could barely tell he was missing a leg at all. Honestly, though, leg or no leg, I don't really think the loss bothered either Steve or Janice. They were both very mature for their age and quite level-headed. I even overheard Steve say one night that he held no malice towards his ex-girl friend. He realized that the whole war experience was probably more than she could handle, and he expressed forgiveness for her. When one can be so forgiving, regardless of how much she had hurt Steve—well, I just knew his future was going to hold many pleasant things for him. Carl had even told me Steve was completing his education on line while working at the shop. Steve mentioned that someday he wanted to have good knowledge on not only working in the shop, but helping to run the business as well. Here was a person who did not let his whole life get ruined by one setback. I was very happy for him.

Chapter Fifty-One

The wedding turned out to be even more fun than anyone would have anticipated. Temperatures for August could not have been better, and the brightly lit sun served to bring cheer to the occasion. All were thankful for the fact that the humidity never materialized until late in the day. Our group of friends always seemed to enjoy themselves whether we were celebrating a big monstrous wedding or a simply elegant one like Steve's.

Prior to the wedding day, knowing we were going to have a small band playing in our backyard, Colleen and the girls made gift bags of goodies packed in colorful packages. Inside each of the bags, Colleen put a little note telling about the wedding celebration and apologizing in advance for any noise that might become offensive any time that day. These gift bags were delivered to our neighbors within a several block radius of our home. The note promised that this was just a one day special event, and it thanked everyone ahead of time for being so understanding. Leave it to the women to think of everything. Most of us men would have said, "If they think we are too noisy, well the hell with them."

As ebullient as my wife always appeared, I could not help but notice a slight tiredness around her eyes, and I was somewhat concerned. Usually, she had the energy of one of those lively batteries we often see advertised on television, hence my concern when I saw her becoming more sluggish. Yet, when asked, Colleen always claimed she was fine and responded that she was not tired at all.

Things did not slow down much after the wedding. The end of summer was near and Aaron was already getting ready to return to college. Colleen was also busy buying school supplies and new clothes for the children who were growing out of everything they owned and sprouting like weeds. The pace of work at the shop became more unhurried, but we were still busy because some of us had to cover for Steve who was on his honeymoon.

A couple of mornings at breakfast Colleen looked downright pasty, and I even heard her upchucking one morning, but she insisted she just ate her breakfast too fast, and it went down the wrong pipe. When this upchucking became more of a routine occurrence, I insisted Colleen make a doctor's appointment, and I told her she was to be sure to notify my work so they could schedule me off on that day. I wanted to be with Colleen when she went to the doctor to see what the heck was going on.

An appointment was made early in the next week. When we arrived at the doctor's office on appointment day the nurse called Colleen to go back, and I started to follow. However, the nurse told me they were just going to do a routine exam first, and when the doctor was ready to tell her his findings they would call me into the office at that time. Upon reflecting on this, I realized that was a good idea.

"What's up Colleen? I haven't seen you in a while," said the doctor.

"Well, Doc, I haven't felt like eating in a while and some days I am quite nauseous. I really think I haven't been eating right because we have been so busy with Steve's wedding and everything, but I did not believe any of this was serious enough to come to see you if my husband had not insisted."

"Have you had a period lately?"

"No, that's another thing. I think I am going through the change, so that probably has a lot to do with how I have been feeling too."

"Well, let's take a look at you and see what we can find out."

The doctor did quite a thorough exam from one end of the body to the other and then left the room while telling Colleen she could get dressed.

When the doctor returned, he had a strange look on his face, and Colleen was almost afraid to hear what he had to say. "Well, young lady, how would you like to add to your brood?"

"What do you mean?"

"I mean you are pregnant."

"No, that's impossible. No way!"

"Yes—way—Colleen."

"Oh Doc, what am I going to do? Who ever heard of having a baby at my age?"

"As a doctor, I certainly have, though I will admit it was more common before all this birth control stuff came into being. They used to call them 'Change of Life' babies."

"Actually, I thought when I missed my periods that I was finally starting menopause and I was one woman looking forward to it. Oh, what am I going to do?"

"That is what I am here to ask you. There is still time to terminate the pregnancy if that is your wish."

"Oh, Doctor Jones, I could never in a million years do that, but doing so would certainly simplify things. I wonder what my husband is going to say. Do you think you could give the two of us some time alone in your office to discuss this situation?"

"Of course, Colleen, I was going to suggest that to you. I'll leave now and have the nurse go get your husband and bring him in to you, and I will return in about fifteen to twenty minutes."

I was starting to get worried that they were going to find something seriously wrong with Colleen and nearly jumped off my seat when the nurse called my name. When I looked at Colleen's face, it did not help me feel any better.

"What's the matter honey? Is everything going to be alright? I have been so worried," I said as I went up and embraced her, hugging her tightly. Colleen burst out in tears. "Oh help me Lord, is it that bad?"

Colleen decided to just blurt it out saying, "I'm pregnant."

I was taken aback, perhaps thinking I heard those words by mistake. I pushed her at arm's length to look her over fully to see if she could in any way be kidding me. She looked at me like a pitiful puppy caught in the act of doing something wrong. That is when the news really kicked in, and I picked her up and twirled her around and around until she claimed she felt dizzy. I was overwhelmed, happy, delighted, scared, a little fearful and unbelieving.

"Imagine us two old fogeys going to have a baby," I said. This is going to be the most beautiful baby in the world.

"Are you really ok with this?"

"Why wouldn't I be? Just as long as the doctor thinks you will not have any problems I think that everything about us having a baby is perfect."

"Oh, honey, you are the best. I should have known you would not react in any other way. Wait until we tell the kids."

At this point there was a knock on the door of the doctor's office, and without us saying come in the doctor entered the room. "Well, guys, how are you doing?"

I immediately asked the doctor if he thought Colleen was going to be able to handle this pregnancy without problems.

Doctor Jones assured me that if Colleen took good care of herself, ate a healthy diet to care for two people, and got plenty of rest, he did not envision a problem at all. He also would be monitoring her frequently throughout the pregnancy he explained. "Now, you two love birds get on home and celebrate with your family," he said as he handed Colleen prescriptions for her to get filled.

The strangest thing of all happened when we got home that was totally unexpected. The girls told us that Tom's wife Lynn had called and said to call her back as soon as possible since she had some good news. Colleen immediately picked up the phone to call Lynn. After their usual chit chat Colleen became silent as she listened and then she screamed out, "You've got to be kidding. What great news and guess what?"

Lynn could be heard screaming that she was not kidding at all and wanted to know what she was supposed to guess.

All Colleen said into the phone was, "Me too!"

"You too what?"

"I'm pregnant too."

Lynn was silent on the other end of the phone, and all the children and even I just stood there in disbelief. Did I hear correctly that not only was Colleen pregnant, but Lynn too?

"The girls were screaming, "Mom, are you going to have a baby?"

Aaron looked at us like we were crazy. After all, his parents were not supposed to be having sex.

"Imagine these two over the hill gals pregnant with little babies," Colleen talked back into the phone."

Lynn responded, "Wait until I tell Tom."

There was no doubt our life was in for a big change, but how much more fun this change was going to be sharing it with two of our best friends who were in the same boat. This was going to be wonderful fodder for the town gossips for sure.

Chapter Fifty-Two

For about a week after finding out Colleen was pregnant that was all everyone talked about at the house, and at the shop, and at Tom's bank. The whole town seemed to be in a tizzy over it. Colleen and Lynn could not resist going into baby shops and picking up cute little items. "We should be buying this stuff for grandchildren at this stage in our lives," was Lynn's take on it. Both women laughed and kept buying.

The coming weekend Aaron was leaving to go back to school, and I was the one chosen to ride along with him to see him hopefully get settled without any problems. We were going to go in two vehicles because I wanted to return the same day, and Aaron was keeping his car at school. Ever since last semester when I spotted my former wife in the college town, I could not feel quite comfortable going back to that campus. Colleen still suffered from a little morning sickness, so we felt it would be better if she did not go along on the trip.

Aaron and I stopped for some breakfast before arriving on campus to unload the cars. That boy could really put down the food. His breakfast was going to be enough to unload five cars if necessary. We arrived on the campus early enough that not a lot of other students were unloading their cars yet which did make our job somewhat less stressful.

There were a few things Aaron was going to need from the hardware store, so I offered to go and buy them while Aaron went to the Administration building to settle something about some books still listed on his previous bill they said had not been returned. Luckily for Aaron, he had the necessary paperwork to prove that he did indeed return them.

When I got back to Aaron's dorm from the hardware store, his car was nowhere in sight, so I knew he had not yet returned. I had to park a lot further away because more students had arrived by now. After parking, I walked down the lovely tree lined street, and my heart instantly started pounding as I felt overcome by another approaching anxiety attack. This was all precipitated by seeing my ex-wife and daughter Tracy carrying some boxes into a dorm a few structures away from Aaron's building. The path where I was walking meant I had to walk right by them. I thought of turning around, but that might even look more suspicious. I was also praying that Aaron did not return then because he surely would have wanted to introduce me to them. Oh, for crying out loud. I started walking with a different strange gait and pulled my baseball cap well down over my face. Fortunately, at about the time I reached the two women, some of Tracy's friends spotted her. The girls started screaming and hugging each other, so luckily no one even noticed me. However, I realized on second thought that I had better go back to my car and drive away for a while to let them fully unload their car. Not knowing how long it would take them to unload the car, I thought it unwise to be there when Aaron returned.

I drove in the opposite direction of the hardware store, saw a little bar, and went in to have a beer. I also turned off my cell phone in case Aaron should call and wonder where I was. This all was getting to be so tortuous and devious I almost began hating myself. Perhaps this was God's way of punishing me for basically living a good life the past few years and pretty much being happy while doing so. Maybe I needed to suffer a lot more. Was my whole life going to reach a peak and then come crashing down on me? That would not be fair to my new family any more than leaving my first family had been fair to them.

After about an hour, I turned my cell phone back on and started to drive back to campus. Please God, I prayed to myself, please don't let them be in the area outside the dorms anymore. Please, I kept saying in my head. I was going to drive right on by if they were still there. What a relief to see they were no longer in the vicinity. I noticed Aaron's car parked by the curve and found a place to park. After getting out of the car, I ran up the steps.

Aaron looked up from his desk and said, "Dad, where were you? You've been gone over an hour, and I couldn't even reach you on your cell phone."

"Oh, I just enjoyed looking around the hardware store and lost track of time. I also didn't know my cell phone was turned off. Sorry about that."

"Actually," Aaron replied, "One of my friends thought he saw you walking near here about an hour ago."

"Nah, it must have been someone else."

We hung those things that needed hanging, and Aaron appeared to be settled. All I could think was that I needed to get out of there and quick. "If we are finished hanging shelves and things, and there is nothing else to be done, I think I will venture on home Aaron."

"Oh, Dad, I was hoping the two of us could go out to eat dinner before you leave."

"Well, if you can take me to a quiet place where you don't expect to see any students then maybe I will stay. I am getting a little headache and don't feel up to a lot of noise." Lies, lies, and more lies. My lies were becoming routine.

"There is this ritzy place on the other side of town if you are willing to put out the dough. I sure would not expect any other students there."

I requested a table that was off by itself situated in a corner where we would not be easily seen. The meal was excellent, but I was on edge the entire time. This would be exactly the type of place Megan and Tracy would definitely eat dinner, so I was not completely comfortable. Half expecting my daughter and ex-wife to come in any minute, I was scared and uncomfortable. We fortunately got through our meal, but then Aaron said, "You really are quiet tonight Dad. Maybe you had better get on home. I just wanted to spend this time with you since we so rarely get the opportunity anymore for just the two of us to be together."

"Oh, Aaron, you are right, and I do apologize for not being the best of company. I promise you we will spend more time together in the future."

I drove Aaron back to the dorm, gave him a big bear hug and started to leave. Just as I was pulling away from the curb, I saw Megan and Tracy park their car and get out. Through my rear view mirror I also saw Aaron try to flag me down to come back. He obviously wanted to introduce me to them both, but I pretended I could not see him and continued on my way home.

Chapter Fifty-Three

Around three o'clock in the morning, I saw a baby driving a car towards my car, and the other car was occupied by Megan and Tracy. The car kept getting closer and closer. People were all yelling for me to stop, and I sat up in bed with a jolt realizing it was a dream while feeling disoriented and covered in sweat. Fortunately, Colleen was so sound asleep she did not even notice. This dream nightmare kept recurring. One night it would be one o'clock, another night four in the morning. I tried drinking some milk or eating a banana. Nothing I did seemed to help me fall back to sleep. Then, I did some work on the computer which only made me more awake and certainly did not have the desired calming effect I was craving. By the fourth night, I went down into the den in the lounge chair and put on a soothing old movie. Eventually, I fell asleep in the chair, and I was still there when morning rolled around. Since I am the first one to awake in the morning, no one even noticed I had slept in the den all night. I went up and took a shower and prayed passionately that these horrible dreams would go away.

Everyone else was so wrapped up with talk of the new baby that hardly anyone noticed my troubled state of mind. For this I was grateful.

The younger children were relentless. They wanted us to pick a name right away and argued if they wanted a boy or girl. No one really asked Colleen or me what we wanted. We were just there to listen to them fight.

When I spent my lunchtime with Tom, I inquired how all of their children were accepting this newest addition. His answer indicated their actions were pretty much in the same mode as our offspring. I wondered if Tom felt as overwhelmed as I did with the whole process. One minute I was ecstatic, and the next worried sick. But then I realized that a lot of my worry was not so much about the new baby as it was my old family. That was one subject I could not even begin to talk to anyone about, so I inwardly suffered. By the third week, I perhaps only had a nightmare every fourth night or so, and going down to my lounge chair in the den seemed to be the best medicine without filling myself with either over the counter drugs or prescription medications to help me fall back to sleep.

One evening, I decided to take Colleen to see a movie. On the way to the theater in the car Colleen was in a talkative, happy mood.

"Isn't it great honey that you are going to have your own flesh and blood baby? No one has been a better Dad than you have to the children. They love you dearly, but I am so thrilled that I am able to do this for you, even if we are older. I hope you are as happy as I would like you to be."

"Anything that I helped to create with you Colleen could only delight me, though I will admit I am still worried somewhat about you, and concerned for the health of both you and the baby."

"Well, tonight, we are going to enjoy this movie and take away all your worries by buying a nice big tub of popcorn."

The movie was great and after devouring the popcorn, we cuddled together like two teenagers. I was rather happy the theater was not crowded so we could feel less inhibited.

That evening I had the first good night's sleep since taking Aaron back to school. I decided I was going to avoid going back to that campus at all costs. Hopefully, Aaron would not decide to bring Tracy home with him either.

When September rolled around, they kept replaying images of the September 2001 anniversary tragedy on television. One afternoon when everyone was gone, and I was home alone for a short time watching television, I was overcome by the somber ceremonies. I believe this was the first time I was ever feeling any guilt for what I had done. Determination was what drove me to leave my family all those years ago that I never really stopped to think of this whole horrible mess of which I took advantage. After all these years, I never really paid a price for my actions until Tracy came into Aaron's life. Now, lately, I was haunted more and more by what I had done. The worst part is that if my state of mind got worse there really was no place I could go. I certainly could not seek the help of a professional psychiatrist. Even if there were doctor/patient confidentiality, how could I really trust that the doctor would not tell, or at least try to convince me that I should reveal this information? I had learned years ago that revealing what I had done was not an option for me. I could not imagine anyone being sympathetic to my plight.

Chapter Fifty-Four

The local college had approached me to teach a vocational course several nights a week on auto mechanics. Even though they were going to pay me, I felt it was also a good charitable thing to be helping others interested in my line of work. First, I discussed it with Colleen because I knew she would have the extra burden of bathing the little ones on the nights I would be working. I felt better when Casey and Susan said they would gladly help with the younger children. How wonderful that everyone was willing to help out simply because a new little baby was going to enter the picture.

Colleen was worried about the section of town where the college was located because she had heard of some muggings in the area. I promised to use caution and to try and park in a well lit area. I really did not anticipate a problem because I had a faculty parking pass and the faculty parking lot was close to the building where I would be instructing.

The work at the college was extremely rewarding. We not only had an area where I could lecture and give assignments, but there was a big warehouse section where the students could work hands on fixing various different parts of old or disabled vehicles like pumps, radiators, ignitions, spark plugs and also changing oil. The cars we used were old cars donated by people who wanted to get rid of them. We even had a car or two brought in whose owners wanted them to be painted and were willing to have the students do the painting for a reduced price. Actually, the students taking these classes were willing participants, so it was sheer pleasure being their instructor.

Some of the students got carried away working on the vehicles, so much in fact that no one would notice the late hour, and believe me; I was chastised for coming home really late many nights.

One night I didn't come home at all. Colleen called Tom and asked him to drive around the campus to see if he could find my car. However, that particular evening I was not parked in the normal parking area because many professors were visiting from adjoining campuses for a faculty meeting, and all the faculty parking spaces were taken by the time I got to work. Tom drove all around the areas where he thought I would most likely be but never found me or my car.

At this point Colleen was scared out of her wits, and Tom stayed with her and called the police for her. It appeared as though they lost precious hours by first coming to the house to hear what the two of them had to say, but while at my house, one of the cops sent out a communication describing my car and my appearance while asking them to cover the entire campus area.

Since I had parked so far away from the regular building where I normally worked, I asked one of the last students to leave to please give me a lift to where I had parked my car. He did so, but kids being kids, he did not stay around to wait and watch me enter my vehicle, nor did he watch me safely drive away. Not being too sensible myself, I set my briefcase on the hood of the car while I searched for my keys. What happened after that I do not remember. Apparently, someone who had been hiding behind one of the many trees surrounding the parking lot whacked me over the head and ran off with my case that held my cell phone, wallet and everything else. I never woke up again until I was in the hospital. The college police patrol spotted my body lying on the road near my car and called an ambulance. They reported finding my body to the town police department at about the same time the other patrol car received the notice to search for me. Of course they had no identification for me, but since they suspected I was the one that Colleen and Tom had called about they chose not to break into my car since the description fit what Colleen had told them, and they hoped to get positive identification by Colleen at the hospital.

There was a huge gash on the back of my head requiring more than twenty stitches, and I had lost quite a bit of blood while laying there on the ground. I was alive though and grateful for that and happy to see Colleen and Tom when I awoke in my hospital bed. By the end of the week, my room was beginning to look like a happy funeral parlor. I say happy, because I had loads of plants and flowers disbursed throughout the room, and just about each one had a helium balloon stuck in the arrangement. I also had more visitors then I really wanted to see. The staff from the college was the most upset and assured me there was no rush for me to get back to work. I knew though that once I was well, I needed to return immediately because if I let fear overtake me, my life was really going to be screwed. I did not bring up the matter with Colleen though until I was released from the hospital.

The morning I was to be released from the hospital the police called saying that someone had found my wallet with my identification in it, though all the money and credit cards had been stolen. The person who found it had been walking their dog in the park and the dog veered off the path to smell around the area, and that is where the wallet was found. Finding my wallet was going to be a big help in not having to go to the motor vehicle administration to get a new license, nor would I have to endure the process of obtaining new identification.

One of the first serious arguments Colleen and I ever had was about my returning to work at the college. She was adamant about not wanting me to return, and I was just as determined to return. Neither one of us were willing to give in. Finally I said to Colleen, "Would you have gotten an abortion when you found out you were pregnant because I asked you to do so?"

"Why do you even ask such a stupid question," she fired back.

"I guess I believe that some personal decisions have to be made by the person most involved. While I would never want you to get an abortion, the decision was really yours to make and not mine. I feel the same way about my decision to return back to work at the college. Only I can decide what is best for me in this particular case. I cannot let myself be overcome by fear, or my fears will nag me the rest of my life making me feel that the only way to solve them would be to always cave in. Do you understand what I am trying to say?"

"Yes and no. My decision to abort a baby would not have a harmful affect on you, but if you are mugged again that could have devastating results for not only you, but for me and the rest of the family too."

"Well, that is true, but perhaps if I ever have to park away from the normal faculty parking lot, I can call security and ask for support in either following or bringing me safely to my car. I will ask the school if they could provide me with this service. I feet almost certain they would comply."

"If you promise me you will do that, and those involved concur, only then will I feel more comfortable about you returning to work there," Colleen finally agreed.

Chapter Fifty-Five

When the semester was almost over, before Aaron came home, I made arrangements to take a few days off from the shop in order to go on a short fishing and camping trip with Tom. I needed male companionship. There were just too many females overwhelming me these days with baby talk, baby shopping, baby showers, baby, baby, and babies.

I was busy getting my camping gear out of the shed when I heard the house phone ring. It was probably for one of the girls anyway, so I just kept doing what I was doing. I loved the long light hours of daylight savings time as it just seemed one could accomplish so much more. I pretty much found everything I needed and hung some of it up on the screened-in porch to get some fresh air. At that point, Colleen came in saying a bunch of kids from Aaron's school were going to be coming for a visit. I froze in position and said, "Oh?"

"Yes, isn't that exciting?"

"Who will be coming, did you get names?"

"Well, yes, he mentioned a Carl, David, Tracy, Judy and a couple of other names of people I did not recognize."

"When are they coming?" I heard the name Tracy and wanted to die right then and there.

"That's the unfortunate part. It appears the only time they can come is the exact time you will be camping with Tom. Though I do know how much this trip means to you, do you think you could change your date?"

Man, I thought fast, "Tom and I had a hard enough time coming up with this date and besides, they will mostly be in and out probably, so whether I am here or not is not going to be such a big deal."

"In that regard, I suppose you are right."

"What day and time are they coming?" I wanted to be sure Tom and I left before Aaron and his group arrived, so there would be no conflict with my still being at home.

"They should be here sometime around five o'clock on Friday afternoon."

"Oh, that's a shame since Tom and I plan to leave around three o'clock that day."

"Maybe you could wait around a few hours?"

"I wouldn't mind doing so, but that would be just the time for some reason they would leave later and upset both our schedules. We cannot be at our children's beck and call all the time honey."

"You're right. I just wanted them to meet you too, but there will be other times."

I hope not I thought, but said instead, "Of course."

I really could not wait to get away now. Actually, I had a hard time convincing Tom to leave around three o'clock that Friday when I mentioned it earlier in the week. He explained that he was really hoping to leave around six o'clock, but I told him we would get stuck in the worst of the rush hour traffic, and he reneged and agreed to leave at three like I requested. I was pretty much getting my way in all these discussions. I knew this was not always going to be the case, and I just wondered how long my luck would hold out.

What made me start thinking of my mugging at this point, I am not sure, but for some odd reason the mugging came to mind, and I could not dismiss it. They never found out who mugged me, and they probably never would find out. To think someone could practically take away your life and never get caught really upset me. In fact, taking my life that evening was indeed a possibility since the doctor had said that if someone had not found me when they did I would probably have lost too much blood and most likely have died. This same jerk was still roaming around our streets probably stealing from others just because he/she was too lazy to get a job. I imagined the person roaming the campus looking for a lone vehicle hoping that someone would arrive to get into it, and of course that night the object of their find was me. Yet, was what I did any better? No, I did not attempt to hurt anyone physically, but I certainly did mentally. I was nothing but a common criminal myself, and I was also getting away with it, at least until recently. I was not roaming around the streets stealing, but I did leave a whole other life for a new one without respect for those I left behind, and in reality without respect for the new friends I found because of my complete dishonesty. It is done now, so why do I keep beating myself to pieces. Some criminals do get caught and go to jail, and after putting in time they are released back into society. For the most part these criminals are forgiven. Everyone in my life seemed to be living quite well, and some of it was because of my decision to leave. For example, my first family was left with a lot more money after I was gone and presumed dead than they ever would have had while I was still alive. I also am a wonderful provider for my new family and helped to make Carl's business grow to where we now had a wonderful partnership. Here I was again trying to justify what I did. I really needed to get that time away with Tom, and I could not wait.

Chapter Fifty-Six

Megan had given the dating scene a good try and there was one individual she really enjoyed for his companionship, but she had no special desire to ever get married again. She had become used to living on her own all these years and doing as she pleased. Megan did not need to be a maid to some man who never picked up for himself and expected her to cook him a big meal every night. Now, she ate if she was hungry and cleaned up promptly after herself. Her home was always in order, and she liked it that way.

She was surprised how well she adjusted to having her only daughter gone as well. Megan slept much better when Tracy was away. When at home, Megan would lie awake waiting for her daughter to return home in the wee hours of the morning, but when she was away she had no knowledge of where she was, so consequently there was no need to worry. Also, there were nights Megan just wanted a nice quiet house with perhaps soft music in the background. This did not happen when Tracy was home. Megan did enjoy having Tracy at home along with her many friends, so that was not the issue. Those children could certainly make any household come alive. However, having Tracy home was easily tolerated because Megan knew it was only temporary. Yet, Megan did hope that someday when and if Tracy ever married she would live much closer to home. She would like her to live perhaps more like a two hour drive away instead of the long drive to Tennessee.

Lately, Megan would often wonder if she did the right thing when she married the first time. She and her husband really had nothing in common, and Megan realized how easy it was to manipulate him when he was young and impressionable. When she met her spouse she found out it was the first time he had been away from two elderly parents. Once she heard that her lover's background was in finance, she pushed him relentlessly, and he appeared to conform so easily. Megan was determined to marry someone who could provide for her abundantly. She was not at all shy about admitting that to herself, nor was she ashamed for thinking the way she did. Yet, she knew this was not something you went about admitting to others. People had to set goals for themselves. Her goals were to never settle for anything less than what her dreams indicated to her that she could achieve. Having a handsome wealthy man for her husband was part of those goals.

While Megan felt attractive, she also felt lucky to have such a handsome man show interest in her. What she realized really happened was that they sort of just fell into being really good acquaintances who sat near each other in math class and developed a bonding friendship. Megan was the assertive one in their relationship, and they only made love when she wanted to and not because her husband showed any interest. She was not going to let this bother her, however. Her intentions were to always be with him constantly so that he would not have the time or desire to seek anyone else. She would ask him to marry her, and she would plan the wedding. Instinct told her that she would not get any resistance, and that is what happened.

After the marriage however, her husband began to rebel, and small bickering arguments would occur which eventually escalated to huge fights. The two of them had been in a combative state of mind on that horrible day in September 2001. There was never going to be a way she would ever divorce him, so as far as she was concerned they were just going to have to continue to fight. However, she had to admit that never in a million years would she have wished for his demise in such a horrible manner. What was done was done though, and now she was quite willing to go on an occasional date to a good movie, or a night at the theater in the city, but never, ever would she marry again. Megan wanted a relationship like the one Jacqueline Kennedy Onassis had with Maurice Tempelsman or what she perceived their relationship to be. Though, Megan never wanted anyone moving in with her. Usually that type of friendship with a man was hard to find as they often wanted to get right into bed, and the older men justified the urge with the statement of wanting to get married.

As for Tracy, Megan could not determine if Tracy liked any of the young men she often brought home with her, especially the group from Tennessee. Tracy did appear to show a little more interest and perhaps an infatuation for the very handsome young man Aaron, but Tracy was very non-committal about that relationship or really any others. Perhaps Tracy's experience with her first love had proved too overwhelming for the present, and Tracy was willing to just take things slowly for a while and enjoy her friends in a group atmosphere.

On the one hand, Megan really thought that Aaron fellow was a fine, handsome, well mannered individual. The fact that Aaron lived in Tennessee however would be a big drawback where Megan was concerned. Most likely that meant Aaron might prefer a job near his family. If that happened, Tracy would not be in close proximity to Connecticut, so Megan always managed to reserve her comments about that fine young man. This was so contradictory to how Megan usually reacted when she especially liked one of Tracy's friends. Her normal tendency would be to rave and carry on about the individual in order to make an even bigger impression on Tracy. In the long run though, what would be would be, and no one knew that more than Megan. At least for now, Tracy was home for the summer. When the two of them were not working, they enjoyed doing fun things together.

Chapter Fifty-Seven

I decided it would be nice to have one more family fling together before the baby was born during one of the school breaks and take the children to Washington, D. C. Not only would they have fun, but they could experience some history as well. I had been so impressed with the area during the time we used to make our trips to care for Steve when he was at Walter Reed Medical Center, and I vowed at that time to come back with my family when we would really be able to enjoy the sights. The children were all excited about seeing the Washington Monument, and some wanted to see the Vietnam Veterans' Memorial because they had just been studying about that particular war.

In the evenings before the trip, we got out all the maps and as much information as we could gather from the Internet about the trip, and everyone got to pick one of their favorite places to go. Unfortunately, taking the trip in our large van that was a huge gas guzzler was going to add to the expense of the journey, but our family was large, and once the baby was born we would not be traveling such long distances for a while, so we felt this time the trip was justified. We certainly could easily afford the trip with our money and standard of living, but it was just an awareness of the world situation at this particular time when gas prices were the highest they had ever been.

We decided to travel on the weekend which meant we would arrive in Washington at the beginning of the week. Our anticipation was that the crowds would not be as intense during the week days. The city was clean, and the monuments awed the children with their distinct impressiveness and architectural style. We were all surprised how close in proximity the White House was to the streets. One day, to give the children a break from touring, we took them to an amusement park in nearby Maryland. Of course that was a huge hit, and they had no problem falling asleep that evening.

The Newseum had just opened in the District of Columbia a short time before our trip and one stifling hot day we all agreed that would be a good place to spend the entire day in the air conditioned comfort of this new fabulous building. This museum featured every form of media communication from newspapers, to television, to radio and movies, so there was something for every member of the family to enjoy. All the children screamed when we were in the 4D Theater where the seats rocked, rolled and shook you into an immersive experience. The children also enjoyed pretending to be newscasters at the interactive newsroom, and we all enjoyed Wolfgang Puck's delicacies in the Newseum's cafeteria.

Towards the end of the day, we went to the 4th floor to view the September 11, 2001 display of twisted metal and then to watch a short movie of what some actual news reporters who had been in the vicinity of the World Trade Towers that day truly experienced. In all this time, the impact of what actually happened had never really impressed me. I was too focused on my move in 2001, establishing a new life, and finding a new job, as opposed to everyone else who would have been shocked by the horror and glued to their television sets. I really had not paid all that much attention to everything that had transpired with the exception of the time I saw my wife's and my picture that had been flashed on the screen. Obviously, this movie was extremely moving to everyone who saw it because they had boxes of tissues available for all to use. I, however, after watching the movie, was drained to exhaustion from simply viewing what had occurred. A stroke of fate had prevented me from being in that building on that day, or I surely would not be here today to tell my story. I broke out in a sweat realizing that because I had planned something sinister by leaving my old life for a new one, I consequently missed the entire horror like the bodies jumping out of the windows and the collapse of those two beautiful structures where I had spent so much of my time interacting with friends, and doing important business, or enjoying lunch and watching the tourists—all of it mesmerized my thoughts.

When I sat there and watched the pulverization of the two towers into a complete collapse of nothing but rushing mounds of dust that covered the bodies of the reporters I felt complete shock. Shame also overcame me. How could I leave my wife and daughter on that day of all days? I really must have been in some horrible state of mind to even consider continuing on my journey at that time. Could one become so focused on what they were doing that they lost a sense of reality? I kept asking myself why I would do such a thing. Why, why, why?

Unhappiness can be the bane of existence. The only justification I can present to myself is that I was so totally unhappy and so ignorantly unaware of the true impact of the situation, I persistently continued with my plan totally naïve and immature that horrible day in September of the year 2001. Here I was a survivor of the horror, yet I was now suffering the same sadness of people who had lost loved ones. This had to be God's way of punishing me, and obviously I was going to have to be punished in this manner the rest of my life.

The show lasted about five to seven minutes, and the family had already exited the theater, but I sat there and watched the entire movie once again completely captivated. Fortunately, no one questioned me when I finally got up to leave because the movie was hard viewing for everyone. When I had planned this trip to Washington, I had not figured on feeling as though someone had punched me in the gut. Was I trying to torture myself when I suddenly wanted to buy any book, CD or video/DVD I could find about that atrocious day? My life was becoming a dichotomy. On the one hand I was consumed with thoughts of the horror that day, yet on the other hand I could not seem to get enough information about it all.

For several weeks after we arrived home from our little vacation, after everyone had already gone to bed, I stayed downstairs reading the books I purchased about Ground Zero and watching the DVD's depicting various people's stories that day of the terror. I found this so hard to comprehend that so much devastation had occurred, and I was so unmindful of it. I wanted desperately to see a therapist to help ease my concerns, but there was just no way that this was going to happen. Finally, like someone with an addiction who finally becomes cognizant of the harm the addiction can do, I realized I had to gather all the purchases I made on the subject of the pulverization of the towers and the personal stories of heartache, pack them into a box, and put them away on a shelf someplace, so I could no longer torture myself into a paroxysm. My jolly, happy go lucky persona was becoming taciturn in nature. Enough was enough. The new baby was due to arrive soon, and I had to get out of my slump. For a few nights after ridding myself of all the books etc., I felt signs of withdrawal symptoms, but after about five days I began to feel some substance of normalcy, and less ambivalent in my every day actions.

Chapter Fifty-Eight

Summer had not even arrived yet, but the days were extremely and unusually hot. My heart ached for Colleen. Her stomach was the size of two basketballs, just so very round and protruding enough that it appeared her tummy might pop at any given moment. Oddly enough, if one were to look at her from the rear you could not even tell she was pregnant. Lynn, on the other hand, had turned into one huge "roly-poly" as the pregnancy appeared to circumnavigate what was left, if any, of her waistline area. The two friends spent most of their afternoon days sitting around the pool watching the younger ones swim, sipping lemonade and occasionally taking a dip in the pool to cool off. Most of us acted like we were in some type of seasonal doldrums, just hanging around waiting for the big baby day to occur. When the women were not at the pool in the afternoon, both women were just as active as ever, and could have easily put any younger pregnant mothers to shame with all their activity.

One evening, Steve and his new bride invited all of us that had helped him while in the hospital over to a party in the condo common area designated for special parties where he lived. One section of the area had a pool table, plus puzzles and other games where the children amused themselves. The rest of us gathered in a room near the food enjoying all the delicacies and the enlightening conversation. The newlyweds looked so happy together they were a pleasure to be around.

Lynn was sitting next to Colleen, when suddenly she grabbed Colleen's arm and held it very tight. "What's up," Colleen remarked, "Did you see a mouse or something?"

"I just had a sharp pain. Do you think I might be starting labor?"

"Your due date is in one week, so at this point anything is possible." Colleen said somewhat anxiously. I had a feeling Colleen was wishing she was the one feeling the pain instead.

The pains kept recurring at certain intervals and enough so that Lynn asked Tom to call the doctor. Tom got the answering service, and by the time the doctor returned Tom's call Lynn's pains were getting stronger and more frequent. The doctor of course told Tom to take Lynn to the hospital, and everyone was in a flurry of activity. Colleen and I told them to get on their way and we would take their children home and get them settled in bed.

"Would someone please bring my suitcase from home before tomorrow morning?" Lynn asked. "It is in the entryway by the front door."

"Of course, we will, now get yourself on the way, pronto!"

By now all the children had seen the excitement and came running and screaming and dancing around Lynn yelling, "Yea, she is going to have the baby. Super!"

Colleen and I helped Steve and Janice clean up the common area before gathering all the children together. Prior to Tom and Lynn leaving it had been decided that we would just take their children home with us and they could sleep there overnight.

After all the children were in bed, Colleen said to me, "Gee, I wish I had been the one to go tonight. I am really getting anxious now." We both enjoyed hot cups of herbal tea before going upstairs to bed, and surprisingly we both immediately fell asleep.

About three in the morning, I felt a slight shake on my shoulder and someone was whispering in my ear. "Honey, wake up, my water broke. I called the doctor and he is waiting for me at the hospital."

I never jumped out of bed so fast in my life and fell all over the place trying to slip my legs in a pair of pants. "Calm down, calm down. We still have time," Colleen interjected. "I already told the older girls we are leaving. They will watch the children and take care of them in the morning, so as soon as you are ready we can leave."

On the way to the hospital Colleen's mind was thinking of all sorts of strange and inappropriate things not related in many ways to having the baby. She was not yet having much pain and thought to herself how great this was to be having a baby to this wonderful man that came into her life when she was not even looking for someone. Colleen had accepted the fact that she would be a widow the rest of her life, and now to have one more child with this new love of her life was to her a miracle.

Colleen's first husband had died in their bed and for a long time Colleen had a hard time adjusting to this fact. From the day it happened she refused to sleep in their master bedroom and chose to sleep down the hall in a spare room. She had considered selling her home, but she really loved the house that they had designed together. Also, the children loved it there, and they were very young at the time. They had their special friends and Colleen felt that by moving them they would not only have to deal with the fact of losing their father, but then they would have to get used to a whole new area and meeting new friends and perhaps even going to a different school. Colleen did not feel comfortable doing that to her children. After much thought, and knowing that her husband had left her quite well off financially, Colleen had built an addition to the house that essentially added another master bedroom and bath. She realized she was very fortunate to have this option. Not a lot of people would be able to build a whole new addition. This solved her problem of not ever having to sleep in the same room she had shared with her first husband again, but yet being able to keep the house that had so many other wonderful memories.

She felt the car brakes slam to a halt and realized they had reached the hospital emergency room area. Before she could say anything, people were rushing all around her with a wheel chair and then the pains started coming fast and furious. She was quickly whisked away noticing Tom as she passed him in the hallway. He smiled and mouthed he had a little girl which brought a huge smile to Colleen's face amidst the pain.

I was beside myself filling out papers and absolutely thrilled when I spotted Tom myself. How lucky he was to have the birth behind him already. It had been nineteen to twenty years since I experienced the birth of a child, so in essence this was almost like going through it again for the first time. Being older did not necessarily make you more experienced, and I was yearning for the confident bravado of youth. Tom had a wonderful idea when he suggested we try and get the two women a room together which turned out to be easier than we would have imagined. They were the only two having babies that night and the only other baby born that week had gone home that morning. I took a brief respite to go in and see Lynn and the new baby girl that Lynn happened to be holding at the time. What an absolute little doll she was, and Lynn was radiant.

I could hear the overhead speaker paging Colleen's doctor, and I quickly went back to the expectant father's waiting area. I briefly went in to kiss Colleen with the intention of staying there to give her comfort, but when I started to faint, I was quickly escorted out of the room. I guess dealing with one patient at a time was enough for them. While the time that passed seemed like an eternity, within two hours the doctor came out with the good news that I had a son, and he further explained that mother and child were both doing just fine. I thanked God and collapsed in the nearest chair. The doctor explained that Colleen was a real pro now at giving birth with all her experience. If she had any more children they would probably pop out in seconds. I immediately dismissed that thought as there was no way we were ever going to have another child.

The two babies were beautiful, and no, I did not feel the least bit prejudice at all. Within a few days, both women and the babies were released to go home and both households were full of joy and excitement. Colleen whispered to me that she almost had more help than she needed. For the first two weeks I don't remember sleeping at all. It seemed like the baby was up every two hours, and even though Colleen nursed the child, whenever the two of them awakened, so did I. Eventually, life became more of a pleasant routine except for all the mounds of things that began to fill the interior of our house that had not been there the month before. A stroller, a baby swing, a high chair, a bouncy, a cradle for downstairs and the crib upstairs, every toy imaginable and rattles galore. Binkies were in all the rooms, blankets were everywhere and diapers too. I had taken off for two weeks, and at the end of those two weeks we had little William baptized, and most of us called him Will. When Monday rolled around, I was ready to go back to work.

Chapter Fifty-Nine

Monday, when I returned to work, I had to really buckle down to eliminate the overload of paperwork that had accumulated. In the office directly next to mine I noticed a very lovely young girl busy at the desk. About mid-morning Carl stopped by and asked me if I had met Marie.

"Who is Marie?" I asked.

"Marie is that young lady in the office next to you."

"I noticed her there, but I got so busy, and she was busy too that frankly I didn't think much about it."

Carl explained that the previous girl had run away with her boyfriend and they were stuck without help until they interviewed Marie and hired her. "I believe she is going to make a good addition," Carl said. "So far, she is right on the ball and very efficient. Let me go get her so you two can meet."

This young lady was extremely beautiful with a gorgeous figure and I could not help but wonder why she would want to work in an auto shop. She could have been a model, and her appearance was very composed and sweet when we were introduced.

Carl assured me that Marie already had a good knowledge of how things were run, and I could probably give her half of the paperwork I had once she finished a project she was doing that afternoon.

I told him I could wait until tomorrow, and they both left. I worked late that evening. I was so engrossed in what I was doing I did not notice that Marie and I were the only two left at the shop. She nodded her head as if to say goodbye and asked me if she could possibly get a ride with me since a friend of hers had come by to borrow her car. I could not help but wonder what she would have done if I had left with everyone else and thought she was being a little forward and cocky to start right out asking me for a ride. Not wanting to sound mean however, I told her I would take her.

I held the door open as she got into the car and I could not help but notice her skirt rise way up her legs. She made no attempt to pull it down and sat with the skirt barely covering her buttocks. "Oh, Lord," I thought, "Why me?"

The short ride turned out to be clear across town and way out of my way, but we eventually got there, and after making sure she got into the apartment I continued on my way. There just seemed to be something very aggressive about her that bothered me, but I also knew I was still quite tired, so maybe it was just my imagination. Carl seemed to be very pleased with her, and I was sure tomorrow would be a more typical day. I couldn't wait to get home.

The little baby seemed to have grown just in one day when I walked in the door and took him from Colleen's arms. What an absolutely adorable child he was, and as I held him upon my chest I never felt so enamored to anyone else as I was to him at that particular moment. Colleen was happy for me to hold him saying she needed a little break from the long first day alone.

The next morning at the shop Marie was wearing this very tight red sweater, and her boobs were of such proportion and so upright that I wondered if they were silicone. The technicians were going wild. Not knowing how she normally dressed I decided not to say anything, but to make notice of what transpired that day. I handed her the remaining stack of papers that I had been working on, and as I was checking something in the file cabinet Marie brushed up against me, but did quickly apologize. Ok, I thought, that does happen sometimes when working in close proximity to someone, so I scolded myself by trying not to make a mountain out of a mole hill. I do remember thinking that night after I gave her a ride that this young lady did not know me, and she could say I did any number of things while driving her. In a courtroom the victim lady would most likely be the one to be believed. I made a mental note in the future to be sure and leave along with everyone else so as not to be put in that same predicament.

Doing little car repairs here and there kept me out of my office and away from the blonde bombshell, yet there were some occasions due to the propinquity of our office setups, and the times I could no longer evade going into my office where we could not avoid each other. I very much tried to limit our conversations, but she never seemed to get the gist of what I was trying to do. One day Marie asked me how my new little baby was doing.

Ok, I thought, that is a fair question, and I assured her he was growing bigger every day and just a joy.

"Well, Sir, if he is even one half as good looking as his father, he has to be one handsome boy."

"He looks just like his mother, who I might add is beautiful," I replied.

"You know sir, I realize your wife is rather incapacitated for a few weeks, so I would be more than happy to help out in that department should the need arise."

Was Marie implying what I think she was implying, or do I have a deep prejudice for this gal where I find everything she says a double entendre?

I turned abruptly to face her eye to eye after that remark to see if I could detect anything on her expression that would tell me what she really was saying. When her expression told me nothing, I just mumbled to her that we were managing just fine and I didn't anticipate needing any help. I hoped I had said it firm enough that perhaps she would lay off with her evocative suggestions or implications.

That afternoon, I went into town to have lunch with Tom. The two of us Daddies needed some of our own time to connect. We showed pictures of our babies and started dreaming about the two of them growing up together and maybe someday even marrying one another. The thoughts were far out, but pleasant enough.

Marie finally became an important topic of our conversation. I had to vent to someone about her and wanted Tom's input on what I was experiencing. Tom sat silently with one hand against the side of his face and the pointy finger rubbing his forehead while he had his elbow on the table and rested the other hand against his chin. For a few minutes I thought perhaps he was not going to respond and then in a very soft voice Tom finally said, "Be very careful with this type of girl. I can't be sure, but it sounds to me like she is up to no good and any slight unusual thing you do that she interprets the wrong way can lead to false claims of harassment and a big time law suit. I saw it happen to another good friend of mine years ago and his life was essentially ruined. I hate to condemn someone on just hearsay, but I trust you emphatically and what you tell me sounds very suspicious. Everything she says may be done meretriciously."

Chapter Sixty

Things were a little more stable back at work. I gave much thought to what Tom said, but all of a sudden it appeared as though Marie was quite busy, or something, and we did not come into much contact with one another for a couple of weeks. I actually stopped giving her much thought, and perhaps this was not a good thing.

Life at home could not have been better. The baby did something new every day and he was the first fixation we all gravitated to as soon as anyone of us entered our home. Happily, Aaron was not mentioning doing things with Tracy as much, but that may have been because they were both busy with their soccer teams. Whatever the cause, I was feeling better about my life and not getting as many anxiety attacks.

After six weeks, Colleen had her check-up with the doctor and our life together became even better than it had been before the baby was born. I thanked God every day I had her in my life, and believe me, thoughts of her consumed me one hundred percent of my time.

One afternoon, Colleen drove by the shop to have me check something in her car that had been making some noise. The girls were watching the baby at home. Colleen purposely waited for them to get home from school so they could babysit. When Colleen walked in to the shop the atmosphere at work became livelier. You could hear the buzz among the technicians who obviously enjoyed her good looks as much as I did. All the commotion got Marie's attention too and she made sure she came out to observe the fuss. My intentions were to ignore her, but Colleen being the sweet person she always is gave Marie a big smile and introduced herself. "You must be Marie, the girl who was hired about the time we had our baby. Carl told us all about you."

"That's me alright. I hope what he said was all good."

At that remark I said to Marie, "This is my wife Colleen." The two women shook hands.

In a most seductive manner Marie followed up with, "Your husband has really treated me so very special since I have been here Miss Colleen. He even drove me home one night to my friend's house."

Colleen was a little surprised to hear this since I never bothered to mention it to her because to me it was of no consequence, but all she said to Marie was, "Well, he is a good man, and I am pleased to hear that."

At that point, I grabbed Colleen by the elbows and asked her if I could get her a cup of coffee as I escorted her away from Marie. When Colleen refused the coffee, I walked her to my car that she could drive home, and I told her I would bring her car home later when I got off of work. I noticed the reflection of Marie in the office glass paneling watching every move we made as the two of us walked away.

I overheard many of the single guys at work saying how they asked Marie out on dates, but she always had some excuse why she couldn't go. This did surprise me as I thought she was just out to get any man she could manage to acquire who would submit to her desires.

"I never knew you drove Marie home one night," Colleen said to me with an inquisitive look. Why would you keep that a secret? I will say she is extremely beautiful."

"One night she was without a car and she asked me to drive her home, except when I tried to take her home she then asked me to take her to a friend's home at the other end of town. I was annoyed, but did so, and frankly once I dropped her off, I never thought any more about it."

"Oh, well, she appears to be a nice addition," Colleen said as she kissed me goodbye, perhaps with the kiss being a little longer than usual.

Marie was right there when I walked back in the shop saying she thought my wife was very nice. I told her thanks and walked in the opposite direction while deciding to go and talk to some of the techs to see how they were doing.

Two days later, at the regular time I would normally leave from work, I was preparing to do so when Marie once again asked if I could give her a ride. I immediately said I just remembered something and was going to stay a little later, so she should probably ask someone else.

"Oh, I can wait for you. There is always some extra work I can do."

Rather bluntly this time I said, "Get a ride with someone else Marie," and closed my office door. Once it appeared that everyone had left for the day, I gathered up my stuff and proceeded to the parking lot, and Marie was waiting there.

"My ride didn't pan out Sir, could you please help me?" I immediately thought of Carl's house nearby, and said I was going to go in and talk with Carl, so I suggested she call a taxi."

"I really don't mind waiting for you."

"Marie, get a ride someplace else as I am not driving you home." I didn't know how to say it any more precise than that.

Fortunately, or unfortunately, Carl and his wife came out of their house at that time and I went up to them as fast as possible before they got into their car. "Carl, I need to talk to you."

"What's wrong, you don't look too good."

"Can you two give Marie a ride? I am not going in her direction, and also I would like you to call me either later tonight or meet with me in the morning because yes, something very much disturbs me."

"We really are in a hurry. Can she make some other arrangements?"

"Listen to me Carl, you have to take her and I will explain later."

The next thing we noticed is that Marie started walking away and actually was quite a ways up the road. I told Carl to just let her walk, and I wound up driving in the opposite direction so as not to pass her. I would just go home on some back roads instead.

When I got to work in the morning Marie was in talking to Carl, so I waited to have my discussion with him later. I was apprehensive, yet anxious to speak with Carl when he called me into his office about an hour later.

"Hey, Bud, I am really disappointed in you. I never in all my life dreamed you would be the type to pander to young girls, especially with a beautiful wife like yours."

Ever since the first time I ever met Carl he started calling me Bud. Since he always said it in an affectionate manner I never really complained, so to Carl I have been Bud a long time. "What on earth are you talking about Carl?"

"Please don't act like you don't know. Marie told me everything you have been doing to her."

"She what? What did she say I have been doing to her?"

With much frustration Carl asked, "Are you really going to make me say it?"

"You damn well better say it because that young babe you hired is about to drive me crazy."

"Are you admitting then that you have been harassing her, asking if you could drive her home, bumping your body up against hers all the time, and saying suggestive things to her that could be taken many different ways? Is she driving you crazy because you can't keep your eyes off of her, and she won't do what you request? Is that it Bud?"

After all these years of our total friendship I could not believe what I was hearing out of Carl's mouth. I got a sick feeling in my stomach and had this urge to punch Carl in the mouth.

"You know Carl, I am so outraged at you right now, I can't even stand to stay here and tell you the truth, something you desperately need to hear. How you could jeopardize our friendship by even suggesting or thinking those things about me hurts me even more than the lies that perverted young lady you hired said about me. You had better give some serious thought to what you are saying to me. I am leaving to go home for the rest of this day. Right now, I can't stand to be in this building, nor can I stand to be in your presence."

"Don't turn this around and make it my fault, Bud."

That statement enormously irritated me. I looked Carl in the eyes, shook my head in disgust, and walked out.

Chapter Sixty-One

Colleen came up from the laundry room as I entered the house. I was happy to know that the baby was taking his morning nap. She asked, "What are you doing home sweetheart?"

"Let's sit down Colleen. I am livid and extremely upset and want to talk to you."

"Oh, boy, this doesn't sound good at all," she responded.

"For many weeks I have been very uncomfortable being around Marie. She had a subtle way of pushing herself on me, asking me for rides, getting close to me in the office when I was getting something out of the files, and suggesting things that appeared to have sexual overtones. She asked me for another ride last night and I told her I would be busy and to get a ride with someone else. Yet, when I finally walked outside she was standing there waiting for me after I hung around long enough to be sure she would be gone. Of course, no one else was around then. I walked over to Carl's house to ask if they could give her a ride, but Carl was going someplace and they were in a hurry. However, by that time Marie had already started to walk on her own, so I just drove home in the opposite direction. This morning when I got to work Marie was already in the office talking to Carl, and everything I am saying to you she turned around to make it appear like I was the aggressor. What makes me even more angry is that Carl believed her without even hearing my side. I just had to leave work because I was ready to punch him in the face."

For a long time Colleen just sat there in shock. To her dismay, she was vexed and had worried thoughts wondering if this girl could possibly be saying the truth? After all, her husband did give Marie a ride one night and neglected to tell Colleen about it. Then, Colleen became immediately ashamed of her thoughts and knew in her heart that her husband would not do such a thing. Finally, she looked up at her husband and said, "What do you think is the best way to handle this honey, especially since it appears that Carl is making it your word against hers? I suppose every time she did these things no one else was around to verify, so you probably don't have any proof that she is lying either."

"Unfortunately, that is true. But, why would Carl believe her without even giving me a chance to respond to her allegations?"

"I suspect that Carl was duped by her wiles too, and he doesn't even realize she affected him that way, she is such an embarrassing little pervert. Do you want me to call Carl's wife?"

"No, I'll take care of it. I just need some time to calm down. Maybe I'll call Carl this evening and talk to him away from the office and Marie."

At this point we could hear the baby babbling in his crib and I went up to get him. What a great smile he had on his face when he saw me. I picked him up and gave him a huge hug then changed a smelly diaper before bringing him downstairs.

I understood later that Marie walked back in to Carl's office after I left and inquired about my leaving. Carl explained that I got very angry and acted as though I wanted to deny everything she said, but walked out instead.

"That's proof he was guilty, don't you think?"

Carl had a few moments to think about what happened between us and said to Marie, "I never saw Bud act the way he did just now. He never before raised his voice to me, or got so angry that he just left the job in all the years he has worked with me."

"Wouldn't you say that his actions are even more proof he did those things, otherwise why would he pretend to be so angry?"

"I don't think he was pretending anger at all Marie. Just give me some time to think this thing through. For the rest of today I don't want to discuss this anymore. You can just get back to your work."

Carl decided to go into town for lunch and just get away from the whole hyped up atmosphere at work. The techs sensed something was going on and everyone appeared to be out of sorts the rest of the day. When Carl walked into the diner he saw Tom who was indicating to Carl to come and sit by him.

"Wow, Carl, you don't appear to be in a very good mood," Tom observed.

"Things got pretty testy at the shop today. Bud got mad and left for the day, so I had to get away too."

Tom sat upright and gave Carl a sharp intense look, "That bad, huh? Do you want to talk about it, or is it private business?"

"I don't know Tom. Do you think all men at one time or another sacrifice everything in their lives when a pretty young girl comes along?"

"Oh, I think some jerks do, but most of the friends I have are pretty straight forward, good family men, and are not willing to jeopardize something good in their lives. What got you started on this topic? It is not that new girl you hired at work, is it?"

Carl appeared stunned at the question and asked, "What made you ask me that?"

"Well, one day last week, or earlier this week, Bud came and had lunch with me and he remarked how very forward the young lady was and he thought her actions very out of place."

Carl put his elbows on the table and clenched his fists over his mouth just staring into space for quite a long time before saying, "Why didn't he say something to me?"

"I believe his intentions were to do just that after making sure he was not being overly sensitive with an inexperienced young adult. Did something happen to cause him to get mad and leave?"

"Young Marie said Bud kept harassing her, and she said he kept saying very sexually explicit things to her, and I believed her as she seemed so sincere."

"Oh, Carl, you didn't. Are you serious? How could you not trust your old friend who has never once done anything unruly since you have known him? How could you? I actually told him this young lady would do something like that, and he had to be very careful."

"You did? You had to hear her to understand from where I am coming. I usually know people pretty well."

"Well, you sure as hell screwed up this time and at the cost of your friendship with your business partner."

"Are you going to turn on me too? Is this a conspiracy? I tried to listen and do my best and I am still not convinced I am wrong. You had to be there."

Tom stared at Carl in disbelief and finally said, "You know, why don't I go back with you and listen to her too? It appears she has you hood winked for sure buddy."

"I've been running my business for years without a problem. I see no reason for anyone to doubt my decision making now. I don't need your help thanks," and at that Carl got up and left.

Tom's head was spinning. He had never known Carl to be so outrageous in his thinking. He was always such a calm and deliberate person who seemed very much on edge today. Maybe all the troubles with Steve were starting to finally catch up with Carl after being so consumed for many months with one problem after another, and he was just acting irrationally. Tom wondered what he should do. He surmised that both men needed time to think things through, so he decided to just go back to work and do nothing at the moment.

Chapter Sixty-Two

Later that evening after we had dinner and the children were in bed, Colleen and I sat in the den talking. "I am so hurt by the way Carl treated me Colleen. We have known each other such a long time. How could he believe that little pip squeak over me? Could he possibly believe when she is flirting that this young piece of—well that she could actually have affection for him at his age, and he let it go to his head? She certainly seems to know how to manipulate men, only in my case it obviously wasn't working for her."

Colleen just kept shaking her head from side to side and finally answered, "I never could understand how older men are taken in by girls young enough to be their daughters. I too wonder if they really think the girls are infatuated with them. The girls either want their money, or someone to take care of them, and the men are stupid enough to think it is their charm or sex appeal. Worse though is that this happened to Carl, and because of this little flirt he is willing to ruin a wonderful friendship."

The phone rang and it was Barbara. "Hi Colleen, did something happen at the shop today? Carl seems most upset, but I can't get anything out of him."

"Yes, Barbara, that new girl Marie has accused my husband of doing inappropriate things to her, and Bud got so upset he just walked out of the shop early this morning."

"Carl didn't believe Marie, did he?"

"I am afraid so."

"What has gotten into him lately? I thought there was something strange about that girl the first time I met her, but not wanting to be an interfering wife, I just let it go. However, the other night when Bud came to us as we were leaving the house and asked us to take her home, I could see he was upset and figured this little ho was up to something. We were in a hurry that night though, so we kind of let Bud down. I am going to have to talk to Carl. This is stupid."

Colleen finished her conversation with Barbara and mentioned to me what she and Barbara had discussed. I sat there feeling a multitude of emotions from hurt to anger. "Either he gets rid of that girl, or our partnership is finished, and right now I don't know what I am going to do."

"Don't make any hasty decisions you might regret later hon. Let me make you a cup of tea, or perhaps we ought to just get up to bed and call this a day."

I spooned my body next to hers in bed while wrapping my arms around her. Her body was a complete contradiction to me feeling soft and yet firm at the same time as it fit perfectly against mine. I inhaled her many different combinations of heavenly odors of Oil of Olay soap, eucalyptus shampoo, and I could even detect the wonderful clean smell of the softener she used to wash the clothes emanating from her nightgown. "God, I love you Colleen and I could lie here and hold you forever."

"I love you too honey."

"I wish this nightmare would just go away. The way I feel now I don't ever want to go back to work in that shop again. I have made enough money that I could easily retire. Sometimes I imagine I would just like to move away. I think of how much I would love to live someplace near the ocean on the east coast, like in North Carolina."

Colleen spun her body around and looked me in the face saying, "Really? You know something? I actually wouldn't mind moving if I didn't think it would upset the children. Aaron won't really care anymore if we move, and the only ones it might upset would be the two girls in high school. The younger children could easily adjust at their age and get established soon enough in another school."

"Wow, Colleen, it was a vision of mine, but somehow with your growing up in this area I never dreamed you would consider leaving."

"Well, of course I will miss my friends, but all my family is gone now so there is nothing to keep me here, and this might be a good time for a new and different adventure. Maybe tomorrow I'll run it by the two older girls and see what kind of reaction I get. In the meantime, what are you going to do about Carl and Marie?"

"I don't even want to give them a second thought tonight. Right now I just want to hold and kiss you and take every bit of you to me."

The rest of the evening was a lover's dream. Sometimes we filter from hurt an overpowering urge for love, and consequently we became lost in our lust for one another.

Chapter Sixty-Three

When Barbara finished talking on the phone, she just stood alone for a while by the cabinet where the phone was placed wondering the best way to approach the subject to Carl of what transpired at his workplace. She was especially concerned because Carl did not mention one word about the whole thing, and this was so totally unlike him. The two of them had finally reached a point where there was not one thing in their lives to disturb them. The children were all doing fine and it appeared that most of their worries about Steve were over. They, of course, would never get over their child losing a leg when he had been born a perfect human being. No parent would ever wish such a thing happen to their child. She felt they handled the whole situation as best they could and their son seemed so happy with his new wife that Barbara thought things were going quite well…..and now this.

Carl walked into the room and saw Barbara standing there. "What are you doing? Were you just on the phone?"

"Yes, Carl, I was talking to Colleen."

"Oh, did she call you?"

"As a matter of fact, I called her. Your actions since you came home have been so weird, and you obviously were not going to tell me what happened, so I called Colleen to see if something happened at the shop today."

"Why did you have to do that?"

"Don't even ask me why. You know you haven't been talking to me here this evening, and I don't intend to get in an argument over it now. I want to know how you could take the word of that young girl Marie that you have only known for a few weeks over someone you have known for years, someone who is your business partner. Just how could you do that?"

"What makes you so sure that Marie was wrong?"

"Oh, you've got to be kidding me Carl. Why do you think Bud stopped us the other evening? Did you think he was trying to have an affair with that girl when he came to us for help? He asked us to get her off his back and we refused him. I now feel terrible about that."

Carl sat down in his lounge chair and covered his face with the palms of his hands and rested his head back on the pillow. "Do you really think I am wrong in this Barbara?"

"What do you think Carl?"

"You know Barbara, Marie actually reminds me of you. You both have the same beautiful face, and I guess I was blinded by this fact. I just seemed to trust her like I would trust you because she was always so sweet to me."

"You are so naïve Carl. I am sure her sweetness was all an act to get you to believe her and to even get you to hire her in the first place."

"What should I do?"

"You need to get rid of Marie tomorrow. As for Bud, I don't know what you can do to repair the damage that has been done."

"What reason can I give Marie for telling her she won't be working for us anymore?"

"You had better just tell her the truth. That you did not appreciate her telling lies about one of your best friends, and you don't want her working at her job anymore. If she threatens a law suit, you have to stick by your guns and tell her you have too many witnesses to testify against her and if she wants to pursue a lawsuit to just go ahead as you and your company will be willing to fight her all the way. After you tell her that, I don't think there will be a problem. Don't even let her have a two weeks' notice. Either you get rid of her tomorrow or you might be getting rid of me instead. I will not tolerate seeing that girl around one more day. Then, after you get rid of her, you had better go over to see Bud."

Carl left the room. For some inexplicable reason he could not see why everyone was so upset, and besides Marie was a good worker. He never had problems releasing employees before, but he began to worry himself sick about telling Marie she was finished. Maybe it was those pleading eyes she had, but he angered himself even when he thought of that. He never let people influence him the way this young girl was doing. Did he hear his wife correctly? Did she really threaten to leave him if he didn't let Marie go? This whole situation was not only ruining his friendship with someone he had always admired, but now he was threatened with the prospect of losing his wife. He quickly realized he did not have a choice. He loved Barbara dearly, and no matter how good an employee Marie was he was just going to have to be firm and let her go. Oddly, Barbara never once in all these years interfered with any of his business decisions—never once. She was adamant about this obviously, and it was up to him to do something about it.

Barbara went to her sewing room and started to hem a quilt she had been assembling. Carl could hear the hum of the machine and knew at that point Barbara would not be going to bed that night. Working at the sewing machine was an obvious release for Barbara whenever she became upset or angry, and it was easy to assume at this point that she was both upset and angry. Carl knew he was not going to be sleeping either, but he at least made the attempt and got into bed. This was going to be a very long night.

Chapter Sixty-Four

The next morning, Colleen noticed I did not awaken at my usual "go to work" time and she gently shook my shoulder. "Are you going to work honey?"

"I told you, I have no intention of going back to the shop as long as that girl is still working there. Absolutely no intention! I am not even going to call in since I already had a doctor's appointment planned for today anyway. If Carl can't figure out the problem of why I am not there, outside of the doctor's appointment, I am thinking I should never go back to work there again."

"Gosh, you really are unwavering in your feelings on this matter."

"You're damn right I am. Even if Carl does come to his senses, I do think I will approach him about selling my half of the business. I am serious Colleen about moving on and doing something else. Actually, I don't have to work at all and can retire even though I am still relatively young. Right now that option seems like a great choice for me."

"Well, if you are going to be unhappy in your place of work, I would not encourage you to do otherwise. If you are not happy doing what you always have loved that would eventually influence our home life, so it is just not worth your staying there. How sad though that all this stuff happened because of one conniving young lady."

As Barbara was preparing to eat breakfast, Carl was leaving his home to go to the shop. He had never been so nervous in a long time about what he had to do.

"Good morning Sir," Marie said in a cheerful voice. "It's a great day outside, isn't it? I can't wait until I accumulate some leave time where I can take an occasional day off."

Carl thought this was as good an opportunity as any to seize the point of her removal when he said, "Actually Marie, you will be getting a lot of days off. I am releasing you from your work here in this shop today. I want you to gather your belongings and leave within the hour."

"Whaaaaat? Are you kidding me?"

"No, Marie, I am not kidding. I have never been more serious. So, please do as I say."

"You told me I was such a good worker. Why would you tell me I must leave?"

Sitting in his swivel chair, Carl started swinging it from side to side like a child might do. He put his elbows on his desk and folded his hands under his chin. He conjured ways he was going to tell her why she had to leave, and finally quickly said, "You told lies about my business partner, and this I will not tolerate."

"You can't be serious sir. That guy was always after me."

Carl stood up quickly and shouted, "Stop talking like that—NOW! Get out of here, and just in case you are planning to tell your story outside this shop, I want you to know I have enough witnesses that will speak against you, and I would take you to court in a minute."

When Carl started shouting, Marie froze for a minute. She no longer had that cocky bearing about her. As soon as she realized that Carl meant business she started mumbling under her breath, but she did proceed to begin gathering her belongings in preparation of leaving. Carl started shaking. By and large he was a gentle man, and in all the years he owned the business he could not remember ever having such a confrontation with anyone. He was also embarrassed that for some odd reason he was the only one of their group that did not have the foresight to see Marie for just what she was.

By the manner in which Marie left the shop, Carl really did not anticipate they would have any more trouble from her or hear any more of her allegations. Had he not been so forceful he was sure Marie might have contrived excuses for a law suit. When Marie saw this new and different side of Carl it shocked her into reality. This only made Carl even more discomfited because he knew that had he set some standards in the shop where Marie was concerned, this whole state of affairs might never had occurred in the first place.

When Carl heard Marie's car drive away, he visibly and uncontrollably began shaking from head to foot and started pacing the area in the hopes of regaining some self-control. He knew the next thing he needed to do was to call Bud and apologize. Prior to this incident they had been the best of business partners. "My God," thought Carl. "Was I out of my mind?" He picked up the phone and started dialing. After a few rings Colleen answered and explained that Carl had an appointment with the dermatologist in town and probably would not be home until after lunch. Carl then decided to call a fifteen minute meeting of all his technicians to tell them what had been going on as he saw a lot of them walking around with questioning looks on their faces. He had told Colleen he would call back later that day. Neither he nor Colleen spoke at all about what had happened over the past few days.

Chapter Sixty-Five

Several years had gone by since I had been in a doctor's office. I must say that this particular office was very elegant with soft couches for the patients to sit on instead of rigid chairs and beautiful mahogany end tables interspersed throughout the very large room. While the room was large, the way the couches were placed you got a cozy feeling of contentment as though you were in your own home. The doors to get in were made of glass, and soft elevator music played in the background. The music was so soft and subtle one could almost not hear it. I had been bothered by a spot on my chest that bled a lot, especially after I showered and rubbed the area, and this seemed like as good a time to get it looked at as any other. The appointment actually had been made before all this business with Marie, so for today especially, they were not even expecting me to go to work. A few of the patients that arrived at the office with a companion whispered softly to one another, otherwise the room was generally quiet. The rest of us were reading, or pretending to. I could not help but notice the eyes of the people sitting in the waiting room when a new patient came in, or someone left, as they peeped over the book or magazine they were reading trying to be unobtrusive but not wanting to miss a thing. I was no exception and was happy when they finally called my name. My doctor was pretty much convinced I had basal cell carcinoma on my chest and took a biopsy. They had a lab right in the building and for some types of skin cancer they would know the results the same day. I decided to wait for the results which indeed confirmed the doctor's diagnosis. I was happy that I had made this appointment because after reading the literature I was given and listening to the doctor's advice, I was pretty much convinced that by treating the condition everything was going to be all right. They set up an appointment for the following week to have a surgeon remove the cancer from the area on my chest.

On the drive home, I kept going over in my mind all that had transpired at work, and I had imaginary conversations with Carl wondering if there would be any way to resolve the issue. The kind of hurt I had was deep inside me. I just could not understand how Carl could take Marie's side in the matter, and I questioned how after working for him all those years Carl did not have the faith in me to know I would never do what he imagined. I really wanted to go at him and give him a big fat piece of my mind, but I knew instinctively that acting in that manner was not going to solve a thing. Like Aesop's Fables of the "hard wind and sun" story of persuasion being better than force, I decided to be gentle when I finally did talk to Carl. I had pretty much made up my mind to retire from the shop, and I wanted Carl to agree to buy my share of the business and perhaps make arrangements for Steve to take over in my place. Steve still lacked the knowledge I had with the expensive specialty and antique cars, but as long as I was around I could mentor him. At the present time, with the price of gas so high, people were not seeking to purchase those types of vehicles as frequently as they did a few years ago anyway.

I also wondered if Colleen was serious when she said she would really consider moving away. This disturbance in our family life, plus the shop lifting problems with Casey, had left a little stain on our once story book existence, and if we were going to make a move, this would be a good time to do so. Tennessee was beautiful, but once an east coast guy, always an east coast guy. The lakes in Tennessee were nice, but I sure did miss the ocean. I interrupted my thoughts when they concerned Colleen and realized I had promised to call her when I left the doctor's office. She was somewhat upset when she heard about the cancer, but I attempted to assure her that everything was going to be fine since I really believed that. That was when she told me Carl had called and said he would call back later, so I went back mentally preparing myself for the conversation. I knew, however, that most conversations don't follow the pattern you might hope they would.

When I got home and walked in the door, the smile on the baby's face when he saw me was exactly the medicine I needed to put me in a better frame of mind. What an absolute little doll he was, and I loved him so much it almost hurt. After wrapping Colleen in my arms with a huge hug and sitting down at the kitchen table with her to enjoy some coffee and pastries, I picked up the little guy and went into the living room. I reclined on the living room carpet and held him over me with my two arms straight over my body. You might know he would drool right down on my face. Yuk! I then brought him down and held him in my arms, and we both fell asleep on the hard floor oblivious of our surroundings. The ringing of the phone brought me out of a sound sleep, and I was not too happy to hear that it was Carl. However, I guessed this time was as good a time as any to talk to him. I handed the baby to Colleen and went off to the den for our conversation.

"To say you hurt me Carl is putting it mildly," I stressed as I decided to dive right in with my feelings.

"I am sorry," Carl replied, "it was not my intention to hurt you."

"How could you believe that girl over me after all these years of us working together?"

"I guess Marie just seemed very sincere to me Bud."

"You know, when you say that to me Carl it is almost making it worse because I can still sense some doubt of your feelings about me in this whole situation. That is why, Carl, I want to sell my half of the business and just leave. You will always be one of the dearest friends I ever have, but there will always be something missing in our relationship that will be very hard to repair. I just don't want to be working at the shop anymore, and that's the way it is."

"Oh, Bud, aren't you being a little overly dramatic?"

"You can think what you want to think, but that is how I feel, and we both better see our attorneys to work out a plan. I was thinking that this would be a good opportunity for Steve to come in and take my place. I know you will enjoy working with your son, and Steve will do a good job. I don't anticipate he'll have any problems coming up with a loan since he already works in the shop and his military background speaks well for him. Besides, we all do have Tom, the manager of the bank, to intercede."

For a while, I could not hear anything at the other end of the line, and then I heard a huge condescending sigh as Carl said, "If that's what you want, I guess that will have to be the way it is."

While finishing our conversation, I could smell the delicious aroma of a roast cooking in the kitchen oven. When I left the den, I saw the table in the dining room was set with all the best china. Just at about the time I was ready to inquire about all the fuss I heard a car pull into the driveway. I looked at Colleen inquisitively, and she said that while I had been talking to Carl, Aaron had called on his cell phone saying they had a few days break and he, Tracy and few of the other friends were stopping by for tonight and then traveling on to another part of Tennessee tomorrow.

"I had already prepared a decent meal for you when I heard about your ordeal at the doctor's office, so since I always make more than enough food for any one meal, I just was happy to invite them all to dinner." I thought we could all use some comfort food.

I could feel the pounding in my heart begin. All I kept thinking was "Oh, my God, Oh, my God, Oh, my God. Help me, help me, please." I told Colleen I would make a quick rush to the bathroom and then come out to greet them.

I splashed cold water on my face and tried to assess the situation. Why now? Weren't things bad enough with Carl? Am I not to get a break? This for sure was God's punishment for me for the horrible—Oh, my God. What am I going to do? Ok, now—I need only to look normal. Even if Tracy sees some sort of recognition in me she will only think herself crazy. Right? Just be gracious, and try not to sit anywhere near her. Yes, I must compose myself. This is what I will do. This is what I HAVE to do. I could hear all the excitement in the entryway. Kids laughing, shouting, excited and happy, the way kids should be. I must not change that in any way. So, I look like her father—well, so what? Jeez—listen to me for crying out loud. I am her father after all. Well, nobody else knows this, so deal with it. I kind of messed up my hair which was grey now, and I did look a lot different than when Tracy was a small child. I tried to brace myself and decided to go for it before Colleen started wondering what I was doing.

When I appeared in the entryway, Aaron came over and gave me a huge hug and began to introduce me to the other three students that were with him. The introductions went rather fast as my other children were steering the group towards the dining room while claiming they were starved. So far, so good. Tracy sat to the right of Colleen at the opposite end of the table, so that turned out well. We said grace and started passing the food around the table. At one point Tracy's eyes met mine directly, and my heart sank. Her eyes were beautiful, and I could sense some sort of detection of something familiar as she looked at me. I realized I was staring so hard into her eyes that she became flustered and looked away. Then I saw her peek at me again with a worried frown across her face. I attempted laughing when it was appropriate, or saying "uh huh," just so I would appear to be as normal as possible, but otherwise I was not very talkative, and I expected Colleen would attribute that to my recent conversation with Carl.

The baby was sitting next to me in his high chair, and I spent a lot of my time attending to him and occasionally trying to get some food into his mouth. His little hands kept fiddling with some Cheerios on the tray and most of them were landing on the floor. Towards the end of the meal, the dropped Cheerios irritated one of the other children. They shouted at the baby to stop doing that, and this, of course, only caused the baby to cry. I saw an exit plan in this situation and quickly picked up the baby telling everyone to excuse us while explaining that the baby was tired. Colleen was grateful I offered to take him upstairs for his bath and put him to bed. I said good night to the college students, told them to have fun that evening and that it was a pleasure meeting them. In my heart, I was hoping this would be the last meeting we ever had, but of course I did not say that. I wondered what was going on in Tracy's mind.

Chapter Sixty-Six

The next morning, I pretended to sleep longer than usual causing Aaron to come in the bedroom to say goodbye to me. I asked Aaron to convey to his friends my wish for a safe trip and asked him to please apologize to them for my over sleeping.

"That's ok Dad. Mom told me you have had a tough week and about the cancer. I hope everything will be ok. She also mentioned something about possibly moving to the east coast and you know what Dad—I think I could really learn to love that. Most of my high school friends are no longer around here, and I loved going east when I would visit Steve at Walter Reed. I am thinking it would be a pleasant change of pace. Who knows? Maybe I'll even transfer to a school on the east coast."

"Well, don't make any hasty decisions in that regard. It does make me feel good though knowing that should we go ahead with the moving plans that you will be right on board with us. Be careful driving buddy. I love you. Take care now."

As Aaron turned towards the door getting ready to leave he said, "Bye Dad. I love you too."

I actually fell asleep again and had the best sleep for the next few hours than I had in a long time. It was Saturday, and when I finally awoke the smell of cinnamon buns permeated the entire house. Since living in this house I could always notice wonderful odors coming from the kitchen, either in the morning, or when I returned home from work. Realizing I had not really eaten a lot of the dinner we had the prior evening, I couldn't wait to get downstairs for something to eat. I immediately walked over to the island with the coffee pot on it and poured myself a cup of coffee and then sliced a piece of the cinnamon bun while licking the icing I had on my fingers. Colleen placed some bacon in the microwave and prepared some sunny-side-up eggs for me.

When she put the plate of food before me, she leaned over and gave me a soft warm sensuous kiss on my neck. I was ready to turn around and go right back upstairs, taking Colleen with me, when the children started entering the kitchen. Our few minutes of solitude quickly disappeared, and the lively buzz of children's voices and plates clattering against the table filled the air.

By now, most of the children had been told about our possible move to North Carolina. I was truly amazed how they were all so willing to accept the news. After the older children took off for their various activities that Saturday morning, Colleen and I took our cups of coffee onto the side front porch and talked more about the move. I mentioned the fact that I was surprised to know she was so agreeable to moving away from her home of many years. Up to that point, I had not realized that in Colleen's younger years she actually had lived on the east coast. I began to realize how very little I knew of her younger life. Her father had gotten a new job at a University in Tennessee and the family moved to Tennessee when she was about ten years old. She explained also that before her grandparents died they spent every summer at her grandparents' beach house on the east coast beaches in Virginia. Colleen remembered those days as being some of the happiest in her life. Perhaps we were both wishing to bring some sort of utopia back into our lives. Perhaps, also, this was really not a good thing since it appeared we both wanted to move to escape some of our own personal difficulties. Nevertheless, the planning felt good, and if it should have, or not, was beside the point at the moment as the plan appeared to come more to fruition.

After breakfast we piled the younger children in the van and went to one of their games. From there we were all going to go to one of the big box stores to stock up on staples which meant we were going to drop a couple of hundred bucks really fast. We saw Carl and Barbara in the store. Colleen and Barbara were discussing a book one of them had picked up and each was urging the other to buy the book while Carl and I rather stood around looking ill at ease. Carl tried his best to act in a nonchalant manner, but I could not get over the hurt I still felt about him not understanding my side of the predicament. Fortunately, one of the little guys knocked over some cans, and I went to the rescue. I began to realize how often I was using the children to avoid awkward situations.

When we finally arrived home and got the groceries and bulk items put away, it just felt good to sit around and do nothing. For once, in quite a few weeks, it appeared our evening would have some sort of normalcy to it, and I was grateful for the break. Colleen and I made plans to go out to dinner the next evening—just the two of us. I needed to talk to her more about the move without the distractions of family.

While we were all sitting in the den the phone rang and it was Aaron saying they arrived back at school safely and he wanted to talk to me.

"Hey, son, how ya doing?"

"Wait a minute Dad while I close the door. It is just too noisy with it open, and I want to talk in private."

I could feel some palpitations again, fearful that Aaron was going to say something about his relationship with Tracy. What would I do if they ever got engaged, or wanted to get married? What would I do?

"I'm back," Aaron said, "and I have a question for you."

"OK, Shoot!"

"How did you know you were really in love with Mom, Dad?"

Oh Lord, I thought as I queried, "Why do you ask?"

"I think I am nuts about Tracy Dad. I am not sure she feels the same way about me though. She's all I can think about when we are apart, and when she is near me I just about go crazy. Is that how you felt when you fell in love Dad?"

Oh how I wanted to say all the cliché types of things like oh it is just infatuation, or puppy love, and you are too young to really know, so don't tie yourself down. Yet, I knew I had to be honest with Aaron. He was putting a lot of confidence in me by being so forthright and sincere. Just the fact that he would confide his concerns to me meant a lot. He was truly like my own flesh and blood son, and I loved him dearly. "Yes, son, it sounds to me like you have a good case of—well, yes, that is exactly how I felt. What are you going to do about it?" In many ways I did not want to know his response.

"Well, I did have a good talk with Tracy and foolishly blurted out everything I felt for her, and now I feel sort of stupid for doing so."

"How did she react to your telling her that?"

"She gave me a whopper of a kiss, but explained she was hesitant to get involved again with anyone. She explained how she had an intense relationship with someone in high school that caused a lot of friction with the families, and she honestly was not sure she was yet over the emotional involvement."

"Aaron, after hearing what you said, I am afraid you are not going to like my answer. I don't feel it is ever a good thing to get involved with someone who is carrying around a lot of baggage. There is a lot of importance for a person in her situation to be able and want to break all ties to her past before starting a new relationship with anyone, let alone you."

"I guess you are right. That is not something I wanted to hear when I especially have to look at her every day knowing the way I feel. I frankly don't know if I can just break away from her."

"Yes, that has to be tough I am sure, but I am certain you know her schedule enough that you can try to avoid the places where you often would meet with her."

"I'll have to give it some thought."

"Also," I said, "While she is feeling the way she is, you might be more of an irritant to her than if you actually left her alone. What is that old saying about absence making the heart grow fonder?"

"I hadn't thought of it that way. Perhaps it is worth giving it a try."

"Before we hang up son I want to leave you with this very important thought while you are making your decision, and that is to love yourself enough to choose a partner you don't have to rescue."

"Wow, that's a pretty intense thought Dad, but since I called and asked your advice, I am going to try and do what you suggest. I love you Dad and thanks."

"Love you too, and I always want you to feel free to call and talk to me. I love our conversations. Get a good night's rest now and continue the good work you are doing in school."

Would my suggestions help Aaron to forget? Would he find someone else eventually, or were those two destined to be together. There is just no way they could ever be together, just no way. How could we have a wedding? I could not continue always avoiding situations by hiding, or being out of sight as I managed to do so far. No way! My former spouse would absolutely know me. I am sure. You don't live and sleep with one another for all those years and not remember once you are back together. My life would be ruined. My story would be told. Every freckle and mole on my body would tell the story even if my face had more lines and my hair had a different color. Can I even think to pray to a God for help? A God who knows that I have done a most horrible thing? How devastating this would be to Colleen and all the children. What have I done? What - have - I - done? I wanted to scream, but Colleen came over to inquire about my conversation with Aaron, so we sat down and I discussed my chat with him while enjoying a beer.

Chapter Sixty-Seven

Colleen and I decided to go into the city to Morton's Steak House for our dining out time together. She was such a superb wife the way she handled all the children with her quiet ease and temperament, and it was obvious they all loved her dearly. I felt she not only deserved to eat a splendid meal, but she also needed the pampering and the total elegance that this dining establishment provided. Sipping our wine, we could not help but be overcome by the fact that no one was running in to interrupt our conversation. This was a little bit of heaven on earth. We had both received a bit of good news earlier in the day when we found out that Tom and Lynn wanted to buy our house. This was a huge hurdle to overcome in the very depressed housing market and the way the economy was at the present time. They had been thinking of buying a larger place to accommodate their ever growing family, and Lynn had always been infatuated with Colleen's home even when Colleen lived there with her first husband and before I ever met Colleen. We settled on a fair price for both of us. Somehow, it made moving out of the lovely structure more bearable knowing our friends that we adored so much would be living in the home instead of some strangers.

"There is so much we have to do prior to moving, I sometimes get overcome with anxiety just thinking about it," reiterated Colleen.

"I think they call that seller's remorse honey, and we will probably get buyer's remorse too once we get to North Carolina and try and find a home there. Let's get a baby sitter and go to look for a house the week after next. During the interim, I will check on different realtors and look at sites on the web to help us make some choices as to what and where we want to live."

"Just the thought of getting new doctors for the children and a new vet for the pets is enough to challenge my nerves. I forgot to tell you about my experience at the vet's office this morning."

Colleen had this beautiful German shepherd dog that everyone loved. She actually got him as a puppy hoping he would make a good watch dog. However, he was just one big loveable creature that probably wouldn't hurt a soul. Though, I do believe, if anyone attempted to hurt Colleen or the children the dog would certainly attack under those circumstances.

"Didn't the appointment go well today? Did the doctor find something wrong? I thought this was just the ordinary time for the dog's checkup."

"Actually, the vet experience was good but a bit traumatic for me. We walked in around eleven o'clock in the morning and were the only ones there at that time. As I was checking in, a woman came in with a little white dog (the kind Dice doesn't like) and the woman was crying, and I could see the little dog's eye was all bloody. The receptionist must have known she was coming because nothing was said. As I was filling out the paper work for Dice, a lady with a big black dog came in. Dice wanted to bark and was getting all worked up, but I got him calmed down. Then another lady came in without an appointment and was crying hysterically as she held her little tiny eight pound dog. The vet's assistant took that lady and her pet directly to the back."

I was becoming fascinated with the story when the waiter came by to take our order. After deciding that we would share a salad, and we each ordered our own special steaks with baked potatoes and another vegetable, Colleen continued with her story.

"I never did find out what was wrong with the second little dog because at this point another couple came in with a little seven week old puppy that was obviously very sick. Right after they came in another couple arrived with a cat in a cage and sat right near me. Dice's behavior was so good with all of this commotion, though I did keep a very tight rein on his leash. The man with the cat who sat next to me didn't appear to mind at all that Dice was sitting on his foot. I tried very hard to keep him away, but with everyone coming in and sitting near us we were limited with space, and he is a big dog. At this point, another lady came in with a little girl and a five month old Akita. Dice was so excited his tail kept thumping on the bench seating, and everyone was laughing at that which was nice as it lightened the mood of the other emergencies. I mentioned to them that it was much better than him barking. After an hour we had our appointment, and when we finally left we again were the only ones in the vet's waiting room. I did ask the receptionist what had happened with the little dog. I was wondering if it had been hit by a car, or maybe it had been attacked by a bigger dog. She said that breed and other breeds that have those bulging eyes are prone to the eyeball just popping out, and that is what had happened when the man and woman took their dog out of the cage that morning. Can you imagine hon? I was close to tears when the receptionist told me that."

"Well, what did the vet have to say about Dice, and were you angry at getting in to see the doctor so late?"

"Truly, I was not bothered by us being late because it made me feel good that if Dice ever had an emergency that the doctor would take him right back too, and Dice passed his exam with flying colors though he may have an eye condition called Pannus. I don't think it will lead to blindness, but we will have to put a salve into his eyes for the rest of his life. You can remember I thought he had allergies, but the vet pretty much confirmed this Pannus diagnosis. I tell you this morning was quite an experience."

At this point the waiter brought our salads, and our conversation turned to discussing what we would both like to look for in a new home. We had been munching on a most delicious warm round loaf of bread, so it was a good thing the salads arrived before we ruined our appetites completely.

Chapter Sixty-Eight

I spent the last part of the week before going to North Carolina taking care of some personal business. One day I was in a neighboring town about an hour or so away from our home. After exiting an attorney's office I was walking to my car that was parked quite a distance away. I guess everyone was seeing attorneys these days since so many of the parking spaces had been taken, but at least my visit to an attorney was for a good reason as I was taking care of some details about selling my portion of the business with Carl. I happened to pass what appeared to be a new Catholic church, and something motivated me to go inside.

The church was more modern than the Catholic churches I had been to most of my life. The interiors of those churches had huge stained glass windows and marbleized altars of white. Collosal pillars used to be situated throughout the interior, and if you were unfortunate to sit behind one, you really could not see what transpired on the altar. The architects that created this flaw would probably be sued today, but what did I know. The pews in this church were smooth and light oak in color encircling the altar like a half moon with a center aisle down the middle of the pews and two side aisles. There was a huge cross with Jesus on it directly over the altar in the crucified position. What I found odd about this particular cross was that Jesus was draped in material that gave the appearance of a robe, instead of the usual mini clothed bare armed and bare legged Jesus. I marveled at the space between the pews. Someone could easily walk in front of you without tripping to get to a seat in the middle of the aisle. How great it would be I thought if all churches had that amount of space between the pews, and better yet if we all had that leg room in a theater.

After giving the setting the once over, I stood there wondering what it was that possessed me to enter the church. I decided to sit down, and the next thing I knew I was kneeling and looking up at Jesus on the cross. "Dear Lord," I started to whisper to myself when I heard the noise of a door slamming near the altar. I looked up to see a young, very handsome priest enter the sanctuary. I immediately wondered, foolishly perhaps, how someone so good looking made it to the priesthood and was not overtaken by some young chick. He nodded in my direction as though in greeting. I returned the nod and bowed my head once again.

The priest had this compassionate look about him, and I seriously sat there considering asking him if he would listen to my confession. What was my obsession with wanting to tell my story when I knew only bad things would come from doing so? I had read once that criminals that got away with a crime after many years often feel compelled with wanting to finally tell someone. One would think they would be grateful for the fact they were never caught and attempt to get on with life, but in many cases they just feel the need to talk about it, to tell someone. Was I overcome by these same strange feelings? I immediately tried to dismiss this in my own mind by saying to myself that I was not a murderer after all, and I did not physically hurt anyone by pretending my own death and changing my identity. But, who was I kidding? How would society judge me for what I had done? What good did I think it would do to go up and tell my tale to this particular priest? Was there really such a thing as priest and confessor confidentiality? I realized he did have a peaceful demeanor and the type of face where people would feel comfortable in telling him their innermost secrets. The more I thought I would go up to him, the more my heart started pounding, and the palms of my hands became sweaty. I squirmed in the pew and nearly stood up to go towards the priest when a group of women entered the church and walked directly towards the priest. The Father greeted them as though he had expected their arrival. I knelt down again in relief.

"Can you ever forgive me God for what I have done? The day I left my other home I did not know our country was going to be under attack. That was not in my plan at all. Yes, I did plan on leaving my wife and child, but our lives were miserable. We were always constantly fighting, and it upset my precious daughter. I suppose I could have taken my daughter with me when I left that morning, but it is possible I could have been accused of kidnapping. I also did not wish to take her away from her familiar surroundings. Oh, God, please help me. Forgive me, please! My state of mind could not have been normal to associate my supposed death with the horrible September 2001 tragedy. Also, God, I do need to thank you for helping me to meet my beautiful Colleen and her children that I love as much as my own two flesh and blood children. I have been trying very hard to lead a decent life. Can you forgive me God?"

Was it the move that was bringing back all my inhibitions concerning what I had done? Let's face it, the last time I made a mini cross country move was the day I left Connecticut and my other family. Perhaps this move had triggered the thoughts of remorse I was now experiencing. I suddenly was beginning to feel claustrophobic, so I blessed myself and exited the church. The sunny bright day startled me at first as I reached for my sunglasses in my pocket, but the fresh air invigorated me. The church experience was not all bad for me I later realized. Kneeling and praying and saying things in church I would not say outside to anyone was soothing in some small way, even though I never got to talk to the Priest. Again, as I had in the past, I told myself to forget ever confessing what I did. I would take the information to my grave with me unless a situation came up with Aaron and Tracy where I would be forced to confront it. Maybe I should have been praying that their relationship would end once and for all. I began to hope I would feel better once we were settled in our new home.

Chapter Sixty-Nine

Colleen and I were walking on the beach in North Carolina. The sand felt good under our feet, cool and damp. We had looked at about fifteen houses that morning and early afternoon and saw about five that we really liked. I spread a blanket on the sand, and we opened up a couple of subs we had purchased to eat on the way to the beach. This was the first time we would be eating since breakfast that morning with the realtor. All of a sudden, a gull swooped down and grabbed a chip right out of my hand, and then took a chunk of Colleen's sub. Colleen let out a loud scream. The gull was so fast it was disconcerting at first, but then we laughed as we covered the rest of the food with our arms and heads until the gulls appeared to go away. The gulls seemed to be so much more aggressive lately than when I was a child.

"You know what used to annoy me hon?"

I inquired, "What?"

"When I was little, there were always a group of inconsiderate people on the crowded beach who used to break up pieces of bread and throw them to the gulls."

"Oh, man, I know exactly what you mean. There would always be that group of people who didn't have any sense of beach etiquette when they would throw the food like that causing the birds to swoop down and often leave a deposit on someone's head or blanket. Those were the same people who didn't have any sense of boardwalk etiquette either."

"What do you mean by boardwalk etiquette?"

"Most people realized that walking on the right side of the boardwalk in either direction helped to have a smooth flow of traffic."

"Oh, yes," Colleen said, "we always did that, but it was such a habit that I wasn't thinking about exactly to what you were referring."

At that moment a powerful combination of salt and sea air overpowered us, and I had a strong feeling of déjà vu.

We managed to get the last of our food down without any more problems from the gulls and sat on the beach going over our notes that we had taken on the homes we had inspected that day. We had certain criteria we wanted in the home we bought, but some of our favorites while maybe not having all our pluses, perhaps had something else we also liked to compensate for it.

One of the things we would have liked and considered was a home near the beach, but not on the beach. We did not want the worry of flooding or hurricane winds that being extremely close to the water, or on the water's edge, would entail. The area where we were looking was a lot closer to the ocean than Tennessee, so obviously, finding a place near the water was apparently not going to be a problem.

Colleen still wanted a big front porch and of course we both wanted a two, or maybe even three car garage. We could use the third garage to store lawn equipment and things of that sort. An upper level that had a deck with a view would have been fantastic, especially if the view could see as far as the ocean in the distance. There was one home that provided that. Some of the homes we looked at appeared to be great on the outside, but the insides were a real mess and very much a disappointment. We were not in any mood to do remodeling of the interior. Colleen preferred her kitchen cabinets to have a light color wood or white. While this was not my choice, I realized she worked more in the kitchen, so I essentially left that decision up to her. Colleen was also not one to want stainless steel appliances, and that is what was shown in most of the homes.

We strolled down to watch the waves lap the shore and decided to take a walk along the water's edge. While doing so, we collected some sea glass and shells to bring back to the children. The sun was setting, and the sky looked like a brilliant pinkish red cloth interspersed with white dots. Everything was glowing and appeared to be on fire. Once the sun settled below the horizon we packed up our belongings and walked to our hotel room since it was situated right on the beach. After showering and enjoying some time alone together (just the two of us), we phoned the children and decided to call it a night. We had pretty much decided on two homes from our list. Tomorrow we were going to look at some more homes in the morning and hopefully make an offer on one.

As exhausted as we both were, it was hard falling asleep. We wanted to be sure of the location of some doctor's offices before deciding on a home and also to see about the schools and any hospitals in the area, and stake out a vet as well. When I finally did fall asleep, I woke up a couple of times full of anxiety while numbers whirled around in my head.

We had scheduled an appointment with the realtor at ten o'clock the next morning, but neither one of us wanted to get up. It helped to open the hotel drapes and see the beautiful ocean and watch some children playing on the beach. Several gulls were dive bombing directly into the ocean to spear some fish, and in the distance we could see a variety of sail boats and a fishing boat. I began to realize just how much I missed living on the east coast. I couldn't wait to get the children here to enjoy the experience of doing so as well.

Kim, the realtor, was all bubbly when she came to pick us up. She said there was a new listing that came on the market late last night that she knew we were going to love. The only drawback was that it was a little out of our price range. What else was new? I could not help but wonder. Kim assured us that since these people were moving because of the husband's job she felt confident that she could get the price down close within our range.

When we drove up to the circular driveway, both of us knew instantly why Kim was so cheerful that morning. At least on the outside the house was perfect. There were porches on two levels of the home and while there was not a deck on the top of the house, the second floor porch provided a spectacular view. The kitchen was extremely modern and up to date, and the cabinets were white with granite countertops, though the appliances unfortunately for Colleen were stainless steel. Since the layout of the kitchen was so outstanding, Colleen was willing to acquiesce on that point. Like our home in Tennessee, the den was in a private area and not so close to the kitchen that the noise interfered with the television as was common in so many of the homes we saw. We both loved this home, but before making an offer we were still going to check out the rest of the homes on the list that morning. We went back to the room for a break and checked out the crime statistics on the computer for this town because we had seen another area that everyone was talking about to be nice and it had a rather high crime rate. This home seemed to be far enough away that crime there was minimal.

None of the other homes really could compare, and we rather lost interest in looking at any others after seeing the first home. The two of us came up with what we thought was a fair offer and let the realtor do her job while we went to spend more time on the beach.

We reneged a little giving our own counter offer. Right before we decided to go out to eat at Dave's Oyster Bar the call came in saying our second offer had been accepted. That acceptance was all we needed to really enjoy a fabulous meal that evening. Better yet, the owners would be moving in a few short weeks so we could look forward to an early closing and a rather quick move. Our expectations were heightened at this point one hundred percent.

Chapter Seventy

The ride back to Tennessee was a bit of a nightmare. There had been a five car pileup on the highway we were driving, and we were situated where there was no place to exit. I suppose we should have been happy that we were not involved in the accident, but instead we were dwelling on the fact that we had to sit there for over four hours with no rest room in sight. Several of the men walked into the nearby woods, and finally Colleen had to do the same while hating every minute of it. I escorted her through the scrub brush to help provide protection and to serve as a lookout so she could experience some type of ease. She was thankful that the trees were there instead of perhaps just a meadow.

Of course, our being held up caused all our plans to get off schedule and we were busy having to arrange for a continuation of baby sitters. Then, as is often to be expected when parents go away, when we did arrive home the baby was sick, and some of the others were complaining of sore throats. Our highly anticipated arrival turned out to be more of a fiasco. One child complained of being hungry. Another said he wanted jello. The others would not give us an opportunity to get settled they were so busy asking questions. At this point we were all short tempered, and the peace and quiet on the beach seemed like only a dream.

Once the children were settled and in bed, we both followed suit to our own bed full of exhaustion. There is nothing like your own bed to help you get a good night's sleep.

Fortunately, the next day the children had school, so we only had to deal with the little Will at home. I had many appointments with lawyers and papers to sign, and Colleen was busy calling utility companies and closing some of our bank accounts. We had already opened up some new accounts at banks near our new home while in North Carolina that would help make the transfer of some of our money a lot easier. The baby appeared to feel a lot better that morning, so that was a big plus. In fact, he managed to dump a whole box of cereal all over the floor before everyone left in the morning, and some of the older kids had fun crushing and sliding on the crushed cereal across the kitchen floor until I finally blew my stack and yelled out "STOP." Once they heard the tone of my voice they quickly and quietly got out of the kitchen and gathered their books to get ready to leave.

We also wanted to be sure and register to vote in the new state once we moved. In the fall a big election was going to take place, and we certainly did not want to miss out on voting. There were some eclectic choices leading up to the primaries that year where for the first time in history there was the possibility we might be voting for a woman president, a black president, or a president who was a war hero among some of the contenders. Aaron was going to be able to vote for the first time, and he was all excited about that. Fortunately, we would have the summer months to take care of registering the children in their new schools. Aaron was thinking about transferring to UNC in Wilmington. I was disappointed he was not planning on playing soccer any more though.

When Tracy heard that Aaron was moving and might be going to another college, all of a sudden this seemed to spark her interest in him once again. Again, I mention that quotation about absence making the heart grow fonder. Aaron had managed the best he could to avoid coming in contact with her, but one day he was in the student union enjoying a coke with some friends when Tracy came up behind him and put her palms over his eyes while saying, "Guess who?"

Aaron was taken aback at first but immediately recognized the sweet smell of Tracy's hand lotion, and he grabbed her hands wrapping her arms around his body. The sensation of her body against his was almost more than he could take.

"What's this I hear about you moving?"

"Yup, that's so. I am looking forward to it to be honest."

"Aw, aren't you gonna miss me?"

"Well, we really haven't been seeing a lot of each other recently, but of course I will miss you Tracy, and all my other friends."

Tracy was stretching her head to see Aaron's face, so he let go of her arms and she sat down on the empty seat next to him. The conversation continued for about twenty minutes when Aaron had to leave. Tracy made Aaron promise to keep in touch. He frowned at that and finally looked Tracy in the eyes and questioned her, "Why? I thought you were the one who wanted to sever our relationship?"

"Well, I didn't mean forever, for goodness sake."

"You know Tracy, at our age you can't have it both ways any more. Yes, we can be friends, and if you are ever driving by our home in North Carolina, it would be great to see you, but at this point I don't see that our relationship from the past few months has changed a whole lot."

Tracy's face showed some remorse, but she was not discouraged. She felt she could manage to change Aaron's mind any time she chose, and perhaps now she would make that her agenda. She gave him a quick kiss on the cheek, and they both went in opposite directions.

Aaron's stomach began turning over after he left Tracy. He was afraid what he was feeling were the same old butterflies of love twirling around in his stomach. Just when he thought he would get over Tracy she had to show up and stir all these feelings inside him once again. He had not been counting on this. Prior to this meeting he was really anxious to start a new life, and now he started having some feelings of doubt. He decided to go to the gym and shoot some baskets. Perhaps the distraction would get his mind off of Tracy and back to more pleasant things.

Chapter Seventy-One

Tracy was full of conflict lately. She sat in her dorm room staring at the posters surrounding the beige colored walls. Stuffed animals and pillows appeared to be taking over her bed. While her room was quiet, the dorm echoed with sounds of doors slamming, a loud random voice, some giggles and footsteps navigating the stair well. It was unusual for Tracy not to have music blaring or her iPod stuck in her ears.

Why was she feeling attractions to Aaron again she wondered. Tracy was so sure her infatuation for him had flown by the wayside. Or, she asked herself, was it that he became more appealing because he was not around as much anymore.

In many ways she knew she would never get over Smitty. The only reason they ever broke up was because they knew that their parents were so much against their relationship. How unfair though, she thought. No one should tell you who to love. How could they? Yes, she and Smitty did foolish things when there were young and together, but they had grown more mature lately, and deep down in the bottomless pit of her heart she knew she would always love Smitty. Aaron was a close second though she had to admit. He also had good parents, and her mother liked him a lot. Her thoughts became distracted when she remembered meeting Aaron's Dad. She always had this sensation of familiarity when she looked into his eyes. Tracy wished she could define or pinpoint what it was about him that made her feel rather weird. The feelings were certainly not sexual in nature. Tracy almost felt unease and frustration about not being able to identify these impressions she experienced when she came in contact with Aaron's Dad.

At that moment her cell phone rang. Her Mom was calling from Connecticut.

"Hi, Mom, how's it going?"

"I'm fine honey. I was thinking the two of us should take a trip to Florida when the semester is over. Do you have any plans?"

"Just to come home and look for a summer job."

"I can probably find something for you to do in my office, so don't worry about that."

Tracy remembered the fun time she had traveling with her Mom when she left for college.

"Yea, that just might be fun Mom. Why Florida?"

"Well, with all we went through after nine eleven I never got to take you to Disney World. Everyone needs to experience Disney World once in a lifetime before becoming an adult. Also, I just feel like getting away for about a month. We can make stops in Charleston, Savannah, Hilton Head and Atlanta…eat at some good food places…maybe even Paula Dean's restaurant. Are you game?"

"Absolutely! Did you ever know me to look a gift horse in the mouth?"

"Why don't we both Google some maps and set up an itinerary. When you get home we'll combine the two with the best ideas from both plans."

"It's a deal Mom."

Sitting on her bed, rather than at her desk, Tracy put her laptop on her legs and immediately began to Google some maps. Her entry did not include Florida, but Wilmington, North Carolina instead. This was one stop she was going to include on the trip. She knew she wanted to see Aaron again, along with his family in their new home. Tracy's confidence told her that her Mom would not object to this little side trip. The more info she Googled, the more excited she became, and the more her thoughts revisited her relationship with Aaron.

Tracy could not help but wonder if it were possible to be in love with two people. Was she really in love with Aaron? He was a real hunk to look at, and she felt good every time she was with him, but with Smitty her love was so deep she could not even describe it. Her emotions for Smitty could almost be described as addictive. Smitty was starting to get his life back on track, and when she was with him everything just felt right. Perhaps some of Aaron's appeal was that he did appear more settled with a supposedly good future ahead of him. Yet, she felt Smitty had good potential though most other people who knew Smitty were not inclined to agree with Tracy. Ideally, society suggests picking the more stable partner. Perhaps though, that is the reason there were so many divorces. People settled for second best ignoring the heightened feelings of passion. After time, they begin to realize that a spark is lacking and they choose to not want to be without that spark. It was something to consider anyway.

However, right now all she was going to think about was planning the trip which was definitely going to include a visit with Aaron and his family in North Carolina.

Chapter Seventy-Two

Colleen was all excited that Aaron would be home for the summer and could help them with the move. She was really happy he decided to go to school near their new home. In the middle of all the moving fiasco the two older girls were both going to the prom, so all the gals were busy shopping for gowns, shoes, and coordinating groups for renting limos. Colleen was pleased the two older girls were taking the move so much in stride. Fortunately, neither of the girls had a steady boyfriend. The anticipation of meeting new guys in Wilmington seemed to be the main focus of their recent conversations. Knowing they did not have steady guys made the fact they were both asked to the prom even more astounding.

The older baby went every place with the girls. He would clap every time the girls came out of the dressing rooms modeling new dresses. Colleen was not sure who loved each other more, the girls loving their baby brother, or the baby loving the girls. He was always reaching out for one of them to hold him, and he would say, "sin, sin," when he wanted them to sing. Just give him a French fry when he got noisy, and that would do the trick. Baby Will loved staying home with me. God, I loved these children so much.

All the flowers were in bloom now and looking beautiful. The sunny, warm days made me think of the beach, and I was getting more and more anxious to move every day. Megan never really liked the beach. She was more of a city girl. Thankfully, Colleen and the children appeared to like the beach as much as I did.

I knew the children would be having pool parties before we left for North Carolina, so I decided to clean the pool while the girls were gown shopping. I spent time removing the pool cover and cleaning up some debris scattered throughout the pool area from a recent thunder storm. I made sure we had plenty of 'floaties' for the younger children. You had to be so conscious around a pool where small children were concerned.

A truck pulled into the driveway, and I was surprised to see Carl get out and walk towards the front door. I yelled for him to come around to the back yard.

"So, Bud. You're really moving."

"Yes, I am Carl."

"We sure could use you back at the shop. People are fussing a lot more about keeping their cars in good running condition in this crazy economy. I guess I really didn't believe you when you said you were going to leave."

"Well, I'm surprised to hear you say that. You know me. I never make 'idol talk.' Of course I'm leaving."

"It's kinda hard to find a good mechanic these days."

"Why don't you inquire over at the Vo-Tech school? They may be able to help you find someone."

"Yea, that's a good idea. I didn't even think of that. I guess you spoiled me when you came into my shop years ago looking for a job. I keep waiting for some other miracle man to appear."

"You say that Carl, but you were so quick to condemn me the first time anything suspicious came along. I'll never forget that. Ever!"

"Didn't take you for the type to hold a grudge."

"Oh, come on! I'd like to know what you would have done under the same circumstances."

"See no point in fussing over it again."

"Yea, sure."

"I'm happy Tom bought your house. I would hate to think of some strange people living in it."

"It certainly helped ease the transition for us. How's Steve by the way?"

"Oh, he's a great kid. Everyone gets along well with him at the shop, and he dang well knows those cars inside and out. I love his wife like my own daughter. What a blessing to have her fall in love with Steve considering........." Carl's voice trailed off as he appeared deep in thought.

At this point we could hear car doors slamming. "Sounds like the gals are back."

The baby ran into my arms and there was a lot of commotion as everyone greeted Carl.

"Come inside guys. Take a break and have a cup of coffee," Colleen was saying as she walked near us to glance at the yard. "Nice job hon, the yard looks good."

"Thanks for the invite Colleen, but I need to get going. We plan to have you both over for dinner before you go."

In unison they both said, “Say hi to Barbara for us.”

“Will do. Bye.”

“Bye,” they all yelled.

The girls kept unloading packages from the car.

“Man,” I said. “You sure are doing your best to put money back into the economy.”

“Look, Dad, aren’t these dresses beautiful?”

“Whoa! Don’t you need a jacket or something over that?”

“Daaaaaad!”

The baby clapped.

The next day Aaron came home and unloaded more ‘stuff’ around the house. Everyone was giving us going away parties and gifts we didn’t need. The days and weeks flew by.

Both Colleen and I were starting to catch mover’s remorse like indeed it was a reality. We had heard the word remorse associated with both buyers and sellers, but we were definitely feeling mover’s remorse. As much as we were looking forward to our move, we both began to suddenly feel a sadness that had been absent up to now. Up until the incident with Carl, I had a wonderful happy life the entire time I lived in this beautiful home in Tennessee. Maybe I did not deserve it, but would God really grant me all this peace and happiness with my amazing family if he didn’t think I was worthy of it? Somehow, I thought not…., but even I had to question myself.

Chapter Seventy-Three

Megan was fluttering around her mini-mansion in Connecticut just as excited as she could be about the trip with Tracy. Her life had been good regardless of nine eleven, even if she had to admit this to herself. Looking back, she realized she had not been so much in love with her husband as the fact she was in love with what she knew his career could offer her. Now, situated with more than enough money, she could care less if she ever had another man in her life. Who needed a man to correct everything she did, to complain about how she spent her money, to use her as a bouncing ball? Who needed to do the extra wash and pick up his clothes off the floor? Who needed to clean up the crumbs he always left on the counter and the dishes he left in the sink all the time? Nosiree, she would clean up after herself only, keep track of her own clothes and do as she pleased. Megan never had trouble finding a man to take her to a show or out to dinner, but most of the time she enjoyed just staying home by herself and watching her choice of television programming, or playing music as loud as she pleased or spending social time with her lady friends.

Of course Megan was sad the day of September 11, 2001. Who wouldn't be? The shock of our country being attacked was enough to play on anyone's nerves, and it was difficult figuring out a way to handle Tracy's emotions. How do you explain to a child that their Daddy will never be coming home again? To just say Tracy's daddy died was really not sufficient because of all the horrible pictures shown on television, in magazines and newspapers of people jumping out of the buildings and hearing tales of such devastation. Megan had an intricate situation explaining to Tracy the loss of her father. Knowing Tracy was so sad only built up more gloom in Megan's heart. Megan had to admit though that her husband worked such long hours the years before the tragedy that he did not have a lot of time to spend with Tracy. This was a major bone of contention between the two of them which often led to vicious arguments, and Tracy would cower in a corner or run to her room when her parents argued. All of a sudden, except for the sadness, Tracy was not witness to any of this harshness in her life after the tragedy and the subsequent loss of her father. Once Megan realized her husband had left her a large estate upon his death, she frankly did not even feel sad anymore. She had never admitted this to anyone, but deep down in her heart she knew this to be true. How great it was to just go out and buy whatever she wanted and not have to worry about a budget, nor did she have to be concerned if her spouse would approve. Her women friends used to talk about sneaking dresses and shoes into their homes so their husbands would not see. This was not a concern for Megan at all.

Yes, Megan could have used a man's help around the house when things broke down. It was a nuisance having to call a plumber, or an electrician, and keeping the cars in good condition was something she absolutely hated doing. Through the years she did manage to find a few reliable people she could hire that were trustworthy and dependable, but it took a lot of hit or miss circumstances before reaching that point.

Life was good. Megan had no complaints. She also had to admit that she enjoyed the sympathy that went along with her situation. Megan was not just any ordinary widow, but a widow of a tragedy of the worst kind. How fortunate she felt also that Tracy was their only child and a girl. The older Tracy got the more fun the two of them had together going shopping and travelling together. Megan's biggest concern was that Tracy was still enamored of Smitty. Of all the guys in this world, why would her daughter settle for someone who appeared to be a loser? Tracy was convinced Smitty was getting better, but Megan could not see it happening. Megan was tickled pink when Tracy mentioned stopping in North Carolina to see Aaron and his family. They sounded like nice level headed people, and Megan was going to try her best to encourage this particular relationship. Everything Tracy said about Aaron's family made them really sound special. The stop in North Carolina would be one of the highlights of their trip together. Megan was sure of this.

Chapter Seventy-Four

Soon after Colleen and I settled in North Carolina, the Catholic Church in our neighborhood was having their summer church camp for elementary school students, so Colleen enrolled the younger children, and it was my duty to take them every day. Coincidentally, or not, I was not sure, our realtor always appeared soon after the children were in the classrooms and while I was outside talking to some of the other parents. The first day the realtor invited me to the local Starbucks for a cup of coffee, and each day thereafter it appeared to be a pattern. By the third day, when I got home, I mentioned having coffee with the realtor to Colleen and telling Colleen how I was getting to know Joy very well just by spending these days having coffee with her. I told Colleen I had a lot of sympathy for Joy's divorce. Colleen was peeling the skins off of some boiled potatoes to make potato salad, and she put the knife down on the table and looked at me strangely, but she didn't say anything.

"Is something wrong?" I asked.

"Did you say you have been having coffee every day with Joy?"

"I sure did. Why do you ask me that?"

"I think tomorrow you will have some place else to go," Colleen replied.

"Why, where do I have to go?"

"You figure it out, and just make sure it is not anywhere around where Joy will be."

"Now, why on earth would you say that? For crying out loud, we were just having coffee."

"Bud, no divorced women just want a simple cup of coffee with a good looking man. Don't be so naïve."

Well, damn it, that is all it was, and I resent you thinking otherwise. What is this about all of a sudden?"

Colleen sat down and starting peeling the skins off the potatoes again as she quietly said, "When I was a young bride and before I had the children, I worked with a lot of men. Every day one of them would ask me to lunch. Now, I don't mean for a special occasion where a bunch of workers go out together, but they would ask me individually to be alone with them. I decided then as a young bride that how things appear can be just as damaging as if they really happened. I had a good marriage to a wonderful man, just like I have with you today. My prior husband and I both decided early on that as much as we both trusted one another, we were also going to be concerned how something appeared. If enough people saw me every day eating with a co-worker, just the two of us, it would not look good. Why give the gossips something to talk about? I could find better things to do on my lunch time. We both felt that we could have friends of the opposite sex, but we were not going to spend time alone with them. Any alone time we had would be spent with one another. People used to admire my first marriage, just like the people in Tennessee admired yours and my marriage together. We are new to this area. I don't want people seeing you having coffee every morning with a divorced woman, plain and simple."

"I think you are being rather foolish because that lady did not mean a damn thing to me, but if you insist, then I will be sure to find something else to do when she is around."

"Let's look at it this way then Bud. I have been asked by one of the neighbors if I might like to help work at the library at the college, and I may consider it. Now, I ask you, would you mind if I had lunch every day with one of the male professors?

"Hell, no, I don't want you having lunch with any professors."

"Why is that any different? I at least work with and near the professors."

"I get your point. End of discussion."

"I would like you to stop seeing Joy, not because I asked you to but more because you understand what I am trying to convey about appearances."

As I grabbed the knife and took it out of Colleen's hand while pulling her up to me and giving her a big kiss I said, "I think you made your point very well, honey. You knocked it to me very clearly with the professor thing. Now, let's run upstairs for a quickie before I have to go pick up the children."

Colleen didn't have to be asked twice.

Sure enough, I began to see Colleen's point. The next day Joy was right up in my face again. I thought of Colleen and the professors and immediately told Joy I had some errands to do. After a few days of this, Joy got the hint because she stopped coming around. I realized then that perhaps she might have had ulterior motives after all. I presume women just have a natural instinct for knowing that type of thing. Men are naïve I guess.

Chapter Seventy-Five

Aaron was making a habit of sleeping late after going to bed at ungodly hours. Colleen and I decided to let him get away with this for a few weeks before he had to go and find some type of summer job. He was such a trooper when we moved. His assistance really helped to ease the transition for us.

One morning about eleven o'clock, Aaron could hear some voices outside his upstairs bedroom window and he got up to see what was going on. Down below were two of the most gorgeous girls in short shorts hanging bathing suits on the clothes lines. One had stunning red hair and the other was a brunette, yet they looked like sisters in their mannerisms and body builds.....and whoa what bodies. He peeked through the blinds for about fifteen minutes thoroughly enjoying these bodily specimens. I walked by the door and saw Aaron standing at the window.

"What's so interesting out that window to hold your attention?"

"Come here Dad and look at those pretty little things down there."

Now he had my curiosity. I had to admit they were two very beautiful young ladies.

"I feel like I have died and gone to heaven," Aaron said.

"Hmm, I didn't think our neighbors had children their age. Why don't you get up and casually walk around the yard and meet them as though by accident."

"You betcha I will. Just let me wash my face and brush my teeth," Aaron said as he rushed to the bathroom and spruced his appearance making sure to splash some musky spice male cologne on his body after running the comb through his hair.

He ran downstairs while grabbing his baby brother as he ran outside pretending to chase him around the house. The little guy didn't know what was happening, but he loved every minute of this time with his big brother. The girls were leaving just as Aaron and his brother reached the clothes line area between the two yards. The baby's giggle caused the girls to turn around. Once they got a good look at Aaron, they stopped short and really gave him the once over. One of them waved and Aaron waved back. He picked up his brother and walked over to the girls and introduced himself. Aaron quickly decided that he was going to like this new house and area a whole lot. Any wise observer could tell that the two girls obviously had the same feelings where he was concerned. The two college girls said they were on their way to work at the ice cream parlor which was their summer job and indicated they hoped to see Aaron again. At that point, Aaron picked up the baby and went inside to down the biggest breakfast Colleen had ever seen anyone eat. If all the children were going to be eating like Aaron just did she just might have to give that job offer at the college library a second thought.

After eating, Aaron decided he was going into town to job hunt and possibly make a little side trip to the ice cream parlor in hopes of seeing the two beauties again.

I helped Colleen clean in the kitchen.

"I think I will write thank you notes to all the people who gave us those many great going away parties," Colleen said as she stacked the clean dishes that were in the dishwasher on the shelves. "Do you think you could watch the two boys?"

"Sure, I'll take them down to the beach. We really had a lot of fun at those parties they gave us, didn't we?"

"Yes, I am going to miss all our friends from Tennessee, but many are already coming here to visit, so we can look forward to that and to meeting new friends too."

"I was pleasantly surprised at how much fun we had at Carl's. Who knows why he acted that way when Marie came to work at the shop? I won't question that situation any more though. I am happy to be living here now, and this might not have occurred if Carl didn't show the reaction that he did about those circumstances with Marie. Didn't Steve and his wife look great? The way he walks with his new prosthetic, it is hard to believe he ever lost his leg."

Colleen grabbed her thank you notes and sat at the kitchen table. "Steve's wife is the best thing that ever happened to him. When do you suppose Aaron might ever get married? I really like his friend Tracy and think they would make an adorable couple."

I nearly dropped some kitchen utensils I was putting in the drawer when Colleen said that. "Oh, it probably won't last with her remaining in Tennessee. I am sure he'll find someone else." Of course, I hoped what I was saying would be true. Oh, God, please let him lose interest in Tracy, I secretly prayed. I just could not picture how it would ever work. If Megan were not around there would not be a problem. Tracy probably would never remember me after all these years and my advancing age. Oh Lord, here I go again. I picked up the two boys and had to leave since I was feeling a panic attack coming on. I bent my arms down and grabbed the boys in a backward position with both boys' heads facing Colleen's. She planted a big kiss on each of their cheeks and off we went.

"Be good for Daddy," Colleen yelled as we bounced out the door.

While Colleen sat there writing, she thought about how lucky she was the day Bud came into her life. She, at that time, had been a widow for a few years and had just about given up any hope of ever marrying again. How strange really. Things happen when you least expect them. Money had never been an issue. She had been left quite a bit of money by her former spouse. The children kept her so busy, along with all her charitable work, that her mind did not even consider another man at that point. God was good to her though, and she now had another good husband. How fortunate for her to have been given two beautiful men in one lifetime. She would be forever grateful.

Chapter Seventy-Six

Back in Connecticut, Megan and Tracy were busy getting ready for their upcoming trip, assembling a schedule and making hotel reservations. Arrangements were made to discontinue any paper deliveries and to hold the mail.

Tracy e-mailed Aaron mentioning that she and her mother would like to stop by for a visit, hoping he would be just as thrilled as she was about the trip to see him. On her way down to the basement to pick up her suitcases, Tracy heard the front door bell ring. Her Mom had just left for work that day to get her schedule in order for the office staff so that things would run smoothly the month that they would be gone. Tracy immediately reversed her steps and went upstairs and to the front door.

Smitty was standing there looking tall, slimmed down, yet with a beautiful buffed up body that would make any girl melt at the sight of him. She reached up and wrapped her arms around him and they embraced with a huge hug. "Oh, Smitty, what a wonderful surprise! What's up? What are you doing in our area?"

He entered the foyer, closed the front door and picked her up in his arms holding her body so close she thought she was going to suffocate. Tracy did not say a word though. It just felt so good to be pressed up against him. Then he kissed her at first softly and then with more passion and determination. "Are you home alone?"

"Just for a short time. Why do you ask?"

"Because I would like to take you up to your room and lie down in bed with you."

"Oh, Smitty, as much as I would like to do that too, we really shouldn't."

He kissed her again harder, and Tracy wondered how on earth she could resist. Lord, she did not realize how much she had missed him. "You look so darn good."

"Yea, babe, and you look even better. What say you take a trip with me starting tomorrow to New York to the Catskills?"

"Gee, I would love to, but my Mom and I already made plans to go to Florida for a month, and we are leaving shortly."

"You mean you would pick going on a trip with your mother over me?"

"To be fair, I didn't even know you were in the area."

"Ever hear the word flexibility?"

"Of course, silly, but I also made a promise to my Mom and I am not going to break it. If you were serious about my going with you, you could have informed me sooner."

"You're right. Sorry. It is just that I got a job interview in the city, and then after the interview I thought I would go to the mountains to relax for a while before I hopefully start work. I just never imagined you would be going on a vacation with your Mom."

"I've grown up a lot Smitty and realize my Mom is not the devil I thought her to be when we were in high school. She's a good friend of mine, besides being my mother. Further, she and I went through a lot together after nine eleven, and that is something we will always share with each other."

"Well, can you come over to my house for a while? My Mom won't be home until after six o'clock tonight, and I sure would like to get you alone."

"Hmm, I think I can go over for a short visit. Wait, while I write my Mom a note. I need to do some errands for our trip anyway."

This was probably not one of Tracy's better decisions. Once they were alone in the house they could not keep their hands off one another, and their session was intense. They left about thirty minutes later, both in a different direction with their spirits buoyed and their appetites satiated. Tracy thought seeing Smitty was a good thing. She felt she needed to compare her affection for him to those for Aaron when she saw Aaron in another week or so, but she surely wasn't going to mention this to Smitty at all. Tracy also decided she would not mention this visit with Smitty to her mother either since she did not want their trip to start out on a wrong note.

Chapter Seventy-Seven

The boys and I had a great time at the beach. They were collecting sand crabs and running in and out of the waves as the tide would come in and then recede. I just sat in a low beach chair reveling in every minute watching the boys enjoying themselves so much. It wasn't long before they wanted me to bury them in the sand. They were going to need a good dousing with the shower hose when this was over. I built up the sand around them to look like two racing cars with steering wheels, and for a long time they twisted and turned their bodies, growling motorized sounds as they pretended racing down a speedway. You could always tell when they started to get tired because soon they started throwing sand at one another and I suggested going to the food bar for something to eat. That appeased them for a while. Hopefully, when I got them home they both would decide to take a nap.

As we were eating our hot dogs and fries, Aaron came up to where we were sitting.

"Guess what Dad?"

"Oh, hi Aaron. What?"

"I got a job working at the ice cream parlor with the two girls."

"Are you serious?"

"Yup."

"Well, it isn't exactly what I pictured you doing this summer, but any job is better than none in this economy."

"Yea, and any job near those two babes has got to be a good job."

"I knew you had an ulterior motive."

"They are both actually going to be at the same college as I am, so that is even more exciting, and it doesn't sound like either of them is going steady with anyone else."

"Sit down and have something to eat with us."

Aaron ordered a cheeseburger, fries and a coke and the boys had fun stealing each other's 'frenchies' as they called them. After eating, we each took one of the little guys and hoisted them upon our shoulders and started for home. Hopefully, Colleen was finished writing her thank you notes and the boys might take a nap.

After putting the boys down for their naps, Aaron went to his room while Colleen and I each got a glass of iced tea and went to sit out on the deck. The weather was just so pleasant, and I was feeling terrific when Aaron came running downstairs and unto the deck.

"Guess who's coming to visit sometime in the next few weeks?"

Colleen said, "Who, honey?"

"Tracy, and her Mom."

I nearly dropped my iced tea as a thousand random thoughts ran through my mind.

"Oh, I think that is wonderful. It will be so good to see Tracy again, and I am anxious to meet her mother. Isn't that wonderful hon?" Colleen said while smiling at me with her wonderful pearly white teeth.

"I thought you two had called it quits?" I evaded any expressions of joy or fear at their coming when I queried Aaron.

"Well, I was avoiding her, but we shall see."

My hand started to shake, so I put the iced tea glass on the table and folded my hands together across my lap to keep them from trembling.

Colleen was interested in knowing an exact date which apparently Aaron did not yet know with the exception that it was going to be within the next month. How on earth was I ever going to make sure I was not around if I did not know when they were coming? Also, how could I even think of not being around? It was not as though I had Tom here to fake another camping trip. I could feel my heart pounding.

"Won't it be awkward having them visit us if you are working at the ice cream shop?" I was desperately trying to think of ways to stop their visit from happening.

"Oh, the girls said if I ever needed time off they would switch with me, so I am not worried. Anyway, you all could come together to the ice cream shop, and I could serve you." Colleen chimed in by saying she would be happy to serve them a wonderful meal and really get to know them.

I wanted to get up and leave the room so much, but I knew this would only throw suspicion my way if I acted erratically, so I forced myself to stay and just listened to Aaron and Colleen talk, deciding not to say anything more. My mind, however, was working overtime. I have got to stop this. It just cannot happen. No way! Oh God! I could feel sweat beading on my face and got up to turn on the overhead ceiling fan.

Colleen finally asked Aaron to try and pin Megan and Tracy down to a specific date the next time he talked or communicated with them since that would facilitate Colleen making some decent plans.

I thought once we moved away from Tennessee, Tracy was not going to be a problem any longer especially since Aaron would now be going to a different school. I had been getting away with my deceit for all these years, and I was almost sure it was going to end with the move, even though that was not the intention when we did move—and now my other wife and daughter had to decide to come and visit us. What were the chances? Oh my God, what am I going to do? Why did Megan have to come? Why on earth were the two of them travelling together anyway? I have got to stop the whole thing from happening, but how?

Chapter Seventy-Eight

The summer weather on the east coast was turning out to be better than anyone would have anticipated. White cumulus clouds formed beautiful images in the cerulean blue sky and there was absolutely no humidity. Megan and Tracy were ecstatic as they started on their trip. First they were going to stop for a few days in New York City and hopefully get to see some television shows as well as some shows on Broadway. Sometimes, if you were willing to pay the price and just went up to the box office at a particular theater there was a good chance of getting not only tickets to the show of your choice, but often very good seats. The presumption was that some corporate offices bought several seats that they were not always able to use on a certain evening. The other choice was to try their luck at Ticketron or through the concierge at their hotel. They were confident they would get some good tickets and started off their trip without a worry in the world.

"Aaron was trying to pin me down for a specific time we might be visiting them Mom. What do you think?"

"Gee, honey. I don't know. After New York, I want to spend some time on the Jersey shore and get a bit of a tan before hitting Florida. I don't want us to look like two pale ghosts. I do suppose though that we should be able to give them some sort of an idea so we just don't pop in on Aaron and his family."

"When I e-mail him, what do you want me to say?"

"Tell him when we are within two hours of their home we will call and let them know."

"I think Aaron's Mom was hoping we would stay a few days, and they could take us to do some sightseeing."

"Well, that is very thoughtful of her, but we don't know them that well, and as nice as you say they are, I really don't feel like killing our good time with relative strangers. I know you are more excited about seeing Aaron, but

I sure as heck don't want the two of you going off and leaving me with the parents either."

"Moooooommmm," Tracy exaggerated the word as though the thought was ridiculous. "His Mom was saying she would like us to spend at least one night with them. They had plenty of room, and she expressed through Aaron that she would be thrilled to have us stay one night. That would be fine, don't you think Mom-hmm?"

Megan's shoulders started to droop and she finally said, "Let's drop the subject for this part of the trip and worry about how long we will stay there when we get closer to North Carolina. I don't want to have any distractions at this point. I just want us to get on with the trip and enjoy this most gorgeous day."

The first day was just going to be a short drive and their hotel reservations in New York had already been made. Their Connecticut home was only a little over an hour drive into the city. Once they made use of the hotel's valet parking, they checked into their hotel and then went looking for what shows they might like to see. They also did some shopping on Fifth Avenue and took a horse and buggy ride around Central Park. In the late afternoon, they had lunch at the Carnegie Deli and then went back to their room to rest before their evening's festivities. This was only day one of their trip, and they were already hooked.

Chapter Seventy-Nine

I began having nightmares again and kept blaming them on the food I was eating. Was I going to have to spend the next month or so worrying about staying in my own house because my wife and daughter insisted upon visiting us? How inconsiderate of them that they could not give us a more specific time. Of course, none of this bothered Colleen or Aaron at all. Aaron especially was not concerned. He was spending every spare minute he wasn't working going places with the two girls he met by the clothes line and some of their male friends. Aaron was beginning to fit right in at our new home as were our own teenage girls. They spent their days at the beach and even managed to get jobs at a hot dog stand a few hours each day. Colleen seemed always busy shopping. With company coming there was a great incentive to get blinds and valances on the windows and new comforter ensembles for the beds. No one noticed I was in a sorry state of mind, and for this I was grateful.

My days were becoming more and more filled with anxiety attacks to the point where I thought I had better find a new doctor that possibly could give me some medication that might help. I was out of luck there though since I was a new patient and the first appointments I could get at most offices were to be several weeks away. I did make an appointment with one doctor just to get myself established in the system and then went instead to a medical urgent care clinic. The room was packed with patients, many of whom had cuts or allergies. One patient had a bad burn. I was beginning to feel foolish even being there, but my heart palpitations convinced me I was doing the right thing. When I arrived at the clinic, and after filling out a ton of paperwork, my blood pressure was probably rather normal, but the longer I sat there the worse it got I was sure. Yet, I was low man on the totem pole where the triage team was concerned. Eventually, the nurse came to the waiting room and called my name.

This time when they took my blood pressure the nurse said, "Whoa, let me take that again. Did you just have a cup of coffee, or some caffeine—anything that might make your blood pressure so high?"

"No," I replied.

"How may we help you today?" she then asked me.

I explained how I had been getting panic attacks, and the attacks were becoming more severe and harder to control.

"Is there any reason you might be having these attacks?"

"Not really," I lied. It was a good thing they weren't giving me a lie detector test.

"I see you just moved to this area from the information on your chart. Were you upset about the move?"

"Well, I didn't think so, but yea, that is probably the reason," I lied again. Lying was getting so easy to do. "Do you think the doctor could give me something for these attacks?"

"We'll see what the doctor has to say. Remove your shirt and put on this gown with the opening in the front. The doctor will be in shortly."

I sat freezing in the cold room in the skimpy paper gown as I gazed at the posters of human bodies on the walls. The bodies had all kinds of veins running up and down throughout the body appendages. So that's what we look like under our skins. After what seemed like an eternity, but in reality was probably only a few minutes, there was a slight tapping on the door which I acknowledged, and the doctor walked into the room. After some light conversation, I realized we were neighbors and we had both been invited to a party that Saturday evening at another neighbor's home. I was not so sure I was happy about this fact that I happened to pick the one doctor where I would lose some of my preferred doctor patient anonymity. As a man, I didn't want to appear weak in having to ask for a pill to calm me which is essentially what I was going to do.

The doctor wrote me a prescription for a generic tranquillizer, and he told me to make a follow-up appointment with my regular physician. When I stopped at the pharmacy to have the prescription filled, I could see dark clouds looming in the distance and hear the rumble of thunder. They were able to fill the prescription while I waited, which made me happy that I would not have to return. I probably did not even have to mention to Colleen where I had been under these circumstances. When I exited the store the wind picked up strongly, and a bright flash of lightening zig-zagged across the sky. Claps of thunder were getting louder and louder, and I was happy to be going home. The sky was turning an ominous black, and I noticed when I pulled into the driveway that the lights were already on in the house though it should have been still light out at this time of day. Dice began whining and was searching for a place to take cover. That place was the bathtub in the bathroom. He hated thunderstorms, and this storm was going to be a 'doozy.' The little guy ran into my arms as another big clap of thunder boomed overhead and hid his head in my shoulder. I was thankful everyone was at home now, and I didn't have to worry about them being near the water or driving in the chaos which was sure to happen once it started to rain. This was not a fast moving storm. We were able to finish eating and were cleaning up after dinner when a bright strike of lightening and loud boom of thunder seemed to have occurred simultaneously. At that same point a buzzing sound filled the atmosphere as though an electrical transformer had been struck by lightning, and our power went out.

"That was good timing," Colleen said. "How fortunate we were able to finish eating before we lost power."

I went to get the hurricane lamps off of the garage shelves while Aaron retrieved some candles for his Mom. We also got some flash lights to keep handy since it appeared the outage was going to be a lengthy one. The sky was filled with pelting rain and the streets filled with torrents of water at this point.

"Wow," I said. "I can't remember seeing it rain this hard in a long time." The rain appeared to be going in all kinds of directions as it slammed against the windows. A phone call to the electric company told us our power was most likely not to return until about four in the morning. It was going to be a long night.

We sat around the large kitchen table and played games by candlelight until it was time to put the children to bed. The teens all went to their rooms to do whatever it is teens do when they are suddenly without any electronic devices. Just imagine, no cell phone (because strangely they were not working either), no texting, no iPods, no laptops. They might actually have to end up talking to one another for a change, or most likely they just might fall asleep early.

Around ten o'clock, Colleen went up to bed, and I stayed down to blow out all the candles. I was going to sit in my lounge chair and listen to some music on our emergency radio FM station. Without even realizing what happened I fell asleep. My sleep was a deep one and very sound. I had actually not been sleeping so well since I heard the news of Tracy and Megan coming to visit. Therefore, I was stunned to be shocked out of my deep sleep by the sound of people's voices and bright lights everywhere. Completely disoriented, I couldn't even figure out where I was. Eventually, it began to dawn on me that the noise was coming from the television set that had been on when the power went out, and of course it was the same with all the lights we had on before the storm that were shining so brightly now I had to squint my sleepy eyes. The power came back on around one in the morning and earlier than the electric company had predicted.

Chapter Eighty

Had it not been for all the fallen limbs and other debris strewn about our yards and even some toppled trees further on down the road, one would never have known there had been such a violent storm the evening before. The sky was such a clear blue without even a cloud to be seen. Colleen and I and those children who were not working spent all morning clearing away all the rubbish. We noticed our neighbor, the one who was having the party that evening, was working especially hard to get his once immaculate yard back in shape before all the guests arrived. When we were finished with our own yard, we walked over to offer him our help, but he graciously declined our offer.

"After lunch, honey, why don't we take the children to the beach so they will be good and tired and willing to go to bed early this evening? That way it will make it easier for the girls to babysit and for us to get away to the party."

I agreed with Colleen's suggestion, and frankly, the diversion with the children was exactly what I needed. They keep us so constantly in motion it is rather hard to focus on anything personal when they are around.

After four hours at the beach and chasing the kiddies around, I was frankly exhausted when we got home, and I was further kept busy bathing the children. We also wondered what to give them to eat for their dinner to appease their appetites since we would be eating at the party. When they noticed we were not sitting down with them when they started to eat dinner they became whiny and irritable, and they wanted to know why we would not eat with them. Thinking it best not to mention the fact that we were going out since their tempers were short, we explained we planned to eat a little later. When we then chose to sit down at the table with them, their moods improved somewhat, and I could not wait until they were finished and we got them into bed.

Just like we suspected would happen, as soon as the children's precious little heads hit the pillows they were out quicker than you could say go to sleep. Colleen and I went in and enjoyed some time in the shower together improving my mood immensely. By seven thirty in the evening we were both dressed for the party, the teens were instructed as to their baby sitting duties, and we ventured across the street.

Things were going great until the doctor I had seen at the urgent care clinic came in with his wife, and the first thing he said to me after we were introduced by our host was, "Oh, we've met. Is that medication I prescribed doing the trick?"

I smiled and said yes and could not help but notice Colleen's odd expression wondering what the heck kind of medicine the doctor was talking about and why she did not know I had been to see a doctor in the first place. I was happy though when she chose not to say anything about his query. Fortunately, some other guests arrived and Colleen and I got separated. Hopefully, the statement would be forgotten by Colleen by the time we got home, and actually the rest of the party went well with no more mishaps. Our new neighbors and friends seemed most compatible and friendly without being overbearing. This is always a good feeling when you know you will be surrounded by nice and friendly people. No one wants to live in a Peyton Place type of atmosphere I thought as I remembered a movie I had once seen. Yet, in reality we all possibly live in some type of dysfunctional environment.

For me to assume Colleen was not going to inquire about the doctor's statement was quite naïve on my part. We no sooner crossed the threshold of our home when the words came out.

"What was that doctor talking about at the party concerning some prescribed medications for you? When did you ever go to the doctor's office, and why did you go to his office?"

"Oh, it was just something minor. No need to be concerned."

Colleen looked at me in utter frustration. "Pulleeeze—don't give me that kind of junk. Why did you see a doctor? What's wrong? And, why on earth didn't you tell me you were going? I thought we didn't have any secrets?"

"I didn't keep it a secret from you on purpose. I was feeling a little gassy too many days in a row and the day of the storm I was near the Urgent Care Clinic, so I dropped in to see if the doctor could give me something for it. I guess I forgot to mention the fact because that was the day of the storm when the power went out, and it just slipped my mind." I prayed silently that my statement proved plausible. "Oh, by the way, it made me realize I hadn't established a relationship with a doctor in this area, so I called around that day and also made an appointment for a physical and to get into the system. We need to do the same for you and the children once you are sure what doctors you want to see for yourself and for them."

By my adding the statement about getting us into the system, Colleen started focusing on that part of the conversation saying she thought that was a good idea, and I managed to divert her attention from my doctor visit.

We sat down in the den and discussed our various neighbors and decided we were lucky to be in such a nice area. We just knew that we were really going to enjoy living here.

At this point, our daughters who had been babysitting woke up from sleeping on the couch nearby after hearing us talk and wanted to know how we enjoyed the party.

We told them about our party, but then we listened to how their evening went and we did not like what we heard in return. Apparently, the baby woke up and vomited all over the bedroom carpet. Once he vomited he seemed to be just fine after the girls held him and cleaned his face and he eventually fell back to sleep for the rest of the evening. However, while they were tending to the baby, and before they had a chance to clean the vomit off the carpet, the dog entered the room and ate the whole mess. I felt I was going to upchuck myself when I heard that story. After the dog was finished, the only thing left to do was spot clean a small stain that was left. In actuality, for the girls, the dog's actions were for them a blessing in disguise.

I guess my tranquilizer was working because I was feeling quite tired and relaxed. That evening I had a very good sleep.

Chapter Eighty-One

While carrying the boys down to breakfast the next morning, I overheard Aaron telling his Mom that he received a text from Megan and Tracy, and they were spending a few days at a friend's house on Long Beach Island in New Jersey. From there they were going to spend a few days in Washington, D.C., touring the city and seeing some of the newer monuments and perhaps visiting some museums. "I would bet they will come here to visit us after Washington Mom."

"Well, the guest room is ready. I just need to buy a bath mat and matching towels for the guest bathroom and we will be ready for their visit whenever they get here," Colleen reiterated. "I think I will go out this morning and buy those few remaining things if Dad will watch the boys."

It was at the point when Colleen made that statement when we walked into the kitchen. I told Colleen I had planned to take the boys fishing, so she was good to go. I looked towards Aaron and inquired if Tracy had given him a specific date as to their arrival.

"Nope, Dad. Sure didn't."

"Are you going to try and pin them down?"

"Why Dad? It isn't as though we are going any place, so what difference does it make?"

I wanted to respond "plenty" but instead thought it best to wave off his statement, and I replied, "No difference whatsoever. Just asking."

I could feel the anxiety coming on again and wanted to take a pill, but I had already taken more than I was supposed to, and I feared I might not have enough pills left when the time came for my wife and child to visit. As soon as the boys finished eating breakfast, I collected the fishing gear and decided I needed to get out of the house really fast and hopefully avoid taking another pill by doing so.

The boys appeared anxious to go fishing, but when we got there neither one wanted to put the bait on the hook, and they in fact yelled they didn't want to touch the worm. As soon as their poles were in the water they started screaming they either thought they caught a fish, or they were angry because they did not catch any fish. I was not convinced this was a good idea after all, and for sure it was going to be a long morning. After, they had more fun throwing rocks in the water while they kept asking me if I caught anything yet. Sitting there with my pole in the water, I was concocting all kinds of scenarios where I could avoid being at the house during the time my wife came to visit. Nothing I could think of appeared logical or believable. The thought of them coming consumed my every thought. The waiting for their visit to happen was surely going to drive me insane. What in God's name was I ever going to do?

It certainly did not help when the boys and I arrived home and I found out that Tracy and her Mom would probably be at our place by the end of the week. The palpitations started, and I began to feel dizzy. I stupidly thought that maybe I could force myself to be so sick that they might put me in the hospital. I was really going overboard now.

The little guys were busy playing with building blocks on the floor. I sat on the couch and put a cold compress to my head—thinking, thinking, thinking! I had to manufacture some type of solution. I just could not be in this house when my other family arrived. It would not work. Oh God, help me, I kept thinking, and then I dismissed that statement by feeling I would be the last person God would want to help at this point.

Chapter Eighty-Two

I was home alone when the house phone rang the next day. I glanced at the caller ID not wanting to answer another 800 caller. I immediately noticed the Connecticut area code and I broke out in a sweat. Naturally, I chose not to answer it, and I was happy no one else was at home. I prayed they would not leave a message, but that did not happen. I decided to take a drive along the coast. Many times when I looked at the ocean there was a pleasant mesmerizing effect on me that I was hoping would occur on my drive. The day was pleasant enough though a lot of rain was predicted for the end of the week. Great, I thought, we'll have visitors and unpleasant weather to boot where they might not even want to spend time outside. I began thinking of ways to cover up any moles on my arms or body that might be recognizable to my first wife. They could easily be covered by wearing long sleeves—in spite of the heat. I would just set the thermostat to make the house colder. I stopped at a barber I had never visited before whose shop was further out of the town lines and asked him to color my hair and then give me a really short buzz cut. If I could not escape meeting with my wife and daughter, the least I could do was make my appearance completely unfamiliar to them. Perhaps I should pretend to have laryngitis so that any unfamiliar intonations with my voice would not be remembered or detected. The problem with doing something like that was that it would be so easy to forget, and I might slip up while doing so.

After I was finished getting my hair cut, and since the shop was across the street from the beach, I left my car where I had parked it and decided to sit on the sand for a while after retrieving a blanket from the trunk of the car. It was a little cooler than usual, so the beach was not as crowded. The peace and tranquility that encompassed me as I listened to the waves hit the shore was almost as good as taking a tranquilizer. I was quite pleased with my appearance after the hair coloring and cut. I hoped I was enough older looking and my style of dress and demeanor would be so different that my wife would doubt any recognition that she might detect when looking at me. Maybe our meeting was going to work after all if I put in place all my little schemes. Glancing at my watch, I noticed it was getting late, so I decided to work my way back home. I actually pulled into the driveway the same time as Colleen and the younger children who immediately got out of the car and came running up to me. They had a way of making me always feel special, and for that I could not help but be grateful. However, none of them seemed too pleased with my new hair style.

Colleen hit the button on the answering machine, and we could all listen to Tracy's voice saying that they were right on schedule and hoped to be at our house that Friday afternoon, and they would stay a day or two depending on our schedule. The teen girls were ecstatic at the news as was Colleen. Aaron had yet to arrive home, but I knew he would be happy too. All the tranquility I experienced at the beach that afternoon was immediately wiped away and those old palpitations came back. I told Colleen I would fire up the grill for supper just so I could get outside where I would not have to listen to all the excitement about our very first visitors in our new home. They would be here in two days, and I had no escape. My thoughts always go right away to, "Oh, God, what am I going to do?" Then my mind does a reality check, and I figure God will just tell me that the whole thing was my problem with which to deal. Oh, Dear Lord in Heaven.

I heard Aaron's car pull into the drive while I was outside firing up the grill. In a while he came out to see if he could help.

"Did you hear that Tracy and her Mom are coming to visit on Friday Dad? Isn't that great?"

"Oh yea, sure. I knew you would be thrilled."

"Well, yes, it will be especially nice to see Tracy again."

I inquired if Aaron still had special feelings for Tracy. Under my breath I kept praying he would say no.

"I have been giving that a lot of thought Dad, and yes, I think I do, and that is why I am so anxious to see her and investigate how deep and special these feelings are."

Unfortunately, that was not what I had wanted to hear. Oh, man, those sweaty palms came back.

Chapter Eighty-Three

Tracy and Megan were spending their last day in the Washington, DC area. Their trip had been a great one, and they were anxious to get on to their other destinations.

"Gosh, Mom, I am so happy you had this idea for us to travel together. It has been special so far, and we still have so much more that will be fun to do. I can't thank you enough for thinking to share this time with me."

"I am so happy you are having a good time honey because I certainly am enjoying it too. I still am not too thrilled about staying with your friend Aaron's family though. I so much more enjoy spending our time in the privacy of our own hotel room. They sounded like great people the few times I talked to Aaron or his Mom on the phone, but still, I hardly know them."

"Oh, it will only be for a day or two Mom. They are great people. I know you will feel different after being there."

Megan ceased the conversation at that point. She thought to herself that her child just did not understand how she enjoyed her own bath and doing as she pleased and not having to cater to the whim of other people. It was not as though, after all, they were trying to save money or anything by staying with Aaron's family instead of in a hotel. Though, what do children know? Kids could sleep on the floor with a bunch of other people and nothing bothered them—especially not their bladders. Oh to be young again, yet she could not remember ever being as nonchalant as her daughter Tracy.

The idea was to spend time in the morning going to the Vietnam and Korean War Memorials after checking out of the hotel then they would get on the road towards North Carolina in the early afternoon.

Viewing the names of the deceased military members on the slick black wall of the Vietnam Memorial was both impressive and sobering at the same time. Strangely, it made Megan think of her husband and the horrible tragedy that took him out of their lives. What would it be like to see his name on the future new Twin Tower Memorial some day? Megan momentarily was overcome with emotion. This was odd for her because outside of the initial shock of nine eleven she never did experience a lot of sadness at the demise of her husband.

"Remember my friend Joanne from fifth grade Mom?"

"Oh my, yes. You girls were like two peas in a pod the way you hung around together."

"Her Dad was killed in Vietnam, and that is why they moved away from Connecticut to go back to live near family."

"I sort of remember that story now that you mention it. Let's look for his name."

They found several names on the wall that had Joanne's Dad's last name, but they were not able to remember her Dad's first name.

At this point they noticed several tour buses with tourists disembarking. This was all Tracy and her Mom needed to go back to their car and find a place to have some lunch before getting back on the road. The sunny sky started to turn grey, but it was still nice and clear outside, and it appeared that it was going to be a good day for traveling south.

When they finished lunch and got in the car, Tracy called Aaron and said they were getting an earlier start than what they anticipated and would probably be at his home around seven o'clock that evening. She was told dinner would be ready for them when they arrived. Tracy screeched with excitement when she realized she would be seeing Aaron in only a few hours, and the screech nearly scared Megan to death.

The gals managed to be ahead of rush hour traffic and got out of the city in good time. They put some CDs on to play, and both women relaxed with their own particular thoughts streaming through their heads. Tracy, of course, could not wait to see Aaron, while Megan was rather dreading the whole scenario.

Chapter Eighty-Four

Back in North Carolina, the house was buzzing with preparations for the invited guests. I, personally, was attempting to come up with some sort of excuse where I would not have to be involved in any of the preparations. In fact, I did not even want to be there. Surreptitiously, I concocted situations where I would be away. So I could have an excuse to wear a hat, I thought of cutting my head a little so I could keep the hat on the entire time and in that way cover my face with the peak of the hat most of the time. I would apologize for wearing the hat while explaining the reason I needed to keep wearing it was in order not to gross them out. I was really beginning to like this idea, but how could I explain getting the cut on my head. Perhaps I could pretend I dropped something on the bathroom floor, and after bending down to pick it up my head hit the sink when returning to the upright position. Was I becoming psychotic to even think of such a thing? Anyone hearing this would definitely think I was a psycho. One did not need an intelligent brain to figure out how stupidly psychotic were my thoughts. Colleen came in at this point. I was momentarily distracted from my bazaar thoughts when she asked for my help in doing some task that involved lifting.

Out in the yard I could not help but notice the ominous looking clouds in the distance, but I did not have a lot of concern at that point because the sun was still shining brightly over our house.

The day advanced, and I had not yet cut my head which was spinning and spinning with untoward thoughts. I tried going for a jog to clear my head, but even that did not help.

I decided to go inside and take a shower. Maybe that would help me to have more lucid thoughts. As I was undressing, Colleen came in the room and remarked that I did not seem my usual happy self.

"Is something wrong honey? You have lost your luster somehow, and I haven't seen you smile in a long time. You appear to have the weight of the world on your shoulders."

"Oh, really? I can't think of anything in particular that might cause me to look so strange to you, nor can I imagine what would give you those thoughts about me. I'm sorry if I don't appear to be my usual self."

"Well, just as long as you are not having any problems, I guess I can tolerate missing your smile for a few days. However, if that look continues, then you and I are going to need to talk."

In the shower, I again contemplated doing something to my head, but I could not muster the courage to do it. Time was running short, and my heart started beating faster. The only thing the shower did was to help me smell a little better, though it seemed to heighten my sensitivities even more. Again, I wanted to go to the Lord and ask for his help, asking over and over again for God to please help me, even while knowing I did not deserve any help. Time was running short.

Chapter Eighty-Five

Driving south was a piece of cake on this particular day. Traffic was minimal. Perhaps this was because the two women were leaving in the early part of the day and not during rush hour. Whatever the reason, they both felt blessed. The CD's started playing some peppy songs and Tracy and her Mom began harmonizing.

"Hey, Mom, we ought to make a CD. We sound pretty darn good, if I do say so myself. We could be our version of the Judd's Mom and Daughter singing duo."

"Wouldn't that shock some of our hoity-toity Connecticut friends?"

"Oh gosh, it has started to rain. I knew things were going a little too good. I hate driving in the rain."

The sky turned completely black, and the rain started coming down faster and harder.

"Oh, Mom, I can't see. I don't know what to do. I want to pull over."

"No honey, you can't do that or someone might ram right into you."

"But, I also could ram someone in front of me. I just can't see for the life of me."

"Neither can I, but just keep your same slow speed, and continue on as best you can."

"Mom, I can't even tell if I am following the road or not. If there is a bend in the road, I just can't see it. I am so scared Mom."

Megan was equally as afraid, but didn't want her daughter to know the fear she was experiencing. The CD was blaring, but all of a sudden the peppy tune became an intrusion and interference in their cognitive thinking.

Both girls could hear loud booms getting closer and closer and they were sure the sounds were not that of thunder….. and then there was no question what the explosive noises were as their car kept getting hit on what seemed multiple sides of the vehicle, and it spun around uncontrollably….swirling and swirling. Both Megan and Tracy screamed and then—and then—silence!

Chapter Eighty-Six

Everyone seemed to be in a festive mood. Unfortunately, I was not one of them. The delicious smell of pork roast and French cut potatoes heating in the oven filled the house in North Carolina. Brownies were also baking in another oven, and soon that odor filtered through the smell of the pork and the whole house just smelled delicious. Colleen was letting the girls do most of the cooking, and they were really enjoying the whole experience.

While cooking, the girls had the radio playing in the kitchen, and the news reports were mentioning that a big rain storm would be reaching us in about a half an hour. Thank heavens we were not planning to eat out of doors.

Seven o'clock arrived, but our guests had not. We actually did not get a lot of rain. Around seven thirty, the young children kept complaining they were hungry. I remarked that it would have been nice if Tracy had called us to say they were going to be late.

"Well, Dad, maybe they are not in a satellite area and they can't get their message through."

"I suppose, Aaron, and today it is not easy to find a phone booth on the side of the road. However, the route to here is not necessarily an isolated one."

We decided to feed the children and put them to bed. We reset the table to just include Aaron, Colleen, Tracy, Megan and myself. The teen girls were disappointed they could not stay awake and eat later with us, but they needed to get up early for work, so Colleen and I ruled against that idea.

I kept sneaking bits and pieces of food here and there because even now I was starting to get hungry. The time was getting closer to ten o'clock, so we just decided to go ahead and eat by ourselves. We were starved, and we felt at this point Tracy and her Mom would understand our not waiting any longer for them. What a shame. Everything had looked so pretty and the food preparation was outstanding for it all to end like this.

Eleven o'clock rolled around. The dining room table was cleared and the kitchen was once again clean with all the food put away. We sat down to relax and watch the news. I began to realize I had stopped thinking about myself for a change and my own personal dilemma. At those thoughts, I got more butterflies in my stomach.

A news flash came on the television telling about a multi car pileup on the highway south. There was no word on casualties at this reporting, but we understood better why perhaps they did not call. We thought that maybe they were stuck in a massive traffic jam. The reporter explained the storm as violent with torrential downpours and high velocity winds filled with fury.

Aaron tried calling Tracy several times, but he kept receiving a no signal sign. He spoke his fears out loud saying, "I hope they are OK."

Colleen assured him that they were probably fine, but then when an accident of that caliber happens everyone becomes disoriented. Colleen suggested they should probably all go to bed. "They will probably be here in the morning, and we'll make them a nice breakfast and hear all about their adventures."

Reluctantly, Aaron agreed with his Mom and went to bed, and I, too, was exhausted. I had not really done a lot of physical activity that day, but my mind had been working overtime, and sometimes those mind games can completely drain you. Frankly, at this point, I was even too tired to consider how I would disguise myself when the company did arrive. As soon as I hit the pillow I was out.

Chapter Eighty-Seven

I awoke to the smell of bacon wafting its way up to my bedroom and the sound of voices coming from the kitchen. After glancing at the clock, I was shocked to see how very late it was. *Oh, crap, NO! Had our company arrived?* I delayed going downstairs by first taking a shower and making the bed when I noticed a big plump juicy looking spider on the floor leading to the closet, but I did not want to step on it with my bare foot. By the time I reached for something to swat it and turned around, the spider was gone. The queasy feeling I had in my stomach about our guests having arrived was now compounded even more by the disappearing spider. This had to be a bad omen. I am deathly afraid of spiders.

When I finally got the nerve to go downstairs, I was stunned to see only the members of my family.

I inquired, “Any news yet from Tracy?”

“No, Dad. I am really getting concerned,” replied Aaron.

“Is it possible you had the wrong day son?”

“No. I even checked my text messages, and yesterday was definitely the day they were to arrive.”

A news flash was flickering from the television screen with breaking news. We all stopped what we were doing to look and listen.

We learned the horrible news of that fatal car crash the day before. Twenty people had been killed. They started naming all the victims that they were able to identify. Several young beautiful babies and a set of twin girls and their older brother were among those killed. We gasped hearing that news and especially after seeing their beautiful faces on the screen……..and then it happened.

The low sexy voiced blonde television anchor was heard saying that a mother and daughter who had also been victims of the nine eleven tragedy were among the fatalities. You could have heard a pin drop in our house at the announcing of Megan and Tracy's names as we all stood there in stunned astonishment.

Colleen glanced at Aaron who flopped down in a chair immobile with shock.

"Mom!" That was the only word Aaron could manage to squeeze out in a guttural voice coming from a bottomless area reaching far down inside the body.

Colleen sat down beside Aaron and put her arms around him as he broke down in utter despondency.

The other children gathered around knowing something was very wrong but not quite sure what to do about it. For once they sensed the best thing they could do was to quietly sit down and not ask questions or be intrusive.

Both numbness and shock encompassed my entire being. There were labyrinths of thoughts swirling in my head. My wife and daughter were dead and there were no words to help me describe my emotions. Nor, on the other hand, could I even explain my hurt, sadness, pain and shock upon hearing what happened. *Family of mine now—do you understand? Could you possibly comprehend what I am going through? I am the one hurting here after all.*

Finally, I snapped to my senses. How stupid of me really. What a foolish reaction for me to have. I went over to pat Aaron affectionately on the back and to tell him how very sorry I was at the loss of his friend, and I was. Then it hit me. They were gone—my once wife and daughter were gone, and my life was about to experience a profound change. Along with my feelings of extreme remorse came a feeling of utter relief. Everything from my past life was over and done, and this time it was for real. I had only now to live day to day without fear of exposure and maybe even without anxiety attacks.

Like my son Aaron, I, too, sat immobilized and in shock comprehending the full impact of what this was really going to mean to my life now and how I would live it for my continued existence. I am a diminutive creature in the scheme of things. Life happens to us all either by happenstance or by choice. Were I to tell my story, some would hate it and despise me for what I had done. Others would care less. However, that is my story, and I am sticking to it. In the long run, only God will by my judge.

Discussion Questions

1. Do you think bad behavior can be justified if no one is harmed?
2. Should Bud have attempted to take his daughter Tracy with him the day he left his wife?
3. In actuality, could Bud's treatment of his new family, by not telling them the truth, be considered as equally appalling as when he left his other family behind?
4. Is the fact that Bud was so "oblivious" to the horrors of September 11, 2001, equivalent to him having an abnormal psyche or being mentally insane…or could it be determined as sheer selfishness?
5. Do you believe there are people in this world who continually do bad things but always seem to get away with it?
6. Do you find that people too often try to please other people instead of themselves? For example, Bud studied finance instead of another field of work because of the wishes of his parents and fiancée?
7. Can the fact that a person caters to other's wishes be detrimental to their having a successful and happy life?
8. Barbara set strict standards promptly for her husband when she heard the news that Carl believed Marie. Could that be a sign of a strong marriage—the fact that spouses of a strong marriage will not tolerate abhorrent behavior in their partners?
9. Colleen thought that inappropriate appearances can be just as bad as actually doing something wrong when she stated, "how things appear can be just as damaging as if they really happened." Do you agree with her thoughts?

10. Realizing what occurred at the end of the story, do you think it possible that Bud might never have anxiety attacks again?
11. Must one suffer the rest of their life for bad judgment previously committed earlier in life?
12. How do you think God would judge Bud?

www.ingramcontent.com/pod-product-compliance
Lightning Source LLC
Chambersburg PA
CBHW020944310726
48980CB00001B/40

* 9 7 8 0 7 6 1 8 5 6 8 1 8 *